too
LATE
to
BRAKE

too LATE to BRAKE

DELANEY JEAN

Content Advisory

Too Late To Brake is an adult romance novel featuring several instances of explicit sex.

Please enjoy responsibly.

For the fangirls.

*I love screaming about these beautiful idiots on the internet
with you.*

CHAPTER ONE

Sunny

The needle climbs the dial at a nerve-wracking pace.

At uneven intervals, the number ticks higher. Sometimes jumping abruptly, then hardly budging for a few long seconds. Not nearly fast enough.

The sharp red arrow creeps closer to the right side of the gauge, but I've got less than a minute. I'm running out of time.

"Come on. *Come on.*" I swipe a bead of sweat and fight to keep my smile wide and face otherwise impassive as my audience watches.

This is it. I've done everything I could. Now it's just waiting to see if all of my effort was enough.

As my last season preview video comes to a close, my active viewer count finally does it—it ticks to 1,000.

My jubilant shouts echo through the apartment as I leap from my creaky desk chair. Rainbow confetti explodes across my computer screen, accompanied by the sound of trumpets.

The upstairs neighbor thumps their floor, showering flecks of popcorn ceiling across the bed behind me as punishment for the racket. I ignore it and cackle as congratulatory messages flood my stream's chat bar.

```
MyHeartisRACING: wooo!!!
GrantColbyluvrrr: Congrats, Sunny!
Mnday: It's finally Riot Racing
   season! *sunglasses emoji*
```

My favorite comes from one of my most loyal subscribers, who began popping up in my streams last year.

```
Macaron91: never doubted you for
a sec, sunny
```

I click that message so it sits above my face on everyone's screen watching at home. "As usual, you're too sweet, Mac. Since I met my goal..." I let loose from the air horn I purchased for this moment. The neighbors are already mad anyway, even though I'm mouse-quiet every other day of the week. "...and broke my record of most active viewers on a stream, there couldn't be a more fitting time to share an announcement."

I queue up a drumroll sound as the chat goes crazy. The most eagle-eyed Riot Racing fans will have guessed what's coming. They'll have seen earlier announcements from other influencers and rumblings from the series.

"My sweet, sweet Rays of Sunshine," I start, flourishing my hand before me. "The generous folks at Riot Racing HQ have invited me to participate in their Creator Crush at this week's Seattle Grand Prix!"

I've been sitting on the news for weeks, but disbelief still buzzes through me as I recite the nature of the program. Riot Racing wants to grant the series' most passionate creators unprecedented access to the season opener so they can share the excitement with their audiences, drawing in new fans and invigorating the existing base.

Riot is a young series, and the one that ignited my passion for motorsports. When they announced Seattle as this season's first race, my heart soared, even before learning about the Crush. Finally, a race was coming to my corner of the US. Prior, I'd had low hopes of attending a Riot race, with none of my few friends interested in spending the cash to get to one. My parents could always be roped into hanging out, but not if it involved leaving our sleepy town. I didn't bother asking my younger sisters. Unless perfect beach weather was involved, they wouldn't be interested.

But thanks to the Crush and the followers who value my content, it's happening for me. Tightness grips the back of my throat. I smack a button to release another rain of confetti across the screen so I can blink away the sensation on the sly.

It's not enough. The feeling spreads. Oh god, I'm gonna cry on stream. I play the promo video Riot sent when they invited me to the Creator Crush, buying myself a full minute.

Pressing my hands to my chest, I breathe deep and slow to calm the storm of gratitude surging through me. I have to look away from the lovely comments rolling along the side of my screen. Desperately, I search the room for a small distraction.

There's a buckler on my bedroom wall, a small prop shield from our local renaissance fair, my favorite place in the world. It's bracketed on either side by a family photo. The oldest is from my first visit to the fair when I was little, wearing a plastic knight's helm and sparkly fairy wings, my sisters' faces blotchy and scrunched with distaste in a double stroller. The most recent is from just last year, when I got my master's. Comically, my mother is wearing the same oatmeal-colored sweater in both, my dad the same awkward smile. Though my sisters got slightly better at masking expressions that suggested they'd rather be somewhere else. The tiny tableau is my room's only decoration, but staring at it gives me a quick emotional detox from the colorful pandemonium of my livestream.

I focus on the gray space between the mementos until I'm sure I won't cry, then turn back to the camera.

Macaron91 has gone weirdly quiet. Normally, they can't make it five minutes without hyping me up. I could use it, honestly.

The video ends. I swallow, smushing the tears down. I need to thank them. "This wouldn't be possible without you all and your support over the last few years. Thank you so much."

I cut the technical effects. "The Creator Crush will feature all sorts of behind-the-scenes access, and I'm taking you with me. Plus, the program's capstone is a short, professionally shot segment on any topic of our choice, so keep an eye out for me on Riot's socials. Alright, we've got time for a few final preseason questions. Whatcha got for me?"

The viewers send a wave of sun emojis flying across the screen as their questions pour in. I take sips of soda between replies, acknowledging and considering different points made in the chat as we try to predict what this year has in store. Who will be the series champion? Will certain drivers settle their rivalries on track? Will we finally learn what's up with the weird vibe between Marco DeFlora and Stevie Dixon?

As we talk, glowing contentment fills my chest. I adore this little community I've built since I began streaming my thoughts on the Riot Racing Series halfway through their first season. Now, a few years later, there are a whole bunch of Rays, as my fans adorably call themselves, who follow me on social media and join my streams.

Someone asks how Luke Boltek, my prediction to win this year's championship, is looking, so I pop up one of his recent interviews where he comments on team Cyber Ward's car development.

"Y'all know Jenna Bow is my GOAT," I say at the clip's end. "So it pains me to say it, but I think Luke's going to catch her this year."

The next clip is from an interview with RJ Savo, who's making her debut with her family's team this year. I could stop the stream—I should; my flight is early—but the quiet that consumes this little apartment after every stream is depressing, and I don't have the energy to fight it tonight, so I keep us going a little longer.

As I read the Rays' different arguments about who will win races this season, I notice a trend in the chat.

I sigh dramatically. "Okay, chat. I see all of you requesting Evan Evans so you can make heart eyes at him." I pull up an Evans interview clip so everyone can see. It's not difficult to find one. His mischief-promising green eyes and wide smile take up most of the pixels of most of the thumbnails on the Riot Racing homepage. It's abundantly clear who the media's favorite driver is. Sticking my tongue out at my camera in defeat, I hit play.

"Yeah," Evan says, scrubbing a hand through his brown hair. He pats at one lock poking over his forehead. He's misplaced his team cap somewhere, as usual. I swear he does it on purpose to show off that hair that everyone's obsessed with. His eyes go a little crossed as he tries to see if he's fixed it, and I snort. "Sorry, what was the question?"

The reporter happily repeats themselves, charmed like everyone else seems to be around the Panache team driver. "How's your confidence in the number eleven car going into the season?"

Hair fixed, Evan shakes out his shoulders. The man never stops moving. "Well, Ol' Rustbucket—" My groan at yet another stupid nickname for his car cuts out a few of his words. "...really pointy, which makes for precise diving into the corners, but that can make it unwieldy, too. Like a possum in a bounce house, if you know what I mean."

"None of us knows what you mean," I huff as the clip ends and cross my arms. "I don't know what you all see in him."

I won't pretend I wasn't transfixed like the rest of the masses the first time I saw Evan on a broadcast, stretching before climbing into his car. "Who is *that?*" I'd wondered aloud on a call with Jackie, which made her cackle with delight. She'd been following him in other racing series for years, and let me know that he made everyone react like that. My initial awe subsided quickly as he dodged hard questions and flirted to avoid explaining his errors in interviews. Most of the fandom was under his thrall, but I knew plenty of guys like him, and I was certain Evan Evans was full of shit.

"Let's do one last question, for real this time. I need to get to bed. Riot is flying me out tomorrow for all the race week action." My voice gets squeaky at the end. "I can't wait to take y'all with me for all the behind-the-scenes access they're granting us. You'll be the first to see what I see, so make sure you're following all of my socials and have your Streamerz notifications on."

Shana_Girl_94 gets to it first. I read her question out loud.

"'Any predictions for how Ev will do this season?'" I sigh and shake my head. There are over twenty drivers in the Riot series, and my people want to talk about Evan repeatedly. "Listen, I think he has an impressive bank of raw talent. I do."

The chat's roiling before I get going with messages like "Here she goes again" and "Hear, hear! Don't believe the Elevans hype!"

And of course, there are many exclamations regarding how good-looking he is.

I mean, he is. Dreamy eyes, a big, goofy smile, and hair that's always perfectly tousled. He's white like me, but with the glow of someone who spends a ton of time outside. There's no doubt that Panache Racing's #11 driver is the most handsome man on the grid. Not to mention, he oozes charisma, so much so that every interviewer that talks to him eventually gets tongue-tied or starry-eyed.

"I reserve my judgment until we see how he drives this year," I say, holding my hands up. "No matter how many times he winks at a camera, it doesn't change the fact that he ended last season with lackluster results. Need I remind you he had five fifth-place finishes in a row? Not a bad record for some drivers, but it is for him. He didn't catch a whiff of a podium in the second half of last season. In the other series he's raced, he's never had a middling streak like this, yet he acts so unbothered in the media pen. He's all talk until he shows me otherwise."

The emojis in the chat turn decidedly negative. Good-natured thumbs down and crying faces as the Rays insist there's a massive upward trajectory for him just around the corner.

"There certainly is potential, especially with Seattle being his home race. It's a track he's familiar with. All I'm saying is, I've watched so many interviews and everyone is so enamored with him... The constant winking to the camera, the bad jokes..." I struggle to articulate my issue with Evan Evans. I chalk it up to a long, stressful week of anticipation and settle on a closing statement. "I'm not buying what he's selling."

The beginnings of bedlam break out in the chat as folks reference different drivers who have taken longer to hit their stride. I need to douse the embers of argument or I'll never get to bed.

My hands fly up in a gesture of pleading pacification aimed at my webcam. "Evan needs a podium ASAP. His Panache contract is only through this season. I know you all want him around for longer than that, so let's hope he can make good on all the potential and promises we saw last year."

I leave it at that. I like to be real with my subscribers, but they don't need to know why I can't trust a man who talks a lot and seems to know exactly how extremely good-looking he is.

"Because every weekend, what?" I demand, thumping the button to allow my followers to share a brief voice message.

"These beautiful idiots show up and RUIN MY LIFE!"

My speakers crackle as the cacophony of many voices at varying internet speeds blares through them. Every time we close like this, I have to laugh with joy. What started as a frustrated expression of my stress levels after a particularly hectic race weekend my first year of streaming has become my tagline. It's a mess, and it's *us*.

I sign off my stream with another reminder to follow me on socials and close it out with my theme song, a punky jingle with lots of drums.

When my screen confirms the stream has ended and the camera's light blinks off, I sag. Within moments, the beige-gray truth of my living quarters creeps in.

The apartment's silence is deafening. It's a growing cloud, determined to press me against the wall so I can't move... or breathe, even. I glance back at the scant mementos nailed to the wall. The wooden shield has a dragon painted on it, and I bring it back to the field that's turned into a medieval festival every summer. This year's fair won't open for months. At least I have the racing season to occupy my free time now. The off-season for both hobbies is wildly depressing.

A silly thought flits across my mind; a wish that I could bring the shield to Seattle with me.

My snort rebounds around the sparsely furnished room. I stand and stretch, running through my mental checklist a final time.

I've already shoved everything I'll need for the week into two suitcases, so I haul them to wait for morning by the front door. Even after all the lugging of laundry and toiletries, my heart races with anticipation.

I putter around. Wash the lingering dishes, dust my dresser. Finally, I flop on my bed and scowl at the ceiling. Anticipation is a low hum in my chest, gradually ramping up. Lately, I've been like an animal in a cage here, pacing and yearning for more room. More *anything*. I'm so grateful that my creator work has taken off in the past year, but I can't help but feel like I'm ready for a next step I can't see, and I refuse to leap blindly.

I'm so fortunate, but something's not right. Most of my time is spent at my mundane day job, which provides income more reliable than content creator money. My coworkers are pleasant. My workload is manageable.

I live five miles from the house I grew up in. I meet my parents for dinner twice a week. My sisters even join sometimes, when they're not off with their bustling school friend groups.

I am so unbelievably lucky and blessed.

But I *want* so desperately that sometimes it's hard to breathe.

I constrict my arms around a pillow, a nightly ritual that I convince myself eases the pressure in my chest.

My spiral is mercifully disrupted by the buzz of my phone.

> Your live views goal has been met at last!

Jackie's token raised eyebrow greets me in the avatar atop our text thread.

> You okay? Got a little sentimental for you in the middle there.

Though I've never met her in person, I can practically feel the comforting weight of her arm around my shoulder.

I swipe at my suddenly runny nose and type back. The tears will demand to be released sometime. Hopefully after race week.

> It was a close call.

The bubble indicating Jackie is typing appears and vanishes a few times, until finally:

> Your followers LIKE you, you know. They're a safe place. You can cry with them.

I shoot back a barrage of green-faced nauseous emojis.

Jackie goes quiet, likely attending to some of her own content creator commitments, and I'm too restless, so I take a quick shower. After, I sit on my bed, absently running a towel over my hair, imagining all the week will bring. When I finally lay down, I check for the fifth time that I've set enough alarms at the correct intervals so I'll be absurdly early for my flight. Additional distractions are hard to find.

The library book on my nightstand is a thick fantasy tome laden with battles and magic and a spicy-as-hell romantic storyline. My mind's too scattered to focus on a plot, but perhaps some fantasizing about a handsome, scraped warrior who fought through a battlefield to find me could slow my racing mind.

And some assistance from a toy could diffuse the restless energy that zings through my body.

A sudden buzz comes from a different device. A new message from Jackie graces my phone's screen.

> And to your point about Evan… He's gotten better about answering questions lately! You're seriously telling me you're not interested in buying THIS?!

The accompanying photo is from Evan Evans' most recent campaign with an underwear brand. He's wearing nothing but a pair of briefs and a smile, his black and white racing helmet tucked under one arm, the whorled pink plume painted on the top showing under the curve of his bicep.

I can't think of a response.

Jackie sends a GIF of a rabbit hopping around with steam coming out of its ears.

I set the phone down, stare at the ceiling, then pick it up again. I reopen the photo of Evan Evans, his pine-needle eyes sparking like he knows something I don't.

With a huff, I open my nightstand's drawer and pull out a vibrator, giving him one last narrow-eyed glare.

Still, the hero in my fantasy ends up having messy brown hair and a mischievous grin.

CHAPTER TWO

Sunny

Despite being significantly faster than race cars, planes aren't nearly as exciting. However, fate wanted to give me a run for my money today, because our pilot took the flight's delay like a personal affront to his mother. Beyond that, I'm fairly certain everyone on the plane except me has a now tight-as-fuck connection for some life-altering event. I've never seen flight attendants so flustered, passengers so tense, or clouds wing by so fast.

It's exhilarating.

"That was stressful, huh?" A guy my age in a vest, khakis, and a fancy watch says as we're spurted from the jet bridge into Seattle's airport.

"Uh," I start, realizing he's talking to me. I'd been digging in my bag for the journal where I keep my outline of content for the week. "I thought it was fun."

"What brings you to town?" He leans way closer than the spacious hallway warrants. I duck left, but he keeps pace with me.

It must be obvious, given the numerous racing-themed buttons pinned to my jacket, but maybe he's unaware. "The Seattle Grand Prix."

"No way! Me too." He adjusts the zipper's height on his vest, like the exact position could signify his peak masculinity. "I'm being featured as a creator for it. They flew me out and everything." He smirks, and it's like the movement is directly attached to my eyebrows with an invisible string. They slam down.

"No way. Me too," I say blandly and fish out my journal so I can review it as soon as I get to baggage claim.

Well, as soon as *we* get there, because apparently this guy is my peer.

"Oh... cool! So we'll be at the same hotel. Maybe we could get a drink or something."

"It seems like they've set us up with a pretty packed itinerary. I'm Sunny, by the way." I stick out a hand.

"Uh, right." His grip on my palm is limp. "Adam."

I check the time. "Well, Adam. I don't know about you, but I want to get to the hotel ASAP so we stay on schedule. Keep up if you can."

My dismissal is effective, evidently, because he stammers and gives me space.

I sniff and refocus. They're like piranhas, some of these dudes. They realize they're conventionally attractive, notice that you might be conventionally attractive enough for their needs, and they swoop in.

After grabbing my luggage, I park myself at the arrivals screen and try to determine how my delay affects my and Jackie's plan to meet upon landing. My phone is being stubborn about reconnecting to cell service, so I'm not sure where she is.

A familiar, warm voice that seems to grate only on me winds through the carousels.

I groan. On a huge screen taking up most of the closest wall, they're playing an ad for some travel insurance that's bagged Evan Evans as a spokesperson. I roll my eyes through the hokey tagline he delivers with gusto.

"Like you've ever needed travel insurance a day in your life," I mutter.

A force made of densely-packed joy, sarcastic comments, and dark blonde hair barrels into me. Arms band around my middle. My name is sung in my ear with all the energy of a Christmas carol.

I shriek and hug Jackie back, Evan's ad forgotten. We're a ballistic ball of glorious girlhood in the middle of the terminal, jumping up and down. "It feels so good to hug you!"

She simply squeals back. I fumble for my phone and snap a selfie, posting to my story with the caption: MEET YOUR INTERNET FRIENDS!

In a flash, Jackie shares it to her story because I get an alert that @carJackiex has tagged me. She added her own text: CAN CONFIRM: @alwayssunny is a real person!

We haul our bags out of the airport and into the fresh air and call a rideshare. Throughout, the speed and volume of our chatter doesn't cease and surely overwhelms the driver, but Jackie and I have been internet friends for nearly two years, and no amount of phone calls can make up for in-person interaction.

"Can you believe when we met," Jackie starts, "I hadn't even launched my channel and you had, what, fifty followers?"

I stretch my legs. "The good old days in the motorsports forums."

"And now we're going to see the actual team garages up close!"

"And ride in a real Riot car," I add. "Interview people who run the show—engineers, organizers, team principals..."

"Drivers," Jackie adds, head bobbing so fast it looks like it hurts.

"And ride-alongs," I repeat. "We get to watch pit stop practice... We get to do segments from the press set!"

"AND RIDE-ALONGS!"

I drop my head to my hands for what must be the hundredth time since Riot Racing's media team reached out. "I can't believe this is happening."

Jackie nudges my arm and points.

We gasp as the driver pulls up to the fanciest hotel I've ever seen. We tip generously as an apology to his poor eardrums.

The gasping and pointing continues into the hotel lobby, which is all black stone and elegant chandeliers, with a real fucking race car parked and cordoned off in the middle of the floor.

An imposing woman in a maroon pantsuit passes us, flocked by a small team of assistants taking notes as she recites a checklist.

"Is... Is that...?" I stammer.

"Yeah." Jackie's response is near-breathless as we ogle Riot Racing's CEO.

She passes us with her small entourage, good-naturedly shaking hands with the passing team principal of the Cascade racing team.

Jackie tugs my sleeve and jerks her head, and both our jaws drop as we spot the two Benji drivers ordering coffee in the corner.

"We died," I say. "We must have. The taxi crashed, and for our efforts in advocating for women in motorsports, we've been sent to racing heaven."

I tear my attention from a group of Manta team mechanics loading into an elevator as we're approached by a woman in a Riot-branded polo, who I recognize from their marketing team.

"Jackie and Sunny, welcome!" She extends a hand. "You're the first of your group to arrive. Cooper here will get you situated."

We learn that the attending creators have been split into groups of four, each with a Riot intern assigned to keep us on schedule. With some nervous mumbling, Cooper hands us welcome packets and room keys and gives a hurried rundown of where food can be found. My head starts spinning. Can adrenaline kill a person? Do I need to see a doctor? Is it safe to be this excited for such an extended period of time?

Our bags are whisked away and we're ushered into a small ballroom to wait for the other creators to arrive. There's fresh coffee and a racing movie on the projector screen, so Jackie and I settle in.

Some time later, we're both entranced by an infamous crash scene when a warm voice drawls. "Ladies, *please* tell me you've been assigned to group three." Jackie and I erupt into squeals again and jump from our seats to hug Gael, another creator friend of ours. We tousle his dark, shaggy hair and exclaim over the mathematical symbols he got painted on his nails for the special occasion.

"How was your flight?" He had the longest travel day of the three of us. He lives not far from Jackie in Pasadena, but was visiting family in Mexico and flew directly here. By the time we're done recapping, everyone else has arrived.

But the fates giveth and taketh away, because our group of four is rounded out with bro-ey Adam from the airport, who won't stop asking Cooper to find him a phone charger.

After much blustering, a charger is found, the larger group of creators is circled up, and we're subjected to a few hours of expectation setting and icebreakers.

Jackie is debating whether or not to try and sneak one of the Riot staff fifty bucks to assure she gets the chance to interview Lex Gotham when I spot a clock and realize it's later than I would have guessed, and even though I feel like I could make it the whole week on adrenaline alone, I'm setting myself up for trouble if I don't get at least *some* sleep.

My eyes are drooping when it seems like they'll finally release us to our beds before the rest of the week's chaos commences. Cooper gives our small group another run-down of the week, as if I haven't already memorized the schedule.

"All of your Riot team interactions will be random-ized," he intones, making me think he rejected Jackie's bribe, "to assure you get exposure to as many teams as possible. But you'll be with your small creator group all week."

Jackie hugs Gael and I close, and awkwardly reaches one arm further to pat Adam on the shoulder. "Talk about a dream team!"

"Speaking of dreams," I hedge. "I still need to publish some content before bed, so I'm turning in." I bid our little group goodnight and worry that I'll barely have the energy to kick off my sneakers before collapsing into bed, but remembering what comes in the morning helps me make it through my work and brushing my teeth.

"I know there are a lot of newbies here, so let's review a little Riot Racing 101." While my audience originally began with a group of other die-hards like me, I love that people are getting into Riot and coming to me for information. Over the past few weeks, I've been posting short segments with bite-sized details about the series, encouraging viewers to stick around for the full slate I'm sharing this week, which will cover Riot's workings in depth. I spin a little, looking for decent lighting in the dim garage we're all waiting in. I grimace. This is the best I'll get, so I look back into the camera.

"There are twelve teams of two drivers—so twenty-four drivers total—and sixteen to twenty races a year. Points are awarded to the top fifteen finishers, and the higher you finish, the more points you get. Wins and podiums at races are a big deal, but drivers are also aiming to accrue the most points over the season, both for their team and themselves. The team championship, for which points from both drivers are counted, is the one with all the prize money that helps a team advance its technology and performance for the following season. But the driver's championship is where the bragging rights lie. That's what these drivers really want, and it's what can make this competition the spiciest."

I duck under the arm of another creator walking and talking, and move to a quieter part of the room.

"Adaptability is the key to success in the Riot series. With a variety of track types and race conditions throughout the season, the team, including mechanics and engineers to strategists and drivers, that consistently excels is most likely to clinch the championship. And—"

One of the marketing people pops up in the corner of the room with a bullhorn, desperately trying to garner the attention of a dozen creators filming content.

"That lesson in adaptability is serving me well so far, Rays, because they have us running around all week, and I can't wait to show you what's next. Stay tuned." I post my video. Jackie clings to my arm and hops up and down. She's gripping Gael so hard on her other side that his hair flops around from her jostling.

The Riot crew must have wanted to start the Creator Crush with a bang, because the very first activity is ride-alongs. After breakfast, they bussed us to the track to watch a safety presentation and hastily climb into custom racing suits. Best of all, current Riot racers will be driving us, when promotional hot laps like this are usually assigned to reserve drivers or retired series stars.

I run trembling fingers over the race suit. *My* race suit. Bright red with yellow accents to match Riot's sunburst logo. They even printed our names across the waistline like the drivers have. Jackie and I aren't squee-ing now, too overcome with nerves and emotion over what's about to happen.

An engine roars to life somewhere beyond our room, and my heart leaps into my throat. The noise is beautiful and so much louder than I imagined.

"Oh my god." Jackie's words are a breathless squeak. "That never gets old." Unlike me, she's at least been to races before, though never with this much VIP access.

My voice wouldn't sound much better, but I'm too excited to speak anyway. I do my best to pay attention as we're reminded of safety procedures, but I'm going to explode if they don't let us out of this garage soon.

Years of fandom, focus, and work have led to this. The entire week will be a dream, but this could easily be my only opportunity ever to experience a ride in one of these cars. This very well could be the best day of my life.

More engines fire out in the pit lane, causing the closed garage doors to vibrate.

Gael tugs at his earring, his always-present, good-natured smile faltering. "I wasn't scared... until, well, right now." Behind them, Adam fiddles with his smartwatch, but his downward glance doesn't hide how his pale features have gone a little green. Even Jackie looks pallid beneath her SoCal tan.

Cooper clears his throat. "They had us do it a few days ago. It's not so bad. It's like a roller coaster, but, you know, without the rails." He swallows, then waves the safety brochure around, giving us a chance for one last peek.

Gael raises an eyebrow. "The rails that the roller coaster cart is attached to? The ones made of industrial steel that keep the carts from flying off into free air? Those rails?"

Cooper blushes a red deeper than his auburn hair and freckles. "Y-yes. Those ones."

"It should be just a few more minutes," someone calls.

I reach for my phone, but Jackie grabs my wrist. "If you *insist* on believing that this is the the only race weekend you'll ever attend, you better spend some time living in the moment! You're giving the Rays plenty of insight."

I itch to jot down the content ideas burgeoning in my head with every passing second, but concede to Jackie's point. I've already posted more than any of the other creators. We were all encouraged to come into the week with a specific focus for our content. I've opted for entry-level Riot knowledge with the aim of bringing new fans to the sport. Gael has a physics background and is diving into the science of race cars. Jackie's opted to focus on the women involved in the series. We met online when I fangirled over her piece highlighting that Riot's safety team is almost entirely women. With a grin, I notice more than half of the creators at the Crush are women as well. Jackie's picked up on it too, and quickly pulls out her camera and pans over the flock of us, finishing with me. I wave and stick my tongue out.

"Given all our hard work," she says, "it's no wonder we're tired of hearing that we only like this sport for the hot drivers." She rolls her eyes and posts the clip to her social stories, her face flushed with adrenaline.

"There's some merit to that, isn't there?" Adam asks. I have no idea what angle he's brought to the program. I haven't seen him record anything, and a quick creep of his socials revealed that he's popular for something to do with sports betting. "There are some girls who only like the sport for the drivers."

Gael's eyes are slits, and Jackie's cut to me. My jaw pops open. A smoking retort builds in my throat like dragon fire. She holds up a hand, not in need of our assistance. "If that's the case, that's a perfectly fine reason to be a fan of something," she starts. "But clearly, it's not true for anyone in this room, right? Not a speck of eye candy to be seen." She looks him up and down.

"Er, right."

Finally, the garage doors heave up and cloud-muted daylight floods in.

Happy to leave Adam's dumb ass behind us, I drag Gael and Jackie into the pit lane after the rest of the group. We're a jumble of appendages and phones trying to see everything at once.

Tarmac stretches off to our right, abuzz with personnel. Out here, the engines' rumbles are joined by the chatter of strategists and the whir of mechanics' tools. More than twenty double-seater Riot cars wait for us in a neat line, matched by color, next to their corresponding team's garages.

"Holy shit," I breathe.

Cooper takes my elbow so I keep pace with the others. My feet move, but my brain is fully occupied processing the smell of fuel and rubber, the whoosh of wind and clank of metal, the flashing color of team liveries as we pass their garages. There's the gray of Cascade Capital, the pale red for Savo, the...

"And uh, here we are." Cooper seems somehow more nervous than usual, practically shaking as he pushes a helmet into my hands.

Dreams coming true do a weird thing to your perception of time, apparently. My brain needs to catch up. My hands shake as I lift the helmet to eye level.

It's black and pink with white detailing.

I stare in horror. There's a fifty percent chance I'm paired with Grant Colby.... The half of Panache's driver pairing that I've *not* spent copious minutes shit-talking online. The helpful voice in my head fizzles. This is the garage on the right. There's a second black and pink car to my left, where Jackie stands. Only one Panache driver is always in the garage on the right.

My toes scrape the pit box, like some deep instinct wants me to run. Cooper steadies me and pries away my phone before stepping away, his arms already full of tripods and miscellaneous gear from the other three in our group. He's going to capture video for us while we're on track. He mutters something that sounds like, "Just know that *I* didn't pick your partner for today."

Oh god. I risk a glance at Jackie. She's standing with—god damnit—Grant Colby, who looks beyond confused because she's cackling at me so hard she's likely to piss her race suit.

It's happening. I thought I'd avoid him easily this week, with the way the media and fans follow him in a near-constant parade. Surely, no other driver has less time or desire to participate in the Crush?

It's okay. I'm okay. I can hoard a few seconds to breathe and compose myself...

"*Sunny Waite!*" That voice again. It's much richer in person, way better than hearing it over a TV's speaker or, on one occasion, imagined breathing harshly in my ear in the dark, dealing out dirty commands and praise. My traitorous head wants to snap his direction at his call, like I'm one of the countless moonstruck, lovesick fans he's hypnotized.

Evan Evans is laughing at me.

At a speed I assure myself is perfectly casual, I look up into the fate I've foolishly tempted. There's a very clear reason for my critique of Evan, and all that reasoning slips from my brain in the moment's chaos. My gaze catches on his name emblazoned across the race suit at his "slutty waist," as my followers call it, which makes his shoulders seem broad, even though he's got the trademark slight race car driver figure. His arms are crossed. The veins on one tanned hand taunt me. My eyes trace up to the prominent muscles of his neck, which all drivers have to protect themselves from the G-forces of high-speed turns.

That goofy grin is way wider than the pictures ever showed, and his eyes are joyful and as green as a patch of four-leaf clover.

Cameras are a menace for hiding how attractive he truly is.

Even when he's laughing at me.

I force a tight smile. This is fine. This is FINE. The Rays will be STOKED at the irony, and let's be real, I'm probably some nobody content creator to him. There's no way he knows what I've said. He's just laughing at the look on my face. He has no reason why it's there.

The most beautiful—and loud—of the Riot Racing idiots, Evan Evans, throws his arms wide and yells for the entire damn race track to witness, "I hear you're not buying what I'm selling!"

CHAPTER THREE

Sunny

"**F**UCK!"

Evan's laughter drowns out my mortified shout. He laughs and laughs, clutching his middle and nearly sliding off the stack of tires he's using as a chair.

My body has crouched of its own accord, my hands melded to my reddening cheeks.

I look away from Evan, away from Jackie. On my other side, Adam gapes, as if worried part of me has somehow been accidentally run over. The mechanics in Evan's garage shrug, faces stoic. They must be used to the chaos Evan tows around like a shadow.

My voice still echoes off the empty grandstands—chased by Evan's guffaws—when a set of pink racing boots stops in front of me.

I blink, and a warm hand takes my elbow and guides me up. "I'm sorry," Evan starts, his striking face far too close for comfort. "I thought I'd make you laugh. I didn't mean to embarrass you." The laughter's gone from his voice, his brows drawn together.

"I–I didn't mean— When I said…" Jesus, this man's smile is blinding. I shake out my shoulders and try again, my voice stern. "I stand by what I've said about you, and I'm okay with saying it *to* you. I just expected to have a bit of warning."

He places a hand over his heart. "All good. I'm giving you a hard time. Everything you've said about me is completely fair. Nice to meet you. I'm Evan."

Completely fair? I mean, I agree, but I'm shocked that he thinks so. I stick out a hand, though he looks like someone who'd default to hugs. It's extra awkward because he's standing so close and has to drop his hand from my shoulder to shake mine.

"Sunny. Really nice to meet you. What I meant on my stream… I don't know you. You're still kind of new, and most other drivers on the circuit I've seen a lot of."

"I can understand that…" he says, rubbing the coating of stubble along his statuesque jaw. "Today's a great day to reconsider, though."

I hold his gaze. Those eyes flash like emeralds in a coal mine.

"We'll see," I say. We stand at that impasse until a Panache team member clears their throat.

"Let's get moving, guys. Earpiece and balaclava are tucked inside the helmets."

Evan grabs his helmet from where it rests on the race car's nose and keeps up a stream of questions as I press my rubbery earpiece in. Even with the two-seater grumbling beside us, he shouts and remains chatty.

"How was your trip here?"

"Not too bad." I shake out the balaclava, searching for the correct opening before I pull the cloth over my head. "Flight was a little delayed, but the views from the window were too good for me to mind."

"Yeah? Nice. When did you get in?"

He's still jabbering as I smush the helmet onto my head. I buckle it snugly beneath my chin and do my best to answer him.

Evan asks something new, but it's gotten louder as cars ahead of us begin to rev and move through the pit lane. "What?" I shout.

"Can I check that for you?" he asks, gesturing to my helmet. The cushioned lining mutes the chaos a little, which allows me to hear my heartbeat banging like a gong. The car is *right there*. I'm about to *ride in it*.

I screamed a profanity down the middle of a crowded pit lane. Not my finest professional moment.

I remember Evan's question and nod, or try to. With gentle fingers, he checks the strap, tugging it tighter, his fingertips warm through the material of the balaclava. He grabs a HANS device and places it around my neck, expertly clipping it to the helmet so if—god forbid—we crash, my head doesn't continue moving at a breakneck speed when my body stops. He steps back, admiring his work.

After a moment, he gestures to the car. "I can help you start getting situated if you're ready."

Somehow, I know I'll both never and always be ready for this. I give a thumbs-up.

I swing my head slowly to take in the full beauty of the car. These two-seaters are older than the single-seaters that the drivers will pilot the rest of the weekend, but they still capture the sharp, threatening beauty of a Riot car. Pointy nose, painstakingly designed front and rear wings to slice through the air as fast as possible, a narrow tub housing the cockpit, and a thick, comforting halo arcing over it to protect drivers in the case of a roll. It's stunning.

Taking Evan's offered hand is the logical thing to do. Getting into these cars can be a feat of acrobatics. Evan has famously face-planted while leaping out at least twice.

I let him help me. It's not like I want to hold his hand. His large, impressively calloused hand... Likely from years of extensive training and weightlifting, and when he allegedly spent summers helping on his aunt's farm growing up...

His palm is warm against mine, and he holds me steady as I swing one leg wide to step gingerly into the cockpit behind the driver's spot. I drop his hand as soon as I find my balance and brace myself on the cockpit's rim to shimmy down and slide my legs into the allocated spaces.

When I look up for confirmation that I've done it properly, Evan's flexing his hand and staring off. I must've squeezed hard. Oops.

I clear my throat and settle in. The idling car sends a pleasant vibration up my spine. The seat's snugness is a comfort, considering how fast we're about to go. I twist to try and grab the seat belts, but the helmet restricts some of my vision and the space is cramped.

Riot staff slowly make their way down the line ahead of us, checking restraints and setting cars on their laps to keep the track from getting crowded.

"Can I keep helping you?"

The giant goofball leans over the cockpit, and I tell myself it's the close quarters and impending rush that have me flustered. "Uh, yeah!"

He seems to understand that I'm having a hard time dealing with the growing noise, because he ceases the twenty questions bit and starts singing to himself as he deftly does up the seat belts.

In the media, Evan's usually shouting, laughing, or sampling an array of terrible accents, but his singing voice is… kind of lovely.

He clips the belts together at my front, then rechecks his work and finally plugs the wire dangling from my earpiece and under my helmet into the radio jack. "Thanks!" I shout.

He gives me that smile again. It really is too sweet to be trusted. "No problem. Everything feel okay?"

I nod, the movement barely perceptible now that I'm strapped in.

"Good." He hands me a pair of black gloves and looks across the pit lane. "We're up soon. They told you we're not going for maximum speed today, yeah? Don't want to mess up anyone's neck by pulling too many G's, but I'll still give you a thrill."

An ecstatic squeak escapes me as he steps back. I watch him pull on a balaclava—Ugh, his hair's gonna be perfectly tousled when he takes it off, whereas my curls are probably already flattened—and then his helmet. It's painted to look like the metallic helmet of a medieval knight riding into a fierce joust, the pink plume on top a tribute to his team's name.

He climbs into the seat ahead of me, his long legs making easy work of the task.

It gives me an amazing, uninhibited view of his ass.

The radio channel buzzes to life and interrupts my admiration.

"Radio check, Ev," a pleasant voice says. I know it—it's Pete Crayley, Evan's main race engineer. Evan made a stipulation when he signed on fully with Panache that Pete would come with him. They've been pals since they were kids.

"Chickity check, *bok bok bok*!"

It takes me a second to realize Evan is imitating the sound of a chicken.

"Always something with you," Pete sighs. "That's a yes, then?"

"Sure is." Evan accepts the steering wheel handed to him. I wish I could watch the process of him clipping it into place up close. The cockpits are so tight that drivers have to get seated without them. From my spot, I can only see a hint of his helmet. "Sunny, this is my best mate and engineer extraordinaire, Pete. Pete, Sunny's my co-pilot today."

"Nice to meet you," I chirp.

"Likewise. Welcome aboard. Sorry you lost whatever raffle they did today and got stuck with this idiot. Feel free to smack him on the back of the helmet at any time."

"That sounds like a safety violation," I muse, flipping the clear visor closed over my eyes.

"Yeah!" Evan adds.

Pete gives a retort, but Evan revs the engine so we can't hear it. I jump, a thrill shooting up my spine as power ricochets through the car around me.

It's our turn with the safety team, and they joke with Evan as they secure his belts and check and tighten mine. "Nice work!" one of them calls to him and pats him on the helmet. The helper finishes the belts that clip between my legs and flashes me an encouraging smile before they all step back.

Oh god, it's happening.

Evan eases the car forward. In my periphery, cars zoom past on the track proper, and somehow, my heart pumps faster.

With a weird turn in my stomach, I realize my legs are on either side of him with no barrier except for our respective race suits. Barring the carbon fiber seat he's sitting in, Evan is basically in my lap. As he tweaks settings and adjusts some sort of lever, his arm brushes against the inside of my leg, firm and confident and—

Keep it together, girl.

I take a deep breath and shift in my seat.

"Any nerves?" Evan asks, his helmet shifting sideways as he turns to try and look at me through the visor. All I can see is the sparkle of his eyes that constantly promise mischief, his well-groomed brows, and the bumpy bridge of his nose, which he must have broken at least once before.

"Nope. This is what I've been most excited for."

"Glad to hear it. Do you want a couple warm-up laps first so you can get acclimated, or do you want me to send it?"

"Are you kidding? Punch it. Drive like it's a race."

His laugh is warm and uninhibited, loud enough that I can hear it through his helmet as well as in my ear. "Copy that, Sunny. Full beans it is."

I roll my eyes but let it slide because that's actually something drivers say... and because it sounds like he's about to make my wildest dreams come true.

We approach the pit exit where a video board blinks red. Pete pops over the radio. "You've been approved by race control. Three other cars on track at the moment. Should get the green light any second now—when they determine there's a good bit of space for you to let it rip."

"Understood," Evan says. His hand grips my thigh, just above the knee, and squeezes once. "This'll be fun, I promise. I've got you."

I want to protest, to tell him I trust him with my physical safety, I just don't like him, or the magnetism of his good looks and charm that he wields without discrimination. I don't get to say it, though, because the light turns green and we're flying.

The tires squeal, and I let out a startled screech. I swear Evan's shoulders shake more than the car's vibrating warrants. He's laughing at me again.

Half the world slows down and the other half speeds up. No research I've done has prepared me for how loud it is in the cockpit once we're going. Wind buffets my head, and I'm pressed into my seat. The world whips by, and once I get my breathing under control, I look around. Seattle's cotton ball sky is beautiful above the blurry gray grandstands.

I'm minutely aware of only a few sensations: the car bucking when Evan shifts gears, wind whistling past my head, and the unnamable, unplaceable feeling of physics happening to me as we hurdle through the world faster than any higher power ever intended.

I have many, *many* questions for Gael when I get out of this car.

Turn one approaches, and Evan slows slightly before whipping us into the more wooded section of the track. I catch my breath and notice Evan's confident movements as he shifts, steers, and brakes. For this first lap, I try to notice everything and commit it to memory because this will likely never happen again.

"All good back there?" Evan's voice is a breathless crackle in my ear.

"So good."

I sink into the bliss of the lap and let Evan drive.

As we fly around the last curve, my driving knowledge catches up with me. Evan couldn't have sent it full beans on our first lap. Not with the tires cold and not if it's his first lap of the day, without giving the track an assessment.

Even if it was a fast one, this was a warm-up lap.

We cross the start finish line, and Evan fully sends it.

CHAPTER FOUR

Sunny

The world is a brilliant blue-green blur. I'm sweating, and screaming, and Pete is patiently citing the status of various aspects of the car. It takes me a minute to realize that my yelling sounds so intense because Evan's shouting along with me, whooping like a drunk college kid, and Pete's talking over us when he can.

Evan slows at another corner. We're at the hairpin so much faster than the first time around, and I have a moment to catch my breath as my brain regains the ability to make sense of what my eyes see. I catch the trees being walloped by our gust of wind and gravel spraying as we fly by. Though the visor shields me from the wind, tears stream down my cheeks.

Evan steadies the car as we fly down the next strip of track, which curves gently. "All good back there?"

"Never fucking better," I gasp. My mouth is dry, my voice an adrenaline-fueled scratch. "This is amazing."

"Tell me about it!" he shouts back as he brakes before the next turn.

The laps fly by too fast, and I can't take it all in. Not the scenery, or the glint of the other cars on the rare occasion the sun peeks through the clouds, and definitely not the glimpses I can catch of Evan working the steering wheel. It's not enough time to stare and make sense of when he glances at his mirrors, or shifts his weight, or tweaks the controls. I've watched plenty of onboard footage, but it doesn't compare to witnessing a racer's skills live.

I'm mesmerized by how the slim bit of the front wing I can see undulates through the churning air when I realize we're nearly finished.

I groan. "This is going too fast!"

"I'm going too fast?" Evan asks, concern in his voice as our speed immediately drops.

"No," I insist. "Our time on the track. I want to stay out forever."

"Hmm." Our speed increases. Evan's voice turns serious. "Pete, I'm sensing an issue with the front right tear-goggle."

Silence. Then, "Why am I not surprised?" Pete sounds like he's speaking with his hands covering his face.

"Should I be worried?" I'm no mechanical expert, but I know the basic issues the cars usually face from my many sleepless nights of deep dives through Riot's engineering videos. I have no idea what a teargoggle is, but each team has some permission to customize their cars, and they often use code names to keep from spilling too much if the other teams are listening in on their radio.

"No, no. No need to worry," Evan assures me.

"Confirmed," Pete says. "Take a few more to work it out. I'll tell race control. Keep us posted." The line pops quietly as he switches channels.

"What's going on?" I demand.

Evan sounds so satisfied when he speaks that I wish there were room to reach forward and strangle him. "I'll tell you when we're done. You okay if we do a couple more laps?"

I put it together a second later. This beautiful idiot. Forget the strangling. In this moment, I could kiss him. "Are you kidding? Let's go!"

Evan takes our extra laps at a flying pace so intense I can't speak or do anything other than relish the adrenaline song in my veins and the track whooshing away beneath us. I never want it to end. I want to fall asleep to the sound of the car buzzing and the tires and track eating at each other, but only if in that soundtrack I can cut out the soft pant of Evan's breath in my ear as he gets caught in the moment, too.

I squeeze my legs together as much as I can in the molded seat and tell myself it'll be okay if I like him for a few more minutes. He can feel it, I'm sure, and he doesn't complain.

Three laps later, we roll back into the pit lane. My body hums like a neon sign, flashing alongside the pink and white of the Panache personnel bustling around us. I feel like I could run a marathon and also maybe fight a shark? Adrenaline is awesome.

Evan holds up a fist over his shoulder.

Several seconds pass—like a too-long pit stop—and I realize he's waiting for me.

My heart in my throat, I reach forward and bump my gloved fist against his.

A flurry of hands descend to free me of the belts while Evan climbs out easily. I catch sight of a small tattoo of a bulb of garlic on his left hand. No one knows its meaning. It's one of the "Elevan" fandom's favorite things to theorize about, besides how good he must be in bed.

It's his hands that hover as I climb from my seat. He steps back when I hop from the cockpit and mercifully stick my landing. But the feeling of solid, unmoving pavement beneath my feet has been made alien by ten minutes in a rocket ship, and I keel to the side.

Evan's there in an instant. I throw my arms around him, and the bastard goes with my momentum, seizing the opportunity to lift and twirl me in an inelegant circle. He laughs like a maniac the entire time.

When he sets me back on my feet, I'm no less dizzy, and my traitorous body instantly misses the firmness of his chest against mine. But then he trips and nearly takes us both to the ground, and it's me who keeps us upright.

It's the most chaotic thirty seconds of my life.

By the time we both get our feet firmly beneath us, I'm sputtering. "Don't you ever stop moving? Y-you—" I struggle to catch my breath. "You're like a... a... A BABY GIRAFFE!"

My outburst sends Evan reeling, and he's fully on the ground cackling at my dismay. Through one strained gasp, he cries, "A giraffe?"

I unclip the HANS device on either side, tug off my helmet and shove the accoutrement inside before handing it off to nervous intern Cooper, who's returned with my phone and is thankfully not capturing this moment. I run my fingers through my hair, my fingertips going cold in the cool air, away from the heat of the car. "Your limbs are like a thousand feet long, and it's like you've never used them before. You're gonna concuss someone, bonking them with those things on their heads, the nubby antler things..."

Still cackling, and hair perfectly tousled as I predicted, Evan climbs to his feet, laughing and fucking arguing with me. "I don't think they're antlers. Moose have antlers, deer have antlers..."

"You know what I mean!" My chest heaves as I mutter thanks to Cooper. "And what the hell is a teargoggle?"

"Do you need a photo for socials?" Evan ducks his chin toward my phone and slings an arm around my shoulders. There's a suggestion in the gesture, a gentle tug, an invitation I'm allowed to refuse.

And fuck, I don't want to.

I allow him to pull me against his side. It's not too forward or familiar. It just feels like... we could be friends. He's warm, probably because he seems to never stop moving for long, and smells amazing—the bastard. I lift my phone, take in our reflection, picturesque in the muted morning light, the rush of the racetrack flushing our faces. I smile and snap one selfie, Evan's megawatt grin taking up most of the frame. As I go to take another, he turns so he can whisper in my ear, "A 'teargoggle problem' is the made-up mechanical issue I cite when I don't want to head back into the garage. When I can't stand to get off the track quite yet."

I step aside to check the photo. I can't bear to be this close to him for another second. I had a suspicion that the issue Evan cited was made up, but to know that he did it so we could have more time out there? "In that case… thank you." I gesture to the car. "Thank you for this. It was a dream come true, really."

Scientists need to study how his smile can always go just a little bit wider. "You're very welcome, Sunny." He rubs the back of his well-muscled neck. "So… are you buying what I'm selling now?"

I bite my lip. It's worse than I feared. He's not only charming, he's potentially actually very nice. I'm firmly in the danger zone here. I know he probably talks to everyone like this, but that tilt to his smile seems like he thinks I'm special, and I can't fall for it. I like to flirt, too, but it can't go a single step further. I'm not looking to get wrecked again anytime soon, not by a guy swamped by a new city of adoring fans every other weekend. I need space, or I'll soon be at risk of becoming infatuated.

I cock my head. "After one drive? I've only known you for half an hour, most of which we weren't doing much talking."

He looks shocked, and I give a smirk as I turn to walk away, hoping my hips look as good as they feel in this racing suit.

A gentle hand catches my elbow, and I spin only to get sucked into those eyes again. "How about an interview?"

"What?"

"We can do an interview. For your socials—only yours. An exclusive. Ask me whatever you like. Get to know why I am how I am."

I study him for a long moment. "Why do you care so much?" For my singular skeptical attitude, he's got a thousand other ride-or-die fans in his corner. My blog and video channel don't scratch the surface of his depths of fans and admirers. Hell, most of my followers are in love with him, no matter what I say.

His lips tighten, his smile gone, but he doesn't answer me.

An exclusive interview with a Riot Racer? I'd be stupid to turn down the opportunity. I snap into business mode. This is a once-in-a-lifetime chance for me and the people who get their motorsport news from my channel. Whatever his motives, he found my catnip right away.

"When?" I demand. "Our schedules are both packed this week."

"What's your first commitment tomorrow?"

I wrack my brain. "I have to be on the shuttle from the hotel at 10:30."

He nods. "I can make that work. How about before? Is there somewhere at the hotel we can do it?"

"I'll find us somewhere."

He digs in his pocket and pulls out his phone, handing it over. "I'll text you in the morning."

I tap out my digits, shaking my head that this is really my life. There's a huge chance my number will get lost amidst the hundreds he has, and he'll forget about this. It'll make a good story, though. I've got plenty to share from the ride-along, and I can tell my community what it feels like inside a race car. That's what matters.

The small crowd around us grows. Cooper returns with Jackie, Gael, and Adam in tow and is shifting from foot to foot, clearly anxious to usher us to our next commitment and away from the race-focused work that needs to happen now that the fun is over. Engineers and mechanics come for Evan with tablets spiderwebbed with bright telemetry lines and other data.

I let myself have one last wistful look at the car—and its driver—before turning to leave.

"I'll see you tomorrow!" Evan calls. "Do you like coffee?"

I spin, walking backward as I call back. "Who doesn't like coffee?"

When I turn around, I'm smiling way too big for the occasion, and I force myself not to look back.

CHAPTER FIVE

Sunny

"Even though some of the teams' cars are generally faster than others, and with a wide variety of experience and expertise throughout the driver lineup, plus changing conditions for every race, one of the most exciting things about the Riot Racing series is that anything can happen. If an accident occurs up front at the start of the race, that opens up a lot of possibilities for the drivers in the back. If there's one slip-up during qualifying, the driver who's been on pole for four races in a row might be starting from the middle and have to fight forward if they want to have a good result. You never know what's going to happen in a Riot race, and it's awesome."

I'm up well before my alarm, and even though the sun's not yet peeking through the curtains, my face is flushed in the glow of a ring light.

I fire off the post and cross it off my list. On the homepage of my main social account, a red bubble shows that

I've got hundreds of likes and comments that came in overnight. I know which post they're from, and I click over to my selfie beside Evan with a sigh. Macaron91 leads the charge with complimentary comments on my other posts from the week, but that doesn't compare to the swarm of interactions on my photo with Evan.

An unfamiliar feeling of overwhelm swamps me as I flick through the comments, tapping the heart beside them but not answering any...

Until I stumble upon one.

```
But what does he smell like??
```

Hm. If I don't reply to some of these, the algorithm will punish me. But how to maintain my skepticism of Evan without coming off like a jerk now that I know he sees my content? After a moment, I smirk, and my fingers fly across the keyboard.

```
Mangoes.
```

There. Cool, calm, and collected. See how they like that. Nothing like a chaotic breadcrumb to start the day. Try as I might, I can't always be above clickbait.

I slump into the stiff hotel desk chair and rub my eyes. I should get moving if I want to have a few minutes to myself before the interview with Evan, though I'm fairly certain he'll bail.

I'm somehow exhausted and exhilarated simultaneously. Between the thrill of the ride-along and the long day of press and presentations that followed, my head and heart are full.

The buzz of my phone interrupts my reverie.

> What's your coffee order?

I know the number is Evan's because he's signed the message off with "#11" and pink and black hearts.

Wow. He's really going to show up. It seems like he's got a smidge of decency.

I type back a response and include directions to one of the smaller rooms in the hotel's conference center that I reserved last night.

Ten minutes of hair wrestling and two spritzes of perfume later, I'm scowling at my suitcase. The fuck does one wear to an impromptu interview with a pro athlete?

A deeply charming, sexy as hell, incredibly unnerving pro athlete.

I settle for not overthinking it and commit to a skirt and one of my own branded "beautiful idiots" t-shirts, plus a rain jacket over my arm.

I wring my hands. I've done a few interviews over the last year and I'm getting the hang of it, but Evan is a huge star, and it's very kind of him to offer me this opportunity. I want to make the most of it.

With a last glance in the mirror, I grab my laptop and head to the meeting room.

The conference center floor is quiet this early, especially with this hotel being booked for folks related to the race and all their business happening at the track. I give myself three minutes of wiggle room so there's time for my nerves to spike and come back down.

The meeting room has a retractable screen and a mini fridge, as well as a conference table that seats eight, but it's the smallest that was available.

I head to the windows overlooking the water and twine my hands behind my back, shifting my weight from one foot to the other.

Evan's humming precedes his arrival. It's off-key and *loud.*

He bursts into the room and sings me the last few words of the song—incorrectly, but with lots of passion and gooey eyes—and sets a paper bag on the table.

"Goooood morning, sunshine!" He's like a farm animal on the first day of spring, all frolicky and flailing limbs. He's somehow resplendent in a gray hoodie and jeans, his feet clad in custom pink and white sneakers. "Woah. I'm underdressed," he says.

I can't help but smile at him. *Dangerous, dangerous, dangerous*, I remind myself.

I flap my hands, fighting a blush. "You're fine. I wanted to be ready to head right to the track." I step toward him, and he offers a hug before I have time to extend a hand. His gentle squeeze feels nice and the whiff of mango I caught yesterday is back.

"Miraculously, I didn't spill," he says as he hands me my coffee. "So this should still be hot."

Our fingers definitely touch, drawing embarrassing goosebumps over my body. After my last boyfriend skewered my heart on a pike, the year since full of mistrust and distaste has left me a little, *ahem,* touch-starved.

I rub my arms, murmur my thanks and gesture to the chairs I've pulled away from the table to face each other. He slides the bag toward me as I take a seat, smile never faltering.

"This coffee place has the best croissants. Not sure how you feel about them..." he starts. "So, I grabbed options."

I peek inside the bag, which smells almost as heavenly as he does. "There are six pastries in here."

Evan's grin turns sheepish.

"Well," I say, snagging a croissant. "The hotel food isn't bad, but the pastry selection is a bit..."

"Sad?" Evan offers.

I nod fervently, mouth full of buttery bliss.

He's moving again, arms swinging as he gets going. "I'm lucky to have traveled all over, and at every hotel breakfast, I give the croissants a chance, but..." He grimaces.

"Nothing dampens a morning like a sad croissant."

"Exactly." I'm learning that every conversation with him feels like a game, every statement a volley of silly unseriousness. It's unnerving, and reminds me why we're here.

"So," I start, pulling my laptop close, "I'm going to record our conversation, if that's okay. It lets me focus on what you're saying rather than taking notes."

Of course, my external microphone is being spotty, so I unplug it, then stick it back in and reopen the program. This takes three seconds, which seems to be about the maximum amount of time Evan can go without talking.

"Have you recovered from yesterday?"

I quirk an eyebrow at him, tinkering with the settings so I'm sure the mic is picking us up.

"Not meeting me. Being in a racecar for the first time."

"Oh my god." Just mentioning it brings all the sensations back. The rush of air, the noise, not having a clue where my breath went. "It was... unlike anything else. I'll never forget it."

"That's amazing." Again, his smile goes wider. "I heard all the people in the Creator Crush get to do a digital segment at the end of the week. That's huge. What are you going to cover?"

I blow a misbehaving curl out of my eyes. "I'm not sure yet. I prepared a few topics to pick from."

"Ooh, like what—"

I accidentally interrupt him because I've got the recording all fixed, and we do an awkward fumble of determining who should speak next.

"This is your interview," Evan insists. "Go ahead."

I take a centering breath and eye my journal, where I've scribbled a few questions. I like to be concise with my interviews and guide and intrigue my guests to share deeply.

Before I can choose how to begin, he speaks. I've noticed this a few times now. Like a question or comment explodes out of his beautiful mouth, whether he wants it to or not. "Can you explain to me what you mean exactly when you say you're not buying what I'm selling?"

I rock back in my seat. It's a perfectly fair question, and it could start us in the right direction for how I want this interview to go if I want to learn more than what all other interviewers have gotten out of him. It really is an interesting angle. His question alone could be a great teaser on socials.

"I'm certainly not the first interviewer—" I stumble over my words. Fuck, something to edit out already. "I mean, fan—er, creator—to talk about your lack of stellar performances recently. Don't get me wrong, all drivers talk a big game, but given a streak of race finishes that are not on par with what you're capable of... You don't seem worried."

Evan listens, head cocked, fingers laced over one knee.

"My impression of you is that you always have a joke, or a charming, deflecting remark. You know exactly how magnetic your energy is, how handsome you are—"

"You think I'm handsome?"

I roll my eyes. "You know you're handsome."

Evan takes a sip of his own coffee, the movement of his lips highly distracting. "That's not what I asked, but I interrupted you. I'm sorry. Please, continue."

His manners trip me up. What was my thesis again? I can't come right out and say, *I've had boyfriends like you and every one has come out and fucked me right over the minute I fall in love.* Douchey Adam would have a blast with my muddled thought process. *Focus on the racing*, my last functioning brain cell commands.

"Uh—" I flounder. "Basically, I guess I think everyone adores you, but I don't fall into that camp so easily because

I don't know you even a little bit. You have a right to privacy, of course, but I'm not gonna fangirl over you and cut you slack because you're charming and know how to wield your smile. RJ is clever. Stevie's fearless." I tick off other Riot racers on my fingers. "Hendrix is a young diamond in the rough. You…" I risk a look into those eyes again and grip the table so I don't get lost in them. "I can't find the truth, the link, between who you are and how you race."

I bite off the end of the sentence. The one that says, *it makes me feel like I can't trust you.*

I drown my silence with another long drink of honestly terrific coffee as Evan considers. His smile is smaller, but not entirely gone. He rubs the trademark scruff growing on his chin.

Seriously, it's trademarked. There are scarves and blankets printed with a repeating design of it in his merch store.

"That's a fair assessment, and an honest one," he says finally. "I guess to start, I appreciate you thinking about it that hard. I know some fans would take the time to get to know me if we had the chance, but, yeah, most people are charmed by me. Which I won't pretend not to like, but…"

He stares out the window, mulling. I wait. This is the chance for the juicy stuff.

"The facade is a defense mechanism. If I'm never serious, no one will know when I'm disappointed."

I wait, hoping he'll continue.

"The goofy, flirty guy is who I am, but magnified a bit. That persona keeps me safe, usually, from tough journalism questions. Riot is a great league, but sports and fame in general are cutthroat, and I decided young..."

I've leaned forward. My elbows rest on my knees.

Evan mirrors my pose. His throat bobs. "Amplifying my likable qualities is how I protect the most vulnerable parts of me. Now that you've pointed it out, I realize maybe there isn't a connection between who I present to the paddock and who I am in the cockpit, because that guy, the one speeding down the track at two hundred miles per hour, is really vulnerable. Have you ever seen an athlete lose it on a live broadcast? Less than an hour and it's all over the internet. All over the world. Nah, I save my breakdowns for the privacy of home."

"You can't be perfect all the time, or expect everybody to like you."

"I don't want everybody to like me."

Somehow this chat has veered toward *too* vulnerable.

"But the downside is that makes some people think you're entirely full of shit."

Evan laughs but doesn't lean back. If anything, he leans closer, unleashing the full power of that damn puppy dog stare. "Sunny, I *am* full of shit, but I like to think it's in a way that doesn't hurt anybody."

"Hm… I suppose I see your logic there."

He squints at me. "Does that mean I'll be seeing you in number eleven merch on race day? Should I have some sent to your room?"

I snicker, but don't break his stare, or give in so easily. I have to admit that I'm beginning to see why people like him. He's not misleading me with flirting or trying to redirect my questions. It's just how his brain works. What could turn me into a fan of his?

I tilt my head and make him wait. "Tell me three true, unfiltered things about yourself, and I'll consider it. No catchphrases, no jokes."

There's a glint in his eye, and he perks up, rising to my challenge. "You're a great interviewer, you know. That doesn't count as one of the three, by the way." His face screws up as he thinks, and he pats a restless beat on his knees. "Okay. I have them."

He ticks them off on his long fingers, and my heart's pounding far too hard for the nature of our meeting. We really don't need to be sitting this close.

"I really do think my name is as stupid as everyone else does, but I love it, truly, because my mom picked it."

He extends a second finger, eyes going from roaming the room to locking back on mine. He's talking slower now, which I didn't know he was capable of. I've gotten to him, the heart of him, and he's picking his words carefully.

"Number two: The only part of this job that I detest is that it doesn't allow me to have a pet. I'd really love to get a cat. And..."

His eyes dart to the floor for a second as he huffs a laugh to himself. His entire body tenses for a moment, like a diver deciding it's time to jump off the board. He licks his lips. The movement has warmth flooding my stomach, and lower.

"And... I think you're incredibly smart and sexy, and I've pictured fucking you over this table at least three different times since I walked into the room."

I swear my heart stops. My mouth forms an O, and I'm instantly, impossibly wet.

My psyche scoffs. *Look at the man.* Listen *to what he just said!*

All my reservations about him have left the fucking building, and instead, my brain gremlins bite at this most recent reveal like a dog with a bone.

He's sweet. And funny. And gorgeous.

And he wants to fuck me.

As I compute, Evan draws back, stammering. "If that was out of line, I'm sorry, I completely misread—"

"I have a condom," I blurt.

The omission freezes us both.

I barge on, desperate to fill the silence. "I do. In my purse, always. That, ibuprofen, Band-aids, a mini bottle of sunscreen, and a granola bar. I like to be prepared. You never know—"

Evan erupts from his seat. He tugs me from mine and interrupts my rambling with a searing kiss.

Oh, *god*, his mouth.

Turns out, I have all his smiling to thank, I think, because the man's finesse with those muscles is divine. He kisses firmly but not forceful, his tongue gently questing along mine, seeking what I want and what I like. His arms are strong around me, one banded across my back, the other wound upward so his hand is twined in my hair.

The sense of steadiness allows me to melt into him. My hands trace his back, following the lines of honed muscle. They twitch with a flash of hesitation, then I plunge them into his hair.

Gently, I scrape my nails along his scalp. He moans and enjoys it for a moment before disentangling us. He shuts the door with a snap, then turns to eye me up and down.

All resemblances to a cute, cuddly animal are gone. He's more reminiscent of a predator…

And he's sizing me up.

"Oh, Sunny," he growls. "Now you've done it."

That bite in his tone. I've craved it for a long time, but no partner has ever given it to me, even when I beg.

"You started it," I accuse, narrowing my eyes, which seems to rile him up more. He's bouncing on his toes as he steps back to me and pulls me flush against him. As I slide my tongue into his mouth, he shifts both hands down to cup my ass. I moan low in my throat and sink my hands back into his hair, his mango-and-man scent a cloud around me.

My head starts to spin as we explore each other. I tug his shirt off, taking a moment to ogle until he does the same with mine.

I half-expect my boldness to fizzle, but I know what I want and I know what to do. I want a hot, frenzied quickie with Evan Evans. An experience to cherish. A story to take home.

I cup his cock through his jeans, thrilled at the rock hardness that greets me. Evan groans and plants kisses all across the skin exposed above my bra.

Anticipation sparks through me, chased by building pleasure. The satisfactory feel of roaming hands that know what they're looking for brands giddy sensations all over my body.

Evan tugs my bra, popping the cups down so my breasts are exposed. He looks at them like they're an offering of gold.

He takes one in his mouth and the other in his hand. Twin pleasures from his tongue and fingertips send my head rolling back. My focus is split—enjoying the pleasure and fighting to remain quiet.

Evan gives me a reprieve from the sharp pleasure, turning to lazy licks and squeezes. One of his arms has my hips locked firmly against his. I squirm against the layers of clothing that separate us. I wrap one leg around him to improve my angle, and he pulls back to catch my calf.

Eyes fixated on my face, then moving down my entire body—my heaving chest, my bunched skirt, my pale leg wrapped around him. He traces a finger down to my ankle and wraps the lace of my sneaker around his finger.

"I like these," he murmurs.

I take the moment to catch my breath. "Thanks."

He traces the skin there back up behind my knee and to my thigh, which he squeezes. God, his hands cover so much of me. My breath catches and I brace my hands on the table as his fingers find the hem of my panties. His expression as he looks up to check in with me is so full of care it's devastating. I nod.

He shimmies them down, and as I brace a hand on his shoulder to step out, he guides me, leaning me back to rest on the table.

The fingers of his other hand trace over my hip and slip beneath my skirt. He draws his fingers over my pussy, growling his appreciation at the wetness he finds there.

"Oh, hell yeah," he huffs.

I tug his hair, making him look at me. "No jokes or taglines, please."

He glides up my body, trailing kisses, and slides two fingers into me. His eyes are locked on mine as he slips in, looking so pleased with my reaction of a stifled moan. "As the lady wishes," he says, and takes my mouth before I can respond.

Evan works his fingers gently at first, then settles into firm, steady pumps as I cling to him. He kisses my neck, my throat, my collarbone.

My pussy starts to clench, and Evan mutters into my skin. "Fuck, you're amazing."

My breath catches. "Almost... *Yes!* Right there, faster."

With his palm rubbing my clit, paired with the steady pulse of his calloused fingertips against my G-spot, an orgasm rockets through me, bowing my back. Evan's scruff is delightfully rough against my cheek. He kneads my ass through my orgasm, not withdrawing his fingers until my throbbing subsides.

"Holy shit," I stammer. He kisses me again before pulling back to wink at me.

"Condom?" he asks quietly, giving my sides a squeeze.

"Right," I manage, breathless.

Definitely on purpose, I flip onto my stomach, bend over the table and snag my purse, fishing a condom from the inside pocket.

With a wicked smirk, I glance over my shoulder, staring through my lashes as I hold up the silver wrapper.

The sound of him unbuttoning his jeans sets my legs quivering, and I spread them wide, bracing on my forearms as he unrolls the condom over his length. I mourn the fact that I don't get a good look at his cock, but it'll be fun to fill in the memory with my imagination later. Evan smooths a hand over my shoulders, my lower back, my ass. "Girl, you are a work of fucking art."

Fire tears across my face, and as much as I love to be worshiped out loud... "We're on limited time here, giraffe."

I glance back and meet his look of warm, wicked promise. He bites his lip.

"Right." His wide palm recenters on my back and presses, sending my torso flat to the table. I wriggle, but Evan holds me there easily. The length of his cock presses against my pussy as he covers my body with his. I bite back a whimper. His free hand traces a lock of my hair away from my cheek, and he speaks low in my ear. "Are you ready? Do you want me to fuck you, Sunny?"

The pressure of him surrounds me, more solid than the table my nipples chafe against, sparking pain edged with pleasure. His face blocks the gray morning light from the window; his eyes demand an answer—any answer. My body's never felt so constricted... or so safe. It's a sensation I don't know what to do with.

But I know what I want.

"Please," I huff. I demand.

Evan gives me the best sloppy kiss we can manage in this configuration, his tongue mirroring the glide as he sets his cock at my entrance and pushes inside me.

He gives me slow, short thrusts to start. I breathe my contentment, my noises misting the table's surface. He doesn't make me wait long before he straightens, grabs my hips, and slides in fully. He pauses as I process the delicious fullness of his cock deep inside me. I affirm I'm good with a contented "mmmmm."

"Yeah?" he asks.

"Fuck yeah."

With that, he holds me steady and starts pumping, and we're both quickly lost in the rhythm. Pleasure coils in my stomach and between my legs, where Evan brushes my clit in time to his thrusts. I have to clench my teeth to keep quiet.

Out of nowhere, Evan spanks me, and a delicious lick of pain races up my backside. I yelp and cover my mouth.

We both chuckle at my reaction. Our bodies' shaking ratchets the pleasure higher. Evan smooths a palm over my smarting skin. "So, no spanking right now, then."

"Probably a good idea," I gasp, and lose the rest of my thought as my orgasm strikes, bliss spiraling out from the intersection of where he's stroking my clit and pumping into me.

It drives him wild, and his thrusts grow in fervor as he follows me into orgasm, the spasms of his cock drawing out my own ecstasy as my pussy wrings him dry.

My brain goes blank beyond my endorphins and his warmth behind me as Evan snags his hoodie and draws it under my head as a makeshift pillow. He bends over me as he pulls out, holding me and kissing the back of my neck. I tangle one of my arms with his and squeeze his hand.

We stay like that for a moment before he straightens and helps me upright, and we start to reset ourselves.

I thought I'd been unnerved by Evan's smile before, but the one he unleashes on me now is like the fucking sun. It carves dimples into his cheeks that make my heart twitch, so I shift focus to straightening my skirt. Evan discards the condom deep in the corner wastebasket, and his smartwatch elicits a chime. He checks it with a frown, scrubbing a hand through his hair.

I give him a cheerful smile, though he looks distraught. "What?"

"I have to go." His tone is adorably forlorn. Then, I can practically see a thought click in his brain, ping-ponging around and drawing his brows together. "Shoot, did you get enough for your interview?"

My answering laugh is tinged with hysteria. "Yes. I won't be writing about..." I rap the table with my knuckles and cringe at myself. "...this. But, yes, thanks for talking with me, and opening up. I mean it."

My phone pings now, and I can practically feel Cooper's anxiety at having to send a first reminder text asking where I am. I fire off reassurances and notice Evan has made no move to leave, still watching me with a dazed look on his face. "We really need to go," I insist.

He literally shakes himself, and, in a flurry, steps close, cupping my elbows. He plants a slow, chaste kiss on my lips.

My heart's heaving, and that's unacceptable, so I pinch my eyes closed.

Evan finally steps back. "I knew it," he says quietly, voice laced with triumph.

His watch squawks, and the impatient face of a Panache staffer appears there, a video call he should definitely answer.

I can't be in his gravitational field another second. He's got my body trapped, and I'll be damned if he captures my feelings, too. "*Now,* giraffe," I mutter and grab his arms, encouraging him to spin.

He complies with a laugh as I firmly shove with both hands against his glorious back. He snags the door frame with one hand, giving me a final look. "See you later, Sunny!"

He leaves as he came, this time singing somehow louder. "Unlikely!" I yell after him, but I doubt he hears.

As his voice fades, I sag into a chair.

My vision snags on my computer, whose screen is glowing gently at the corner of the table.

Our whole encounter was recorded.

I swallow a string of curses as another text from Cooper lands. Rubbing my forehead, I haul myself from the chair, push it in, and check there's no more evidence of our dalliance. I kill the lights, allow myself one lingering glance, and shut the door behind me.

It's only as I'm in the elevator down to the lobby, rubbing a finger over my lips where Evan's scruff has chafed them, that I mumble, "Knew *what?*"

CHAPTER SIX

Evan

"You're going to fall."

At least, I think that's what Pete says. I'm not paying attention.

I've got my phone out, which isn't a best practice when you're on a track run, but I just remembered that I saw and promptly forgot about a social notification when I woke up. Sunny tagged me in a photo before our interview—that interview, wow—and I need her to know I saw it.

"You're going to fall, have a scab on that ugly mug of yours that shows up on TV, and then we're both gonna get texts from your aunt."

"Uh," I start. There it is. My heart leaps seeing the photo of us. Sunny's dark curls all tousled after the hot laps I took her on. The syllable fades to nothing as I share it to my account and search for a giraffe sticker to accompany it. Perfect.

"You are the world's worst multitasker. I don't know why you're risking it." Pete dabs sweat from his face with the sleeve of his Panache tech shirt. Mirrored sporty sunglasses protect his eyes, and a durag is tied around his close-cropped curls.

"C'mon, I'm a high-performance athlete. I'm perfectly—" My protest is in vain because I trip and go rolling across the tarmac.

The world eventually stills and my elbow smarts, but otherwise, I think I escaped bodily harm.

June blocks out the light, staring down at me with her muscled arms crossed. "Seriously, man? With only one turn left."

She and Pete help me up. The moody gray sky blankets the whole course, and while some people might find it grim, it makes me feel at home. There's comfort in the pokey tops of pine trees along the mountainous horizon and the occasional whiff of salt water.

The Benji drivers hoot and poke fun at me as they whizz by, electing to tour the race track for any sticking points from their bicycles.

Pretty much everyone else is walking or biking, but we're jogging, because June said so.

My trainer is no-nonsense and muscled all over, with steel gray hair and nerves to match. She wrangles me and Pete like her own sons and is a master at dealing with my wandering attention.

She brushes a stray piece of gravel from her palm and points, guiding us back into a brisk jog around the track's banked final corner. "I don't know why you bother warning him. He's gotta learn for himself."

It doesn't bother me when they talk around me. I'm cloud-headed on my best days, and I wouldn't have a successful racing career without a solid team supporting me.

"Sorry, guys. Pete, what's the deal with this corner?" It's a long one, the curbs slightly raised and striped red and white. I raced here a few times in other series, but it's been years.

He sniffs, barely breaking a sweat. "Do you really want to know what the data says, or are you too busy making heart eyes at your phone?"

I flip to run backwards in front of him, determined to show I'm coordinated when I try. "Aw, come on, buddy. Don't be like that. You know you love me." I jab at his ribs in rebuttal. He swipes and secures me in a headlock.

"You're such a stubborn doofus," he growls, drawing us up short.

I smack at his arms. "A doofus who appreciates you very much. A doofus who, despite how he comes across, is desperate for your insight on our first visit to this track with Riot."

"Admit you're a great pain in the ass."

"I have a *great* ass."

"Boys!" June snaps.

Pete flips me the bird as he crouches to feel the track. I follow suit, pressing my palms into the texture to try and determine how it'll grip my tires.

Properly cowed, we get back to jogging.

Pete flattens his hand and glides it through the air, mirroring the turn we're nearly out of. "On turns similar to this one, you lift too much. You need to carry more speed through here."

"Enough speed to crash, hopefully." Dean, a driver from Cascade Capital with a weaselly demeanor and a real mean streak on track, says from where he's huddled with his team at the turn's apex.

We ignore him. He's a pain in everyone's ass, and unfortunately, decently quick in some races.

"Let's sprint to the finish," June says, and I hop to obey. As I churn into my fastest clip of a run, I commit what Pete's said about the last corner to memory, adding it to my mental run plan for practice, qualifying, and Sunday's race. As my lungs catch fire and my breath comes hard, though, my mind shifts to Sunny.

She's so fun to talk to. More clever than I could ever hope to be. And even prettier in real life. My phone's screen never showed me the way sunlight bounces off of her curly brown hair, or the small scar on her forehead that tints paler than the rest of her skin when she raises one eyebrow. Her smile is dazzling, the reward of it amped up because you have to earn it, and *I* did. She's always warm on her streams, but they must feel safe for her, because I've noticed that in person, you have to prove your mettle before her face opens like a flower on a bright spring day.

And the way she came around my cock? I think the word I want is *sublime*, but I'd have to double-check the definition. Sunny would be able to confirm it means what I think it means, I'm sure.

I want to know everything about her. What's her family like? Does she have a pet? What's her favorite food? Favorite color? Favorite animal? God, I hope it's giraffes.

I shake my head and push harder, pump my arms faster. Sprinting with a hard-on everyone can see? It happens. Still, not ideal.

She gave me a shot. That's the part I can't believe. I'm smiling like an idiot, but everyone in the paddock is used to that. As I approach the painted line that marks where the race starts and finishes, I try to keep an eye on the track's grading. Then, the condition of the first couple of starting boxes outlined in paint on the asphalt—where I hope to start the race from—but my mind keeps circling back to the fact that I'm pretty sure Sunny would like me if she got to know me.

And at best, maybe love me a little.

I'm ten-thousand percent getting ahead of myself, but I have this gut feeling about Sunny and me.

I cross the finish line with a final gasp and slow my steps. I shake out my legs before resting my hands on my knees.

Pete and June finish not far behind me. June eyes her watch. "Really good stuff, there. Do a thorough stretch and you can be done for the day, okay?"

I wave as she leaves.

Pete pants beside me, and we stretch out our aches and cramps as we eye the growing bustle of the track. Race week technically doesn't start till tomorrow, but there are lots of extra festivities for the first race of the season, and teams want to get in early to try and catch any sort of mechanical gremlins that might be lurking in the cars.

"You can break that habit in the faster corners, Ev. I know you can," Pete says finally.

I nod. Making the same mistake cost me in a few races last season. I can't afford to make it a habit that carries into this season, too. My contract is up this year, and there are a bunch of Panache bigwigs around this weekend who would be all too happy to call for a new driver if they think they could perform better than me.

My mouth has been in the unfamiliar shape of a frown for five whole seconds, but I feel it naturally start to tilt back up.

"I've got a good feeling about this weekend, Pete. My curse is ending."

He claps my shoulder and guides me toward the track wall, where we dumped our stuff before starting our run. He tosses me a towel and I hand over a water bottle, a dance we've perfected over the years. "I trust your instincts, but let's maybe execute the turn properly in practice a few times before you start shouting that in the media pen, okay?"

I'm doing a little dance as I drink. "You bet, Petey Bird." Doling out nonsense nicknames is one of my favorite things.

He slings a drawstring pack around his shoulders. "How was your interview this morning? Did Sunny throw a latte in your face because you annoy her so much?" He's heard me talk about her for months.

I stretch my arms high, holding my wrists to keep from jumping and pumping a fist in the air. I'm fine with attention, but that doesn't mean Sunny is. "Quite the opposite, actually. I think it's fair to say I'm winning her over. Though..." My forehead crinkles as I realize something. "She looked amazing this morning. She always does, but, she was wearing this nice skirt and... I wore this." I gesture to my t-shirt. "Not really befitting of our first date."

Pete snorts. "Important question—did Sunny know it was your 'first date'?" He kills me with the quote fingers.

"Ugh, you're right." I'm a dumbass. I made the first steps. Sunny's interested, and now she deserves my full effort to woo a woman. I fire off a text to her after taking a few moments to delete and reword and make sure it's absolutely perfect. That done, I grab my scooter from where it leans on the wall, as well as the helmet draped over the handlebars.

Pete watches, chewing his lip. He's got an engineering meeting, and he's always more concerned with being on time than I am, so it's weird that he's stalling. "Please know that what I'm about to say is a dispassionate, nonjudgmental statement," he says finally.

"Oh, boy."

He rubs his arm. "You want her so bad you're at risk of looking stupid in front of this entire paddock. Just... be careful."

As I consider what he's said, I plop on my moose helmet, the plastic antlers nearly poking him in the eye as I wiggle it to fit and fasten the snap.

It was a gift from a fan after I biffed it off one of the paddock scooters last year, landing myself in the med center with a head injury that needed several stitches and a badly bruised knee. I like it so much that I have a replica covered in disco tiles hanging from the ceiling in my living room.

"Good thing I've never had a problem with looking stupid."

I hop on the scooter and swerve to face the direction of our hospitality suite. I zoom off, feeling light and fast as a hummingbird and a little bit like one has made a home in my heart.

CHAPTER SEVEN

Sunny

My eyes nearly pop out of my head when my phone buzzes and I see the name, and more so, the message.

> Can I cook you dinner tonight?

I flip the phone over on the table with a decisive *slam!*

"That isn't how this is supposed to work," I mutter, trying to recollect my attention for what I was working on before Evan threw a wrench into my day.

The morning is bright and cheery, the air crisp. Abuzz already but not crushingly busy. I'm beyond content to sit at one of the high-top tables situated in the seating areas scattered along the outdoor space, do some work, and listen to the roar of engines and whine of brakes as Riot's support series of younger drivers gets their practice underway.

The paddock is the central hub of off-track action at any race weekend. I scribble myself a reminder to make a post about it because motorsports newbies might not have heard the word before. Maybe Gael or Jackie will be willing to film me so I can have my hands free and a better shot than with my tripod. I jot down some quick bullets, editing until I've got what I think are the true basics of the concept, what a new fan would need to know.

If the track is where the actual racing occurs, and the various grandstands are where fans watch live, the paddock is where Riot and all the racing teams work to make the whole spectacle happen. At most tracks, the paddock is an open area directly adjacent to the garages, giving the teams easy access. Come race weekend, the sprawl fills with elaborate motorhomes that expand and connect to create lavish hospitality centers for each team, the tire providers, Riot's staff, and more. They house the drivers' prep rooms, offices for personnel, as well as catering for the myriad team members hustling all weekend. Some lucky fans are able to gain access through special ticket purchases or offers from teams, and it's the best chance to see the drivers and other key players up close.

My lips purse as I read the lines over to be sure I'm happy with them. With a relieved sigh, I set down my pen and scrub my face.

I'm tucked close to the entrance gates where a coffee truck's been set up. There are a few other sleepy media reps and photographers milling around, ready to report if any big names show up. One side of the main thoroughfare is edged by the rear entrances of the garages, the other by massive hospitality suites. Riot has its own glistening red headquarters that towers above the rest at the far end of the path.

I click through the sections of the video I'm editing that outlines the format of a race weekend and tick off each session against my list.

Race weekend kicks off tomorrow with media sessions and a community service project, plus a test and tune session teams can enroll in if needed. Friday is when things really get going with two official, mandatory practice sessions, one in the morning and another in the afternoon. Saturday is qualifying, where each driver sets their fastest time to determine their start in the lineup for the race on Sunday, before everything is packed up and this traveling circus makes its way to the next city to do it all over again.

That's the end of my content schedule for the day, and as such, the end of my distraction from Evan's text. I read it again and scowl.

Was this not a one-time thing? He's a professional athlete with everything he could possibly want. We had our fun. Don't we now go about our weeks?

But the spanking, his voice's dark undercurrent that ramped up the physical sensations he made me feel... It's a lie if I say I don't crave more.

Jackie sets a coffee on the table beside me and eases into the seat. "God, I'm tired already. You must be exhausted from this morning." She grips my shoulders and shakes me giddily. "How was Evan? Did he win you over?"

Thinking about this morning makes my brain screech an early 2000s internet dial-up tone.

I relax back in my chair with a wry smile. "You're not going to believe how well it went."

"You had sex with him, didn't you?"

I gape like a fish.

Jackie's entire upper body scrunches in her seat as she elicits the most visually loud but audibly silent scream I've ever witnessed.

"How did you know that?" My heart stops at the horrific thought that somehow our orgasmic audio got leaked, but I tucked it securely in the corner of a hidden folder on my drive.

Jackie plants her hands on her hips. "You're wildly intelligent about his favorite sport in the entire world and you're all beautiful curves and a stunning face that men have to work to make smile—who *wouldn't* want to sleep with you?"

I shove back a curl that the wind keeps whisking into my face. "I don't know if that's it, but thank you. Yes, he answered my questions thoughtfully and then we had mind-blowing sex."

There's a metallic scrape as Jackie drags her chair somehow nearer to mine. "Tell. Me. Everything."

I huff. Bite my lip. Then decide to indulge her. "You know how fingering is just like a throwaway foreplay action?"

"No. Who the hell have you been having sex with?"

"Anyway, oh god, Jackie. He's so attentive, and strong, and... communicative. Complimentary, really."

She bounces in her seat. "Do I look smug? Because I feel smug. He's terrific, and now you know that better than anyone. Are you going to see him again?"

Her question incites a clash of conflicting thoughts. She waits patiently as I untangle them and show her the text. "He wants to make me dinner. I don't think it's a good idea."

She surveys me with all the patience of a kindergarten teacher talking to a kid who doesn't want to play outside after the pizza party. "Okay... why not?"

"I don't want to be his plaything of the week."

"Did he treat you like a plaything?" She shakes her head. "Most importantly, did you have a good time? Do you want to have more of those good times?"

I hedge. "I did vow to myself that I'd take full advantage of this trip, in case I don't have this level of access ever again."

"Yeah, girl. Access to that dick is pretty priceless. And since this is his home race you can see where he actually *lives*."

I cackle. She's right. More mind-blowing sex with a pleasant hottie? And maybe a nap in a bed more comfortable than the hotel's? Hell yeah, but... further exposure with Evan means more risk. The best way to avoid being annihilated by men like Evan Evans is to avoid them entirely.

But... Maybe it's not the only way. I've learned from fuckboys before, and can shore up my defenses now.

"Plus," Jackie continues, index finger in the air, "it isn't all or nothing when it comes to seeing him again. If you change your mind, leave."

"You're so wise." I pat her on the cheek and glance at the clock in the lower corner of my laptop screen. "Shoot, we should go or risk giving poor Cooper a heart attack. Who are you talking with next?"

Jackie bounces in her seat. "Riot's head of DEI. This is a big one. I get a whole hour with her."

"I can't wait to hear all about it. Regroup at lunch?"

"Absolutely. I can tell you all about Riot's inclusivity plans for the future, and you could tell me what kind of underwear you're going to wear to Evan's tonight."

"Deal. Womanhood contains multitudes." We giggle together and traipse through the paddock to our next activities.

CHAPTER EIGHT

Evan

Sunny holds up a giant wrench and explains that this specific type is also called a spanner. Behind her, a mechanic wearing the full baby blue kit of Sno-fall's team cackles at something she said. Sunny navigated the interaction perfectly, using every second of her stream to maximize the information and personality she could get from this mechanic as she walked Sunny through the various work they do on the race cars any given weekend. Sunny's made the expansive, complicated job of a race car mechanic bite-sized and comprehensible.

She's an adorable genius. No one does it like her.

Her focus while she asks questions draws out a line between her eyebrows and a fierceness that overtakes her entire face. The same line appears when she's about to come.

"Who's got you twirling your hair like that?"

Johnny eyes me from where he's sprawled on the ground, stretching his hamstrings.

Across the indoor court, Grant and RJ warm up, practicing their swings and joking.

A small group has gathered outside the court's transparent walls to watch four race car drivers attempt to trounce each other at a *different* sport. Grant is in a Panache-branded tech shirt like me, while Johnny's kitted out in Savo team gear. RJ races for Savo, too, but she's elected to sport her personal merch today, a trendy matching set with embroidered roses and flames.

RJ split us up so no one would have the advantage of working with an on-track teammate. Even as far as athletes go, that girl is competitive.

I don't mind the teammate switcharoo one bit. Of all the Riot drivers, I'm closest with Johnny, and I need advice. I show him my phone.

"Of course," he says. "You got to meet her?"

"She's incredible. I'm trying to see her again."

"Outside the paddock."

I shove my phone in my pocket. "Yep. Waiting to hear."

"How long ago was that?"

"An hour, maybe?" I pull it out again, checking the notifications.

"Didn't she just finish a segment? Give her a minute."

"What about you?" I ask. I don't specifically ask how his love life is. We've been friends long enough that he knows I care and I know when the going gets tough, he shuts down. I won't be hearing about the state of his marriage until it's resolved one way or another.

He gives a noncommittal shrug.

"I'm here for you, man. If you need a place to stay–"

"Hey, gossip hounds, are you ready?" RJ calls. She organized this outing since we're all in town early. It's rare that we get free time when we're together, and it's early enough in the season that we're not sick of each other yet, or too close in the standings to be friends for a while.

The first serve turns us into a pack of hyenas, sprinting, leaping, and cackling as we smack the ball back and forth. The good-natured ribbing starts about halfway through the match.

"Quit making up rules, Evans."

"I don't think he is," Grant offers quietly.

It's not that I make up rules—I don't understand the actual rules, no matter how many times Grant has explained them to me when we're stuck in the garage between sessions. "There are too many paddle-based sports and I can't remember the difference between all of them!"

Johnny and I maintain a narrow lead until I think my phone buzzes in my pocket. Abandoning my defensive stance, I whip it out, only to be disappointed. RJ cheers and Johnny shakes his head as the ball bounces easily within my reach and rolls off the court.

"Sorry!" My phone's halfway back to my pocket when it buzzes for real this time.

You cook?

One moment, then another typing bubble appears. "It's important," I promise as I wait for Sunny to finish typing her second message.

Okay, what time?

Triumphant, I throw my arms in the air. "She said yes!" I sprint across the floor and jump on Johnny. We do a terrible imitation of the *Dirty Dancing* lift. My left foot nearly gives him a head injury. He's a good friend.

"For fuck's sake," RJ mutters.

"Come on, man." Grant smacks the ball right into my ass, and I ignore the sting.

Johnny sets me down. "I'm happy for you."

RJ grumbles and continues to score points as we're distracted while Grant scratches behind his head.

I do the math. Besides the usual meetings, I've got a sponsorship meet and greet thing this afternoon, plus training with June.

How about 8?

As we return to the groove of the game, I can't get Sunny out of my head. I don't want to.

"This is my chance. How do I make one shot meaning-ful to her? Especially when we've only got so much time together. I only know so much about her."

Johnny grunts as he returns the ball with an expert stroke. "That sounds a bit dramatic. You don't think a person would want to take up a whirlwind romance with a famous race car driver?"

I rub my chin. "I want to be more than her celebrity hookup story."

I smack the ball back while Johnny mulls this over. "I know it sounds basic, but be yourself. Your intentions are pure and you adore her. That's either going to be enough or it isn't. There's plenty of race week left. Give it time."

Grant whips the ball near my face, and I barely make the save. I glare at him. "Don't forget to *communicate* with her," he says.

I nod, syncing into the groove of hitting the ball back and forth, my entire body tracking its trajectory on autopilot. This was the feeling, the hunch, I had about Sunny. That we'd get along great, easy as breathing. It's the same way I feel on the track when I'm doing well. The way I should feel taking corners right on the edge, millimeters from too fast and crashing out.

I shake off my anxiety, because the feeling that's been growing in my gut all week pulses louder. Everything's going to be fine.

The round ends and we lose miserably because of me. We step aside to towel off and grab water. I take the time to message Sunny more details.

> Disclaimer: I don't have a wide repertoire, but there are a few things I cook well. On the road I mostly eat out of a microwave, or the Panache catering, which is better than anything I can pull off. Do you have any allergies? Foods you don't like?

Cool, now I'm blabbering. I swipe the sweat from my forehead.

> No allergies, and I don't love mushrooms. That's about it. See you at 8.

Shoving my phone in my pocket, I give our next match my entire focus even though, in my mind, I've already won.

The fire alarm blares through my apartment.

My arms ache from holding a fan pointed directly at the smoke detector for the last five minutes. "I haven't even started cooking yet!"

"Maybe that's the problem, kid," Aunt Cat says patiently from my phone, set to speaker on the kitchen island. "Do you have a hot pan just sitting there? How long has it been sitting there?"

I look over my shoulder and swear. "I definitely left the corner of a kitchen towel on the stove and it got crispy."

I turn off the burner, get the towel in the sink and somehow finally get the smoke alarm to stop screaming. I buzz the front desk to let them know I'm not actually at risk of burning the building down and tell them to let Sunny up when she gets here.

By the end of it, I'm sweating and worried I need to change. I check the time. Hopefully, a few minutes will be enough to disperse the smell of smoke before Sunny arrives.

"All good, Ev?" My aunt pipes in. She's used to all levels of chaos whenever talking to me, and patiently waited while I resolved this issue.

"Yeah, crisis averted. Do you think she'll find it charming if I order pizza?"

"Come on, don't throw in the partially burned towel. Pause. Regroup. Get it together and make her a nice meal."

I do as she suggests, taking a slow, centering breath and attempt to clear my mind. "You're right, as usual."

All that comes across the line is a huff that I know means *obviously*.

I stare blankly at the fridge. "I know, I know. I'll call you tomorrow, yeah? Are you all set with tickets and everything for Saturday?"

"Blair sent them over. I'll meet you in the garage before quali. I'm just sorry again that I can't make the race, but this equipment auction has been on the calendar for a year."

"No worries," I assure her. Aunt Cat and I got close when my little sister's health issues got intense right after she was born. I stayed with her whenever my parents had to spend weeks at the hospital, and loved her farm so much that I eventually spent my summers there, too. I don't begrudge my parents prioritizing my sister's meets over my races now that she's a healthy and prolific college swimmer.

They came to a decade of my karting races before she was born. The pendulum of their attention will swing back my way eventually, or better, even out. At least that's what I've come to believe with the help of Panache's team therapist. "I'll make a race later this season extra entertaining when you can make it."

She assures me she'll attend multiple races this year before we hang up.

"Love you, bye-bye."

I take a deep breath and survey the room. Aside from the smell, it doesn't look like a near-catastrophe. I open the small top portion of the windows to let out the smoke lingering along the ceiling and change my shirt. After, I focus very closely on cooking us nice pieces of fish.

My phone buzzes with another text from Sunny.

> Which floor?

Eleven, I shoot back.

> Of course.

She also includes the eye roll emoji.

I smile, set down the phone... then snatch it up again.

Does she find me exasperating in an adorable way? She wouldn't have agreed to dinner otherwise, right?

I set the phone back down. My mouth twists and I fixate on a blank portion of wall, my eyes narrowing.

Oh my god, do I annoy her?

I annoy many people, but not on purpose. It's hard to stop talking sometimes, and I'm often unaware of my own volume.

My energy makes me feel like a kite most days, with excitement whipping me around. Sunny has this grounded energy...

I didn't imagine the spark between us. I couldn't have. I've never felt anything like it. It's like flirting with someone at the bar who catches your eye, but cranked up so far the volume knob falls clean off.

A firm knock on the door pops my bubble of racing thoughts. My entire body zeros in on the space on the other side of the door, where it knows she is.

"Coming!"

My steps to the door are quick, automatic. I fling it open and barely halt the momentum before it slams into the wall.

Sunny stands on my checkered welcome mat wearing a pretty blue dress, eyes wide as she takes me in, arms full of flowers and wine.

"Hi." Her voice is breathless. Is it nerves? Nerves are good, right? Or are they bad? I don't want her to be nervous...

"*Look* at you. Wow. Here, let me help." I take the gifts and step back, welcoming her in. She steps through, taking in my space. She's so calm and unfazed all the time. I wish I was like that.

I follow her and have to gulp. Yes, her dress is pretty but it's also downright sinful now that I can see it in full. It hugs her body, accentuating her perfectly smackable ass as she makes her way toward the kitchen. I'm hypnotized by the rhythm of her hair swishing as she walks.

I wonder if she sees my home similarly to how I do. Warm, soft light floods from the corners. Sad boy indie rock croons from hidden speakers. I sniff, assuring that my simmering garlic and butter have chased off most of the burnt smell.

Sunny stops in the middle of the rug that marks the boundary between the kitchen and living room. She spins in those adorable scuffed sneakers of hers. As I set her gifts on the counter, I realize I took what occupied her hands; now she links and unlinks her fingers.

"I wasn't sure if red or white would go better with dinner," she says. "But I figure extra wine is never a problem."

"I like the way you think." I step close, sidle behind her, and set my hands on her shoulders. She shivers. "Let me take your jacket."

She does and calls to me while I tuck it into the front closet. "Where do you keep your bottle opener and vases?"

I send her to the drawer left of the sink and fetch a vase myself. "Thanks for accommodating my hectic day. I'm sorry it's so late."

She toys with a fallen flower petal as I snip the stems. Her gaze has been roving since she got here. The cycle starts with her looking me full in the face, holding my gaze, her smile small but open and warm, then it drops downward, and those brown eyes trace my body like chocolate syrup. But, at the end, she looks away and seems to make a concerted effort to focus anywhere but me for the duration of a deep breath.

I nearly ask about it, but her eyes focus on me again, and I snap to attention, ready to serve. Hungry, thirsty, horny? In need of a human doormat? I'm her guy.

"Thanks for having me. I was able to sneak a nap in." A circuit in my brain fizzles because napping usually takes place in bed, and Sunny in a bed makes me think all sorts of very specific things I hope will happen this evening.

The garlic pops, and I move, lowering the heat before eyeing the wine. "Yeah! Tell me about your day. But first...

I don't know anything about wine pairings... We're having fish."

"In my expert and highly cultured opinion, the label on the white one is more fun," she says from where she examines the photos I've got framed on the wall. My heart squeezes as she takes in the frozen memories of my family and friends.

I tear my focus away from her to focus on the much less interesting task of opening the bottle of white. The label features a zebra.

I raise an eyebrow. She's looking at me, and her expression's turned mischievous. "Sorry, they didn't have a giraffe."

Without breaking eye contact, I tug the cork out with a loud, satisfying pop and set the bottle gingerly on the counter. I eat up the space between us and plant myself before her. She turns into me. I grab her hips and tug them against mine. The contact is so sweet but not even close to enough, and I like that her eyes heat when she feels what her teasing does to me. "You really think you've got something on me with that nickname, don't you?" I dip my head so my breath breezes through the curls alongside her ear. "But maybe I really like it." The growl in my voice is not for interviews or radio messages, and by her quick intake of breath every time I use it, I think Sunny is a fan.

With the wall of my chest before her and the row of pictures behind, Sunny doesn't have a lot of options for looking away from me. To my immense pleasure, she doesn't try. I watch as she feasts on the lines of my chest beneath my thin sweater, the broad expanse of my neck, watch the hint of something—it's akin to joy but blended with something else—that blooms in her when she takes in my face and her instincts read what mine are projecting, that I like her a whole fucking lot, and that, more than anything right now, I want to take care of her.

Her hands trace up my neck, then tangle in my hair and tug my face to hers.

I brace one arm on the wall and use the other to hold her to me as she explores this kiss, *her* kiss. For a few moments, I simply mirror, giving back the pressure and movements she exerts.

Her sweet little mouth, that tongue boring into me—*fuck*. A needy noise rises from her throat, and I turn the tables. I lash my tongue against hers, massage her lips with mine—

The fucking oven beeps with the single most jarring noise I've ever heard in my life.

She withdraws with a laugh, but I don't loosen my grip on her body. *Girl, this is just the beginning*, I want to insist. Instead, I press my forehead to hers. I need a minute to swim up from this torrent she summons within me. When my head breaks the surface, I can use reason again.

"I should get that because I had a minor culinary mishap before you got here and I'd really love to serve you food that's not burnt."

With a giggle, she lets me guide her to one of the chairs at my small dining table.

I didn't know she giggled. It must be another facet of hers that she guards, so I won't bring it up for fear of deterring her from letting me make her do it again.

She sits on her hands as I get back to work. "What did you think of the garage? I'm dying to know. It was Sno-fall, right?"

I can't resist looking back at her, even with half my arm in an oven. She's bouncing in her seat, a grin eating up her face. "I've never been in one before."

"What?" There's a clang as I fumble the tray. It takes me a second to get it out, salmon filets and my skin intact, but I do it. "I'm good. Never? Like, never *ever*? But it's your job."

"It's my side hustle," she corrects. "My real job is less fun, but the pay is better and there's health insurance."

"Your Riot stuff sure seems like a real job..." She shakes her head, so I change the subject. "So what did you think?"

I prop my elbows on the counter and oven-mitted hands beneath my chin, staring at her with my giraffe eyes that she pretends exasperate her so much.

Sunny's passion for motorsports is a living thing that takes over her entire body. She mentions a thousand different details she noticed, which spawn a million questions I can kind of answer. For the ones I can't, I want to call every industry contact I have to provide the answers for her.

By the time we're caught up on the events of each other's days, dinner has been set, eaten, and cleared.

I sternly tell her she's not helping with dishes, so instead, she props a hip against the counter beside the sink and talks with me while I clean.

I tease her. She bumps me with her hip. And I swear it's not in my head the affection coupling with the attraction here. Feeling reckless, I lean over from the sudsy water and press a kiss to the top of her head. Her answering smile is small.

"I have bad news," I hedge as the suds drain.

Sunny cocks her head.

"I didn't think about dessert. I think I have some stuff for yogurt parfaits."

She snorts. "That's not a real problem. We'll live."

I take her hand, draw it up to lay a kiss on the back.

"I have an idea for dessert," she says, withdrawing her hand.

Her tone sends warmth spiraling through my stomach. "Oh yeah? Better than yogurt and natural peanut butter and chia seeds?" I snag her hips and haul her up. She squeals and wraps her legs around me. "Should we have this dessert in my bedroom?"

I take a step and she squirms. "Yes, but you can't carry me there! Not with how infamously clumsy you are."

With a frown, I set Sunny back on her feet. I free one hand to tangle it in her hair and make her look at me. "Not when it comes to things that matter." I give her one chaste kiss, but bite her lower lip before I pull back. "Not in the car, and definitely not when I'm carrying a beautiful woman to my bed."

She crosses her arms and gives me an assessing look that raises goosebumps, then finally nods. I swing her over my shoulder with a laugh and head toward my room, my mind racing with ideas for how to fill a full, uninterrupted evening with this girl.

CHAPTER NINE

Sunny

Evan is true to his word, and my ride to the bedroom is smooth. As we leave the kitchen, I notice over his shoulder that we both barely touched our wine.

It's not like me to neglect a nice glass of wine.

Plus, I've been giggling.

There's a pinch in my stomach—my nerves reminding me that I'm continuing to move toward an area I find deeply uncomfortable.

Dinner is not a date. Flirting is not feelings.

That's what I keep telling myself. This is an extended hookup in which Evan's being a terrific host. He probably weaves this fantasy with a new person whenever he's bored. The sex is where I'm comfortable. In bed, it's so easy to draw my boundaries and control my own vulnerability; to decide what I give and take. To choose what I want to experience.

It's cute that Evan seems to want to get to know me, but I'd prefer he didn't. This week already requires so much of my bravery.

Evan sets me down, and my feet sink into plush carpet. His bedroom is sparse and feels too big for one person, even with the subtle lighting and warm wood accents. There's a large, low bed with crisp sheets and marshmallow-y pillows, two chairs on either side of a small fireplace set in the wall, and above a wide dresser, Evan has tacked countless Polaroids.

The pull of the photos is strong, but they can't beat the glow from the floor-to-ceiling windows that make up the wall behind his bed. The sparkling city lights and the muted behemoths that are the mountains behind them draw me forward. I gravitate to the glass as if in a trance. One of my hands stays in Evan's as he follows in uncharacteristic silence.

The vanished sun left everything in shades of purple, and the buildings that hug Evan's are lit up like holiday trees. On the sidewalks below, clumps of people roam between bars and shops.

Evan aligns his body with mine. His warmth washes over my shoulders. One of his dimples flashes the window's reflection.

"What a view."

"Agreed." His fingertips trace the back of my arm, drawing goosebumps. "I wonder if I'd take it for granted if I got to see it every day. But traveling so much assures that I don't."

My focus turns fully to our faint reflections. I'm still reeling over Evan in "normal" clothes. On TV, he's usually in the Panache team kit or his race suit. I'm sure the paparazzi has caught him out running errands or going to dinner before, but I'm not an Elevans die hard; I haven't seen those.

He chose a light sweater in a green that matches his eyes. Its fit is loose, and it makes him look like... just a man who really wanted to make me dinner.

Those jeans though? Criminal. They hug his ass and offer it up like a cupcake whenever he turns around. His tousled hair is still slightly wet from a shower, and the faint smell of smoke lingers in the air.

Somehow, I've been here for two hours already. Time flew as we chatted, easy as breathing. After a thorough—somehow hilarious because Evan makes everything hilarious—debriefing of our days, we moved to more random tangents; hobbies, my work, our childhoods, our families.

I nearly fell off my chair when he told me a story about getting a pencil stuck up his nose in the third grade.

Despite my intentions to be reserved, he's easy to talk to. I thought he was fake and people-pleasing with the goofball act, but it seems that's another quirk of his brain. No wonder reporters love him. He's extremely fun to talk with. I like sharpening my wit against the whetstone of his silliness.

...Maybe I'll make it out of this fling with a new friend. The sentiment sits uneasily in my chest, like an incorrect puzzle piece.

Evan squeezes my hip.

"Sorry, what did you say?"

He traces a finger through my hair and tucks it behind my ear so he can speak close. "Where's your favorite place you've ever traveled?"

My brows draw together. "I haven't, really. I visited London in college, but not for nearly long enough. Don't laugh, but I also really want to see Los Angeles..."

He kisses my ear and moves to my neck, speaking between the touches of his lips to my skin. "Why would I laugh? L.A. is cool." A lingering kiss where my neck meets my shoulder, and the softest touch of his tongue. "Maybe I could take you."

I squeeze my eyes shut as my stomach plummets. I've had enough empty sentiments from silver-tongued boys for one lifetime.

I turn, tilt my face to his. "How about we travel to your bed?" I shove a little against his chest, forcing him a half step backward in the direction of the comfy behemoth.

His eyes spark and he catches me around the waist, hauling me against him. He trips, of course, and we go sprawling to the mattress, his arms a careful cage that keeps me safe and prevents our heads from bumping.

With a laugh that melts into a sort of growl, he flips us over, landing me breathless on my back. Without prompting, I wrap my legs around his waist, already desperate for any friction he'll give me.

Slow as a drip of honey, he lowers his mouth to mine. I moan already because kissing Evan is so fucking good. He slides his tongue against mine, a firm, curious exploration. I bury my hands in his hair and playfully nip his tongue.

He pulls back with a stern, devoted look that turns me molten before he dives back for more. The kisses are hungrier this time, and our tongues clash. His hands shove under my dress, kneading my hips and ass and pulling me against the bulge at the front of his jeans.

I'm lightheaded when he pulls back. We're both panting. My body feels deliciously on fire, and Evan's lower lip is plump from our back-and-forth. He's got my dress crumpled around my waist. Both straps have fallen off my shoulders, and I've been pawing at his clothes.

He surveys me up and down. "Is this okay with you?"

It's a fight to keep from clapping my hands. I want to climb him like a tree. "More than okay."

I see the flash of his smile before he's on me again, one hand holding my neck and the other cradling my ass as we kiss. I run my hands over his sides until I find the sweater's hem and can insistently draw it up his torso. Something shifts, and suddenly it's like we're in a race to tear off each other's clothes.

Evan wins.

I pout as he kicks off his jeans but leaves his briefs. With a knowing smile, he tosses my dress and underwear over his shoulder. He sits back on his knees between my legs and takes me in, his eyes darkly serious. The spark of playfulness there is dimmed but lingering.

"You're really beautiful," he says.

"You're—" I start. "You're as gorgeous as you claim to be in interviews."

Evan's laugh echoes around the room as he presses me to the bed and tangles me up in his arms. "Beyond everything else, you're clever as hell, too?" he huffs. "I'm a goner." I can't respond. His mouth takes mine. He kisses me breathless, then carves a path with his lips down my body, leaving waves of goosebumps in his wake.

He takes one of my nipples in his mouth, twirling his tongue around it as he mimics the motion on my other nipple between his fingers. He pinches one and flicks his tongue over the other, and the warring sensations send my back arching off the bed. I gasp.

Evan laughs and switches to lick my other nipple, repeating his attention. I'm too far gone to realize he's trailing a hand over my stomach until he slips a finger inside me, pushing deep.

I grip his chiseled shoulders, trying to leverage more pressure where I need it, but Evan has other ideas and withdraws his hand. He slides down my body and sinks to his knees at the end of the bed, then hauls me closer. I squeal and my arms fly up with the force. All I hear is half a throaty laugh from Evan before he spreads my legs and draws the flat of his tongue over my pussy.

He licks again, this time with more precision, exploring every inch and testing where I react the strongest. I'm no longer on this planet. A few more luxurious strokes of his tongue and he sucks on my clit.

The noise this man emits when I pull his hair... It's going to be the death of me.

An unintelligible cry of pleasure bursts from me, and a second later, Evan pauses just quick enough to speak. "*Yes, baby. Tell me all about it.*"

He smacks my ass and I yelp. When he resumes eating me out, it's with a fervor and focus I assume he usually saves for the race track. Pressure coils in my core, building with each draw of his tongue. My orgasm rockets through me, a delicious release that leaves me seeing stars.

I blink and Evan's making his way to the bedside table. The sound of a drawer and then he's back, climbing on top of me and covering his body with mine. He plants kisses on my cheek, my temple, my neck, my mouth. His scruff smells like my pussy and it's almost enough to send me spiraling again.

"Wait." I pause with a hand on his chest, which heaves almost as hard as mine.

He stills immediately, his eyes narrowing in concern.

I glance through my lashes at him. "What about my dessert?"

I push him into a plank position and shimmy downward and catch the tail end of his grin as he realizes what I'm after. He braces himself on his forearms so I can slide down and get his briefs off as I do.

I hum with satisfaction at the complete sight of him. Evan Evans has a beautiful cock.

I get comfortable beneath him and grab his shaft with one hand and place my other on his ass, guiding him to my mouth. The low groan he gives as I immediately take him deep is immensely satisfying. I realize how long it's been since I've had sex where my partner seemed really present—in all the various steps of the dance, not just their own orgasm. The way Evan makes me feel when I touch him is intoxicating. And honestly, it's wonderful that he talks a lot, because he keeps saying in a dozen different ways how good I make him feel.

Exploring his cock with my mouth, I bob my head and show him how deep I can continually take him, guiding him into a rhythm. It's wet and messy and loud and *fun*.

It only takes a minute of sucking him deep and savoring before Evan trusts me enough to begin fucking my mouth in earnest. I match his appreciative moans with my own as his thrusts become more sporadic. "Sunny, I'm going to come," he grunts.

I squeeze his ass to let him know I want it all, and he comes on his next deep thrust.

As soon as he's spent, Evan rolls off me. He hauls me up the bed, then collapses on his side with one muscular arm draped over my waist. He slips the other beneath me and pulls me close, nuzzling the side of my neck while I wipe my chin.

"Did you like that?" I ask with a satisfied grin.

He mutters something unintelligible against my shoulder, his scruff tickling my skin. He smacks my ass again and

I squirm against him. The snap of pain is a fiery, addictive sensation that grounds my body amidst all the floaty pleasure.

He does it again, and a noise I've never made before squeaks from my throat.

Evan's head pops up, his eyes molten. My insides melt to match.

"Hands on the headboard, Sunny."

CHAPTER TEN

Sunny

The headboard is smooth and sturdy beneath my shaking hands.

When the calluses of Evan's palms scrape my outer thighs, I jump.

"You love being spanked—when *I* spank you—don't you, Sunny?"

I gulp. In these intimate moments with Evan, he's toed a line of kinkiness that ignites hope in my chest. His words follow a formula I've read many times in books but never practiced myself. The idea of exploring kink has excited me for years, but past partners were, at best, not interested, and, at worst, dismissive.

Evan leans over my body. His hand finds my chin and gently urges me to meet his eyes again. "Tell me."

The subtle shift in his tone summons a trickle of wetness between my legs. The goofball I'm getting to know is still there in the set of his chin, the twist at the corner of his lips, but he's donned a half-mask of dominance...

And I'm aching to obey.

"I—I think so. Yes." My nerves sizzle with anticipation that he's going to give me more of the pleasure elevated with pain, and that if we communicate well, I get to ride along with all the delicious sensations he's going to orchestrate for the both of us.

At least, that's how it goes in the books I've read.

"That answer didn't sound super comfortable."

I clear my throat. "I said *yes.*"

He pauses, considering me. "Do you have a safe word?"

My palms have gotten sweaty. "No, but I can come up with one."

Evan grabs my waist and pulls me into his lap, his strong arms like the coziest cage. "Have you done something like this before? Things that require a safe word."

I stiffen. "I've read a lot about it, so I know the mechanics. I want to try it."

His answering smile is warm, the bossy side banked for a moment. "Then I'd love to teach you."

"Are you like a—a dom, then?"

One of his eyebrows quirks. "I can be. I'm no professional, but I think I do okay. It's often what my partners want, but I don't mind doing the submissive thing, either. I just like to play."

"Got it." Instinctually, I lean into him.

"You're sure? We can still have great sex without treading into kink territory."

"I want to," I insist. I nearly tell him my hopes for a kinky time were the driving factor in my agreeing to dinner. Especially with this double-checking on his part, and having learned that he's experienced, and also terribly sweet. "I trust you."

His breath hitches, I think. Silence stretches, then a bite on my lower lip demands my attention. "A safe word, Sunny, then I'll teach you all sorts of fun things."

My thoughts whir. Images flash, all related to my comfort space, a fantasy land of knights and jousts and magic. "Halt," I say finally.

He repeats it to confirm.

I don't know why I feel the sudden urge to defend myself. "I like to go to the renaissance fair. It's how the actors say 'stop'."

He lights up. "The ren fair, really? I've always wanted to go to one but none of my friends do and I'm not going by myself. Plus, we're usually racing all summer. Do you dress up and everything? Do they really do the attack each other on horseback with sticks thing, and have the beer in those big cups and the people in the handcuffy stand things who yell at you? Do you do like the princess maiden flowy dress thing, or, OH, you'd be a great wizard..."

I think he's forgotten I'm naked in his lap.

I poke his chest, and he stops. "Yes to all, I think? And I usually go as like a... warrior fairy type thing."

He practically has anime eyes. "That's so cool."

"Actually, a lot of the kink I've read is in fantasy books. There are some pretty spicy ones."

In a whirl, he moves us again, till I'm splayed beneath him and he's braced above me. "Right. Tell me what you want to try." His body certainly hasn't forgotten what we were up to before this sidebar.

It's not a list we can get through in one night, but... "Impact play, like spanking," I start. Why is it so hard to say these things out loud? Evan nods encouragingly. "That's the big one. Um, subbing in general, I guess? I like the idea of obeying orders. Not like, major humiliation, I don't think, but that standard cocky, bossy thing doms do... The 'punishments' that aren't really punishments... Maybe some light bondage? Among other things..." My voice trails at the end.

Evan's smile sparks in the dim light. "You got it, Sunny." He stands, eyes anywhere but me as he circles to the foot of the bed, leaving me feeling suddenly extremely exposed. When his voice sounds next, it's silken and soft, his trademark playfulness dressed in leather. "Now be a good Sunny girl and show me you know your safe word."

I'm immediately wetter than I've ever been. "Halt." My voice is quiet but steady.

"Very good." He bends slowly and cages my ankles in his hands. I begin to shake. "Do you have a safe word?" I blurt.

A dimple appears. "Rutabaga."

"Why on earth is your safe word 'rutabaga'?"

"I spent a lot of time on a farm growing up. Remind me to tell you all about it." He points to the garlic tattoo on his hand.

"Do you have any other produce inked on you?"

That incites a full-throated laugh. "If I did, you would've seen it by now. Maybe I should get a bunch of carrots on my lower back."

Now I can't hold back a laugh. "Rutabaga. Got it." That seems to remind him why we're here.

He eyes my body hungrily. "You say that word at any time, and we pause and decide how to continue together. Do you understand?"

"Yes." Too late, I realize I could've mutely nodded and maybe gotten a taste of delicious 'punishment' because he'd prompted me to confirm verbally.

"Perfect." He dips his head and plants a wet, lingering kiss on my hip bone. He trails a finger up my leg, through my sex so I hiss, then draws the wetness up to circle where his lips just were. "Let me ask you again. You like it when I spank your sweet ass, don't you, Sunny girl?"

I shiver but make myself pause to eye him warily. To see if I can eke out a little bit of punishment. I don't think I have a huge bratty urge like those I've read about, but a spark ignites in me when the scenes get to a little give and take.

I wet my lips, then decide on a fib, to see where it gets me. "Maybe."

His eyes narrow as he catches on.

He reclines on the bed beside me. Keeping one hand on me, he places the other behind his head and shrugs. The movement draws wildly captivating movements from the muscles lining his arms, neck, and shoulders. "You're getting spanked either way tonight. Either while we fuck in a few minutes, or right now, a little bit slower, and I'll treat you with an extra orgasm from my fingers before we get there."

Yup. Yeah. Yes. Any further syllables would be a struggle.

Some logical bit of me acknowledges that what Evan said is technically a decree, but there was a twist in his tone, a promise and reminder in his eyes, that I'm safe with him and that I'm the one in charge. Though he's issuing commands, I have all the power because I'm the one allowing him to—granting him the privilege of touching my body and guiding my pleasure.

As I process, his face comes close to mine again, soft, with beautiful lashes. My bossy, dommy giraffe set aside for a moment. "I think you know this already," he stage whispers, a stark contrast to the commands he's throwing around. "But you can always stop this entirely. Or ask for something different, or—"

I'm shaking my head before he can finish his sentence. "Spank me now."

He gives me a stern look that would ignite his fan base into a frenzy if they saw it.

"Please," I breathe.

"'Atta girl. Hands up." I reach and find that I can grab the lower edge of his headboard from this position. The stretch arches my breasts high. Evan rolls to his knees and slips one forearm beneath my thighs, where my legs lie flat against the bedspread. He hauls my legs up and kneels so his knees rest on either side of my ass and... spreads my legs. My breath stutters. I close my eyes and breathe, knowing Evan's looking at the most private part of me. A contented noise bubbles up from his throat as he draws one thumb up the side of my pussy, his other arm holding my legs back and exposing me to him.

He's drinking me in, his face appreciative and devotional. His fingers move with slow focus, drawing through every fold, tracing around my ass and back up my center, until he slides one finger inside me.

My eyes close. I moan. Then the smack comes, a firm strike against one of my ass cheeks. My entire body shakes. It's *so* good. Evan pumps his finger devastatingly slow, till I'm mesmerized by the rhythm, then the next strike lands. This time, on my other cheek, closer to my pussy. I cry out.

"Are you good?"

"*God*, yes."

"You can just call me Evan."

I scoff, but he cuts off my rebuke with another spank that makes me yelp and forget my plans to admonish him.

Evan continues, and the pain and pleasure melt together into a warm bath of sensation. I sink, until Evan curls his fingers to rub my G-spot, and his thumb mirrors the pressure on my clit.

This orgasm crashes over me like a wave, sucking me under. I didn't even realize the crest was around the corner. He built me up so slowly. I can't breathe. I just feel.

Evan's body presses over mine and he kisses me back to reality. He's rubbing my ass, smoothing the soreness from where he spanked me. I moan and he moves to massage my thighs, which were starting to feel tight from the position he'd held me in.

Sleepiness tingles in my fingertips, my feet, ready to crawl up my body. I sit up on my elbows. "You said we're having sex next, right?"

He snorts. "I'd like to, if you're up for it." He slips into his dom tone again. "You've certainly earned it."

"Please," I breathe, the word more enthusiastic this time.

He kisses my thigh and climbs off the bed to find a condom. With a contented sigh, I roll onto my stomach, drawing a pillow beneath my head. They're as soft as they look.

Off to the side of the bed, I watch Evan move. Unfortunately, it's not just my sex organs that respond to him. My heart lurches at the fond look he gives me after he's rolled on the condom and approached the bed.

Get a grip. Keep it light. This opportunity is too good to ruin with feelings. I press my knees to the mattress and wiggle my ass at him.

"Am I pink?"

"Mm." His warm palms roam my ass. "You're lit up all over for me. You feel okay?"

"Better than okay."

He guides the head of his cock to my entrance and I bite back a moan. He doesn't make me wait—just presses in. It's intoxicating, how warm his skin feels against mine... his rough strokes juxtaposed against his tenderness in holding on to me.

"Now," he says, thrusting deeper but still slow. "The real torture in that conference room was not being able to see your face while I fucked you. I only caught a glimpse of your expression when you came. I've been thinking about it all day."

My heart pounds harder in reaction to him. I can't bear it. I bury my face in the pillow.

"Aw, c'mon, baby." One of his hands runs up my back and freezes. We put it together at the same time. Our sex this morning. The blowjob from below. How I've squeezed my eyes shut for every orgasm, to try and keep him from getting that vulnerable part of me. My efforts to contain this as strictly lust and nothing more.

Evan... kind of gets it.

He presses, flattening me to the bed. His dick's still inside me, but he cages me in so I can't move or get friction. His laugh is a little darker than any of the others tonight, like it's hiding something.

"Oh no, Sunny. You don't get to fuck me and pretend you still don't like me." He pulls the pillow from the cradle of my arms, and I bury my face in the comforter instead.

I'm reminded this man is a top-tier athlete as he maneuvers me easily, pulling out to flip me over. He grabs me behind the neck and brings his face close as he slides back into me. "Admit it." He places a gentle bite in the middle of my neck. "Tell me."

I moan as he stretches me, desperate for movement. I keep my eyes open; it's the only way he'll give it to me. The earnestness in his eyes nearly chokes me. In shielding my own feelings, I've accidentally hurt his.

I lick my lips. "I like you."

It's the truth, and I promise myself it's harmless.

His smile blossoms like a daffodil in spring, but he tries to tamp it down. "Can you say that again? I didn't catch it."

I roll my eyes. "Evans, we're the only two people in this room."

"Yeah, but my hearing's shot from the years I spent racing V8 engines."

I narrow my eyes.

He rocks his hips, sending a spiral of pleasure up my spine.

"Fine!" I take his stupid face in my hands. "I like you, Evan, really."

He whoops. The sound has hardly reached the corners of the room before he's kissing me with abandon.

After a long moment, he pulls back, taking his cock with him. I pout, and he stretches like a contented cat. "I want to bask in it, you saying you like me."

I scowl. "You're the absolute worst."

"Yeah, but you *like* me."

I'm halfway to coming up with a retort, but as he processes the realization, his face has gone dreamy. This really mattered to him.

I don't want to explain to him that it's not personal; it's a defense mechanism. "Do you really think I'd be here if I didn't like you at least a little bit?"

His gaze bores into me, trailing from my face, down my body, between my legs and back up. "I'm going to make you come again."

His promise is like the most tantalizing touch, and I squirm a little, my back arching.

"Do you like the sound of that?" he asks. "Me fucking you until you come?"

I'm relieved we've settled... whatever that was. "You know I do." My voice is breathy, like I've run a long way.

I reach for his hips, but he stops me with a lifted finger. "Hands at your sides, Sunny." There it is again, that mild steel in his voice. A subtle, dark imperiousness that's only present during sex. The fact that he's phrasing these things as commands sets every nerve ending in my body tingling.

Obediently, I rest my hands in loose fists at my sides on the bedspread, biting the inside of my cheek. I want him inside me now, but the delay spins the pleasurable tension so much higher.

"That's good," Evan says. His voice is a soft rumble that sends shivers up my spine. He notices, and his smile inches a bit wider.

He glances up to take in the desperation on my face every other second. Just as I think he's about to push into me, he reaches above my head and grabs a pillow. "Lift your hips for me," he says. I obey without thinking, shivering further where his skin brushes mine as he situates the pillow beneath my ass, lifting my pussy a few inches. Putting me on display for him again. He rubs his chin and uses his other hand to drag a thumb over me, sighing appreciatively. Now, he bites his lip. "Do you want me to be gentle, or more rough? I have a guess." He runs his hands up to my breasts and twists both nipples between his fingers, working them to perky points. The small part of me that can focus appreciates the openness on his face.

He genuinely wants to know what I prefer. The warmth that permeates my body sinks somewhere deeper and more private in my chest.

"*Tell me.*"

His hoarse command draws my focus. He's as desperate for this as I am.

"Rough," I say. "Really, really rough."

He cocks his head, slight redness gracing his cheeks. "Anything for you, Sunny. If you change your mind, tell me."

"Absolutely. Same to you."

His answering smile crinkles his nose, and then his mouth is on mine. The kiss is deep and sensual, his tongue sliding over mine. He brushes his hands over my hips, then grips them hard. He breaks the kiss and leans back a little so he can watch my face as he slams into me.

Evan's cock brushes roughly against my G-spot, and I see stars again. I cry out, and he looks concerned for a split second before I manage to find my voice.

"Oh, *fuck* yes."

He grunts in agreement and shoves deeper into me, catching my mouth with his and leveraging one arm beneath my shoulders. He fucks me with abandon, bruising strokes that hurt so incredibly. As he does, his breath turns harsh. I wrap my legs as high on his waist as I can. He takes my cue and lifts one of my legs to his shoulder, then the other.

I relegate any concern for my heart to a dark corner of my psyche and enjoy the best sex of my life.

CHAPTER ELEVEN

Evan

Sunny comes like fireworks.

She carries herself artfully poised, but orgasm lets it all go loose.

I help her come undone like that.

I'm not on this planet for at least three minutes. I land back in my body with her beside me, her skin deliciously warm in the places it touches mine. Her chest rises and falls, slowing gradually. I brush her mussed hair from her face and keep my other arm around her.

This quiet moment is perfect, but the urge to care for and pamper Sunny has me antsy.

I roll up to sit, trailing my eyes down the curved lines of her body. Gently, I clamp her thigh like I did when she was in the car with me. "How about a shower?"

One arm thrown over her eyes, she utters a long, appreciative sound.

I huff a laugh. "Is that a yes?"

She lifts her arm and nods. I'm pleased at the way her eyes go wide whenever she catches sight of my face, my chest, like she can't believe I'm real. It's a look I'm used to from all sorts of incredible fans, but I try not to take it for granted or let it go to my head.

With Sunny, it's totally going to my head. It's tying balloons around my arms and threatening to carry me away.

I offer a hand and haul her to her feet, catching her as she stumbles, my chest squeezing with pride that I gave her a good time.

"Woah," Sunny says appreciatively as we enter the bathroom and she catches sight of my wide, pristine shower. I start the water and chuck a couple of towels into the warmer as Sunny leans against the counter, crossing and uncrossing her arms after she ties up her hair.

I test the water, then extend a hand. She allows me to help her in and step in behind her. She hums beneath the hot water, the noise getting deeper when I wrap my arms around her and join her beneath the spray.

She blinks, and I follow her stare to my little shelf of products.

"That's why you smell so good."

"What?"

She shakes her head. "You smell like mangoes all the time. No wonder, with a luxury product line like that."

I tilt my head back and laugh.

She turns around to face me, her expression indignant. "What's so funny?"

I don't like the way the movement pulls her away from me, so I draw her back in and press a kiss to her nose. "My sister got me those. And now..." I snag the bottle of body wash. "...you can smell like mangoes, too."

She lets me soap her up, content with my slow movement over her limbs and especially pliant when I begin to knead her shoulders. "That's nice," she says. Her muscles tense beneath my thumbs. "You're really nice."

I frown, but don't stop my movements. "You didn't think I'd be nice?"

She pauses for a long moment before she continues. "I tend to distrust handsome men. Especially the confident ones."

Of course it's not about you, idiot, I chide myself.

"Ah," I concede. "Someone hurt you?"

She shakes her shoulders, a sign for me to ease up. "Bingo."

I drop my hands and she turns, using the mountains of suds from her own body to soap me up in turn. I'm curious, but her body language tells me she doesn't want to share any further. She seems to return to herself, drawing a smiley face in the bubbles across my chest. I grab her hand. Time slows down. She goes on her toes and kisses me. I pull her close, probing her mouth with my tongue and stroking her ass, delivering a wet slap to it beneath the spray. She squirms, rubbing her body along mine as best she's able.

I pull back. "You know, I brought you in here with the intention of helping you relax, but now I've seen you all incredibly wet and I would very much like to fuck you again, if that's alright."

Her voice goes breathless. Her fingertips dig into my shoulders. "It's more than alright."

A cozy bonfire builds in my chest as I watch Sunny paw through my things. The apartment feels less lifeless with her around, asking questions about my photos or the pattern on my towels.

It's when Sunny asks for body lotion that I remember, unfortunately, that this is not my life, not really.

Our season is busy and during it, I'm barely home. I don't know where most of my belongings are because I'm not here frequently enough to remember. I live out of a suitcase and usually smell like a plane and I'm not often in a hotel long enough to unpack. The price of living my dream as a racing driver is to not constantly be surrounded by things I love that make me comfortable.

As I brush my teeth, some part of me that wants to be helpful but isn't sends a pouting thought my way.

There's no way this will last.

I stifle a grumble. We've hardly had time to determine that.

But if she's only here through the race... our short time together is winding down fast.

I shake off the thoughts. A towel wrapped around my waist, I lean on the bathroom doorframe and watch Sunny. It takes me a moment to realize she's searching for her clothes.

"Stay the night." I blurt. Thank god my flapping jaw selected that option. Sometimes my mouth feels like a fun wheel of comments and I never know what I'll get. The other plea churning just behind the first was *don't leave*.

I'm too nervous to be more eloquent.

Sunny wipes a towel over the damp ends of her ponytail, her face thoughtful. She tied her dark curls up during the shower to keep them dry. I feel bad that in my seduction, I messed up that plan. Maybe I have a shower cap somewhere...

Is it just me, or is she taking kind of a long time to decide?

"Okay. Your bed looks amazing."

It is. But I was hoping *I* was the reason she'd stay.

"I'll raid my closet for something you can use as PJs."

As I toss her some options, I catch her hiding a huge yawn.

"Bedtime, sleepy girl."

She mumbles what I think is agreement as she tugs on a pair of my sweatpants that are comically too long and a worn t-shirt.

I scoop her up. She only playfully pushes at my chest as I dump her in bed, then wrestle with the comforter to get her under it.

She looks up at me with those eyes. "What time do you usually go to bed? I'm not used to this schedule. They have us doing so much. Amazing things. But there's not a lot of downtime."

I'm already shaking my head as I climb in and extend my legs with a groan. "I'm not a good role model for a sleep schedule. I have to seize the chance whenever I can. And now that there's a beautiful girl in my bed to cuddle, it seems like a perfect opportunity."

"Charmer," she accuses.

"Honest relayer of facts," I argue.

Her smile flashes before she tucks her face into my chest. She lets me pull her tight against me. Usually, when I can't sleep, I get up and wander the apartment, fiddling with different distractions until exhaustion comes for me, but there's no way I'm missing a moment with Sunny, because who knows how long we have.

Sunny rolling in my arms and the faint shaft of light through the curtains wake me the next morning. Blessedly, it's before either of our alarms.

She wakes and blinks, and the expressions on her face flicker as she makes sense of where she is, ending on an adorably confused pout with her eyebrows drawn.

"Hi," I laugh.

She grumbles and wedges her face between my bicep and the sheets.

"Is that noise of dissatisfaction for me?"

Her head pops up, nearly bonking me in the face. "Absolutely not." She shakes herself. "The noise is because I'm exhausted, and I get to do such cool things this week so I shouldn't complain, but still I'm *so* tired."

I pull her on top of me. "You're allowed to be tired," I insist. "Sorry I kept you up late."

She's shaking her head adamantly, stray wisps of hair twining around her cheeks. "No, no apologies from you. Not after what you did."

I cock my head. "What did I do?"

She wriggles, grinding her hips against me and encouraging my already mostly alert dick. "Gave me several mind-blowing orgasms. That's what you did."

"Mmm." I kiss her, just a peck, and add one to her nose right after. "You could sleep a little longer."

"Please don't make me."

I roll us over and pin her hands above her head. "I like it when you say please."

She huffs, and it's got to be to purposefully shove her perky nipples against the fabric of the t-shirt of mine she's wearing. It's one from a karting championship years ago, and god, the price I'd pay to see her sleepy in it every morning.

"Giraffe man, please tell me you have coffee."

I scowl and rub my scruff over her cheek. She tries to escape but giggles at the contact. "I've got an automatic brewer set up, and I added enough beans for both of us." Thanks to multiple sticky notes, a reminder on my phone, a text from Pete, and another one in all caps, like he does whenever I ask him to please help me remember some-thing.

I lean in. She closes the gap to meet me. It's like she's blasted lighter fluid over the spark in my chest. I kiss her. I want her to remember me all day amidst the amazing things she's going to do. As her dreams are realized at the race track, I hope she remembers me, here.

Pleased with myself, I break the kiss eventually and watch her flushed face.

Her eyes spark with that brilliant, unbreakable focus of hers. It clicked on within moments of her waking. This woman is a machine. She's gonna take over the motor-sports world someday, I swear.

Her eyes dart and her jaw works, her brain on fire. I'm desperate and eager to hear what she'll say.

This has been so fun, Evan. When can I see you again?

You're actually a pretty okay cook.

Please let's have sex again, Evan. I want to bounce on your impressive—

"What time is it?"

I deflate a little but hide it, I think, and tear my focus from her to squint at the clock, a nemesis I'm not used to having outside the race track. "5:30."

Her shoulders relax against the mattress. Her wrists loosen beneath my hands, and she smiles at me, though the corners of her eyes are tight. I want to fight whatever it is that has her stressed so soon after waking. I free her wrists and draw her close. She curls into me again. "What time do you have to get moving?"

Her lips move against my skin as she thinks, presumably figuring out the math of her day.

"I want to be back at the hotel at seven," she says finally, with the confidence and regality of an empress.

Keeping one arm around her, I grab my phone from the nightstand. "Seven," I confirm, typing it into my favorite reminder app. Sunny's schedule will not be thrown off on my account. While I'm looking at the app, I've got the opportunity to tackle a looming reminder. "Give me a minute."

I roll from the bed, immediately decimated by the lack of Sunny beside me, and traipse to the kitchen, my brow furrowed at the coffee maker as I make sure I did indeed add more coffee and that it'll brew at the regular time, which will give us time for a cup before I need to take Sunny to the hotel.

I'm hit with that familiar itchy feeling as I realize this wasn't the reason I got out of bed—it was a logical step along the way—and swear. I jog back to the bedroom, enjoy Sunny's smile for a second, then look at my phone again.

Pack neck trainer. That's the reminder.

I scuttle to the closet and dig in the tangle of training equipment in the corner—my designated spot for this mess. I emerge, on a clear trajectory out of the room again...

"Can I see that?" Sunny's sat up against the headboard, a blanket around her shoulders.

"Is it too cold in here?"

She shakes her head and gestures for the trainer, fingers grasping. I don't know if there's anything I wouldn't give her.

I hand her the bundle of nylon, neoprene, and D-rings, the hilarious-looking harness that racers use to train their necks to withstand G-forces. Sunny explores it with the focus and discernment she's directed toward every aspect of race week so far, like she'll never see it again and needs to understand and document it now or never. I frown. She belongs here—in the racing world, I mean. Anyone can see that. She hands it back to me with murmured thanks.

"Do you like doing the neck exercises? Like, are they more or less miserable than burpees?"

I consider and take a moment to duck into the hallway and toss the harness on top of the bright orange bag that lives beside my front door and goes with me everywhere. I return to Sunny in bed, crawling toward her from the foot.

"I don't mind the exercises. They hurt, but the benefits are worth it."

Her eyes go wide as I tug the blanket off her. "Withstanding G-forces, you mean?"

"That," I say, and grab her ankles, drawing her slowly down the bed. She lets me. The friction drags the shirt up her body, revealing the delicious curve of her stomach, the lower halves of her breasts. I dig my fingers beneath the waistband of the sweatpants she borrowed, remembering she's not wearing anything underneath. "And it gives me the strength to spend hours with my head between a woman's legs."

A breathy "oh" escapes her as I draw off the sweats and settle between her thighs, giving her delicious pussy a thorough lick.

She moans, and her hands move to my head, tangling in my bedhead. It's gonna be a baseball cap day, for sure. No way am I fixing the mess she's making of me this morning. She tugs sharply before my next pass through her heat. She's already so wet for me. "We don't have hours."

I kiss her inner thigh. "We have enough for this, for coffee, and to get you to the hotel. I'll drive." I cut off her protest with a wink, even though the hotel is so close. "Now, be good, and let me make you scream."

Pleasure, and more importantly, trust, floods her face, filling my chest with something else. "By all means, don't let me interrupt your plans." Her voice hitches as I press a kiss to her clit. "I don't want to miss an opportunity to see your training in action." Her nails scratch my scalp, the sensation amazing, and I get to work.

CHAPTER TWELVE

Sunny

I've never resonated with that quote about two wolves inside of every person, but this morning, I might finally understand.

One of my wolves has me by the scruff, reminding me that this thing with Evan is strictly casual and has to remain that way. The second wolf is infatuated and smitten with Evan Evans.

They're going to tear me apart.

"Does your head hurt when you do that?"

"Hm?" I glance at Evan. His eyes flash at me from beneath a Panache cap, and I've never noticed how someone's hands on a steering wheel could accentuate their forearm muscles.

He laughs as he guides the car out of the parking garage. He insisted on driving me back to the hotel. I'm thankful, because it's early enough that there won't be too many people to witness my slightly too big, borrowed sweats and the dress from last night tucked under my arm.

That latter wolf—she's thrilled to have more time with Evan.

"When you focus so hard like that," he says. His eyes flick to me every other moment, even while he's navigating the road. "Your forehead scrunches. It looks like it hurts."

My palm finds my face, smoothing the ruts. "I'm fine."

My anxiety spikes when we pull into the drive before the hotel's grand glass doors. Emerging from the Evan-scented cloud of pleasure, I miss my computer and my notes, my carefully curated plan for this week. As a bonus, it'll be a salve for the hurt of not seeing him again.

My hand curls around the handle before he's even touched the brakes.

"I want to see you again."

My mouth drops open as the car stops. Evan's focused on me. His hopeful eyes match the color of the forests I flew over to get here.

I stammer the first thought I have. "How would that even work?"

"Um..." Evan speaks slowly. "We could go out to a restaurant, or maybe do a fun activity. Like... bowling?"

I close my eyes and draw a slow breath through my nose. "I meant, how would that work in terms of our packed schedules? We're both extremely busy."

And we both need to focus, I almost add.

But...this is my first chance at experiencing kink, and I'd like to make the most of it.

And that's the only reason, my first wolf nips at the second.

Evan opens his mouth to respond but is interrupted by another buzzing alert, this time from the watch I assume is synced up to the genius system of reminders on his phone. Text scrolls across the small screen, asking DID YOU EAT BREAKFAST?

He swears. "Guess I missed that one... I was busy doing something else." His smile is small and knowing and sly, and it makes my stomach somersault.

The watch buzzes again. SERIOUSLY, DO NOT FORGET TO EAT SOMETHING.

He reaches past me with a sigh and opens the glovebox, which is full of granola bars. "How about this, can I text you later and we can figure out a plan, together?"

My head turns at the sound of voices. Two people are coming around the hotel's corner. They don't look like race personnel, but the longer I sit here, the higher the chance someone from Riot sees. While there's no fraternization policy in the paperwork they sent for the Crush—I checked immediately after my interview with Evan—I'd rather not talk about this with anyone but my friends.

The people pass, not entering the hotel and—more importantly—not glancing through the windshield. I need to get out of the car. Evan stares at me so intensely, I could trick myself into thinking he's got feelings for me beyond lust. I can't risk entertaining that notion.

"Okay." I spare a small smile for him, because last night was fun, and if it's logical or not, I still do maybe want to see him again. And texting is harmless, right? Right? "Text me later. Thanks for the ride."

I duck out of the car and sprint to my hotel room, like the wolves warring in my chest are snapping at my heels.

I stare at the weird abstract artwork in my hotel room, heart pounding and ready for my day, even though it doesn't technically start for another ninety minutes. I definitely added far too much wiggle room when giving my estimate to Evan for what time I needed to be back. I got ready in record time, anticipation driving me faster.

And now, weirdly, I've got nothing to do. My socials are updated, the day's agenda set, and somehow, I've managed to create a pocket of precious free time.

A grin explodes across my face. I know exactly what I'm going to do.

The shuttle driver seems pleased to make a run this early. I'm joined by a few team staff covering yawns as we're driven to the race course while the sun peeks over the mountains.

As we trundle along, I take a moment to settle myself. It's time to decide exactly where Evan will settle in my sphere of focus. His easy smiles and doting attention withered my logic last night, sending me giggling and opening up.

Unacceptable.

The first and last priority of this trip is my media career. It's the entire reason I'm here.

Evan's purpose is this: a clandestine quickie with a handsome goofball that together we've decided has turned into a weekend fling.

He's respectful and attentive and incredibly fun to be around. Delicious fantasies I'd never hoped to play out are the perfect addition to an already terrific week.

The tightness in my chest eases slightly as I set these boundaries in my mind, being extra careful to lay cement around the ones surrounding my heart. No feelings will be allowed beyond fond friendship.

I stretch the anxiety out of my spine. "Glad that's settled."

The bus eases to a stop. There's a hiss as the door opens, and the driver calls for us to have a nice day and reminds us of the last time the shuttle runs home in the evening.

I step foot into another beautiful day in the Riot Racing paddock. I've got a media badge and a plan.

The entrance gate is a beautiful red and orange arch, and the stile emits a chime that sends my heart soaring when I scan my credentials. There's no on-track action for another hour, and there's no guarantee that the session will feature any cars at all. The early session on Thursdays is a brief window of track time that teams can apply for if something seems wrong with their car that may affect safety procedures during the race. It's not televised, and there's no publication of which cars will be out. Usually, there's only one or two teams that need to take advantage of the session, and the drivers and other team staff would much rather use the opportunity to sleep before the long media sessions on Thursday afternoons.

I'm happy to spend this time simply wandering and staring, taking in every aspect—the smells, the sounds, the myriad colors—and attempt to etch them deep into my memory.

I enjoy the sleepy morning mist before the chaos starts. I walk up and down, jotting notes to myself for later and snapping photos. Not for any content, but just for me.

When I get to the Panache garage, I feel... giddy.

I'm having a fling with Evan Evans. The sex is... god, I can't even think of words. Transcendent, maybe? My traitorous mind slips to thinking of the cuddles after, the sharing about our lives. Can't have that. No. Feelings. Allowed.

Because affection grows like a weed and before I know it, I'm in love. Love is quicksilver that can slip through the tiniest crack in your defenses, and then some guy has access to your fragile insides and doesn't exercise caution.

So, again, I remind myself, I'm having strictly a fling with Evan Evans.

I spin, lifting my camera for a selfie so it's me in front of the splashy pink-and-black wall with Evan's racing number printed huge across it.

Almost as big as my smile when I snap the photo.

"Sunny?"

I spin to find a giant, helmeted moose of a man barreling down the hallway from deeper in the garage, coming straight for me.

I'm swept up in a hug so fast it takes skill to not bonk my own head against Evan's helmet.

He swings me in a circle, and between my cackling, I try to admonish him to stop before I get dizzy. He plops me down but doesn't let go.

"You're out early."

I tap his helmet along the slim opening that reveals his eyes and the bridge of his nose. "I could say the same about you. You're driving this session?"

He shrugs, and the movement drags his thumbs up my sides, drawing a shiver through my clothes.

"There's an electronics issue with my steering wheel we need to iron out."

He looks amazing in his black race suit. I cock my head. "The session doesn't start for like... a while."

"Yeah." His laugh is sheepish. "Sometimes they have me get dressed early because I can get distracted..."

As such, he leans closer, taking me in.

My insides flutter.

Without thinking, I fist my hands in the front of his suit, drawing him a little closer.

He's just staring at me with those eyes. They're wide with what looks like... wonder.

I hope—no, I'm determined to confirm—that he's as frazzled and preoccupied by the thought of me as I am of him. He caught me off guard this morning with his attention, and I refuse to be the only one walking around in a post-orgasm daze.

I glance sideways. We're alone in this corner of the paddock, except for some staff heading into another team's hospitality center.

"Do you know somewhere we could have a private moment?" Also on my list of kinks to explore… semi-public sneaking around. The risk of being caught sends a flash of heat through me.

Evan's eyes spark, and he pulls me into the hall, then elbows a wall panel, which pops open a small supply room.

"Odds of us being interrupted?"

"Minimal. It's spare team kits and stuff." I know he's telling the truth. All of the plastic bins are dusty except for handprints from when they were moved in.

I tug him in. Eager hands trail over my body, but I scan the room and nudge him against a sturdy-looking rack.

He's got one arm wrapping me close, the other already rubbing between my legs, but I have to focus. So I lift my arms to make some space and grab the zipper at his neck, tugging it down.

He reaches for his helmet, but I grab his hands. "Leave it," I command quietly, pressing a kiss to the carbon fiber right in front of his mouth. His eyes somehow go wider as he realizes my plans. He helps me shimmy his arms out of the suit so it hangs at his waist, and he hauls up the hem of his fireproof shirt so it's out of my way. I drop to my knees and tug down his fireproof underwear, allowing myself one second to take in the majesty of his cock, all hard and jutting for me, then take it into my mouth.

On my first plunge, I take him deep into my throat until my lips brush his stomach, and there's a quiet *thunk* as his head collapses back against the shelf. His hands sink into my hair.

I pull back, taking a moment to nip and lick and kiss and tease after my intense initial barrage.

We both freeze at the sound of passing footsteps and chatter of mechanics, but they dim quickly. The moment wets my panties further, and given the hitch of Evan's breath, it seems he shares the thrill, too.

Then I get to work. I've made peace with this decision, but I'd still prefer to not actually get caught, so I establish a rhythm, sucking hard and pumping his shaft with one hand.

Evan's gone from affectionately caressing my hair to holding on for dear life. I go fast, choking a little and working him into a frenzy.

The twitches start coming, and Evan's bucking into my mouth, matching my pace. He moans my name, muffled through his helmet.

"Yes, like that," he huffs, his words melding with the sound of an engine firing down the hall. "Oh, Sunny, I'm almost there."

I speed up, chasing his orgasm, desperate for his pleasure to peak. My knees and back ache, but I don't care. He gave it to me so good this morning, and ever since, despite my anxious boundary-setting and strategizing, I've been yearning to return the favor. To feel him come undone in the same way.

Evan makes a guttural groan and comes for me. His salty taste floods my tongue, and as I swallow, I glance up. With the angle of his helmet, I bet he's barely able to see me, but I can tell in this moment that I am his queen.

It swells my chest. At the end of this, I'm determined to leave as monumental an impact on him as he's leaving on me.

I sit back on my heels and tuck him away, fixing his fireproofs with a satisfied smirk as his chest heaves and his eyes refocus.

I've got the jumpsuit's zipper halfway up his stomach when he jolts into action, catching me under the arms and hauling me up. One arm wraps my waist as he nearly pulls me off my toes. The other grips the back of my neck as he gently leans his helmeted forehead against mine. His eyes are heavy-lidded, his breathing harsh. "Holy shit."

I allow a breathy laugh and wriggle so he sets me back on my feet, but he doesn't let go completely.

"I'm serious," he says. "New catchphrase. All for you. Holy fucking shit."

I roll my eyes. "That's not a catchphrase. That's just a thing people say!"

"Fuck, I love it when you yell at me." He practically growls this sentiment, and it takes my breath away. It's captivating, the lightness of his spirit and the darkness of his desire all swirled together and focused on me. He leans closer, intent on my mouth.

Drills whir from the adjacent garage. The din of a waking pit crew has been slowly growing louder as we've cavorted.

"We don't have time..." I insist weakly. My fingers dig into the many colorful logos emblazoned across his suit till they feel the heat and the muscle of his chest underneath.

He tenses beneath my hands. His eyes dart, calculating something.

"Fuck it," he says, and rips off his helmet.

Evan kisses me into delirium, leaving no part of my mouth unattended. He clings to me like a knight returned from war, like against all odds, we've triumphed against some threat to humanity, and this is the moment before the backdrop of a burning sunset and a ravaged fortress that we realize we've made it, and we're going to live to see another day.

"He's probably taking an exceptionally long shit."

We both freeze. Pete's exasperated voice comes from beyond our hiding spot.

"We have to go," I whisper, my lips swollen from his ravishing.

Evan's blaring smile cuts through the dimness. "More. More of this later. I'll text you. I'll be thinking about you all day."

I swallow past the sudden lump in my throat. It's all I can manage.

Evan heads for the door, almost forgetting his helmet before I remind him. He shoots me a grateful glance and slips into the hall.

"All clear," he whisper-shouts. I smack him on the shoulder as I follow and turn the opposite direction. He gives me one lingering wink before he turns and jogs to the garage.

"I'm here, I'm here!" he yells, and is greeted with shouts of relief. "You know me and my stubborn bowels!"

With a groan, I scurry from the hall and back into the paddock proper, attempting to look casual. No one from Panache is around, and the slowly growing flock of people outside don't pay me any mind.

I sag against the nearest wall, checking my boundaries. They're intact, but feel terribly flimsy in the face of the alluring force of nature that is Evan Evans.

I am so fucked.

There's a massive grandstand near the pit exit with a breathtaking view of turn one. I climb to the highest bench. My stomach sloshes with warring triumph and misery.

A memory of my mom's voice from when I was little comes to me. *They call it a crush for a reason.* She'd say it with the same laughing tone now, but there's no way I'm calling to fill her in on this complication to my race week. She's not great at boundaries and would immediately try to start planning a wedding.

My mother teems with good intentions. Unfortunately, that good often doesn't extend to her execution, mostly in the way words come out of her mouth. She wants grandbabies. I want a man who doesn't expect me to believe that he hasn't looked at his phone once in a sixteen-hour period.

I perch on the chilly aluminum bench. The sky is bruised gray and the air feels heavy, but there's no rain yet. I tug up my jacket's hood and sigh, my mood the same color as the clouds. My mom—both of my parents, really—want that same thing I want for me: to be happy. Mom is absolutely certain she knows the answer to what would fulfill me (a husband, then babies) and Dad, while wildly supportive, has zero suggestions, which leaves me alone in the murky middle trying to figure it out. My sisters are too young for this specific flavor of pressure and rarely pick up their phones long enough to hear an opinion from anyone.

The bleachers vibrate as Jackie appears at the bottom and begins to climb, and also shouts at me. "I knew we'd find you somewhere! I texted the group chat. Have you been avoiding me?"

I cup my chilly hands around my mouth. "Good morning, beautiful!"

"Right back at you!" Gael appears behind her, waving. Jackie huffs, taking a break to lean on a railing halfway up the steps.

Eventually, they plop at my side, stretching their legs out on the bench below us. Jackie blows her hair out of her face, which is frizzing in the slight drizzle. "Don't get me wrong, girl, this view is beautiful. But you couldn't have done with an hour more of sleep? Especially after what I assume went down at your sleepover last night?"

I can barely conceal my responding grin. "I just gave Evan a blowjob in one of the garage's storage rooms."

I have to clamp a hand over her mouth because her answering shriek would have drawn security if it had gone on any longer. Gael's mouth is open, but thankfully silent, with awe.

When I let her go, she returns to normal volume. "Oh my god, you guys are going to get married."

I snort. "Only if that's some publicity stunt scheduled for the end of this brand trip. It's a hookup. Temporary."

A knot in my chest aches. I massage over the spot, willing it away. Maybe I pulled a muscle last night.

"Did he say that?" Gael asks.

"No."

"Well, did *you* say that?" Jackie prompts.

"Do we really need to? He's a globe-trotting pro athlete. I'm here for a week. This is how it works."

Jackie glares at me. "You're no fun."

"A fling is plenty fun," I argue.

"I bet you he'd like it if we started referring to him as your boyfriend."

"Of course he would," I scoff. "He's a cocky flirt. That doesn't mean he'd like the actual implications that come with that title."

Jackie rolls her eyes. "Tell you what, I get a faster lap time than you at karting later, and I'm calling Evan your boyfriend for the rest of the week. You beat me, and I'll drop it."

"Deal."

She doesn't mention it again for a full two minutes, then sighs heavily with her head between her palms. "You're living so many people's literal dream—do you know that? To attend a race and catch the eye of a beautiful driver and start a whirlwind romance..."

"That will end," I clarify. "He probably does this with a new girl every race weekend."

"We don't know that," Gael offers, tugging a beanie over his unruly hair as the rain picks up.

"Listen, call it whatever you like, but know that Evan Evans is the last person I'd get into a serious relationship with."

"But consider if—" Jackie's thought trails off as someone steps onto the stand above the starting line, a green flag dangling from their hand. As the time ticks to the hour, they step forward and flourish it over the track.

Marco DeFlora's car erupts from his garage with a squeal of tires.

"Interesting," Jackie murmurs.

I agree. Matthews Global Racing Excellence, as their team is formally called, rarely has mechanical issues. Their cars are famously reliable. Their driver pairing, on the other hand...

"Potentially volatile" is the phrase one motorsport journalist reported, citing an anonymous source within the team.

"Gonna be spicy in the Matthews garage this season," Gael quips.

"Incredibly," Jackie agrees.

Teammate dynamics in motorsport are complicated. Riot teams field two drivers so they have more chances to earn wins and podiums and points toward the team championship, but a single racer wins the driver championship based on their results alone. Nearly every driver will say that the person they want to beat the most is their teammate, and that includes teams that aren't fighting at the front. No one wants to be the slower driver on a team, especially when contracts are ended early all the time. There have been plenty of pairings in the past with infighting and close calls in races. It makes for especially interesting seasons.

I've covered the topic before, but it's been a while. I make a mental note to add a refresher piece to my content schedule.

A red car with purple detailing, the same paint scheme as Marco's but inverted, departs the Matthews garage at a more measured pace. That's Stevie Dixon, nicknamed "Sparrow" for her impressive dive bombs in tight corners.

"Both Mattys out," Jackie murmurs.

"Must be something with both cars, then."

She nods, chewing her lip. "Should we be capturing this?"

"I could use a break from content, honestly." I rub my eyes, and Gael nods in agreement. "But content is what got us here..."

She groans. "Tell me about it. We don't have the time for that existential crisis. Or the alcohol or the therapy, for that matter. Let's just enjoy."

I sling an arm around her and tug her close. "You're right. I do want a memory though. Scoot in, Gael."

The ensuing selfie is so adorable, I can't wait to frame it. My heart swells. "I'm glad we got to meet in real life."

She squeezes my hand. "Come to another race. Come see me and Gael in Cali, or we can pick a different one and meet up there."

My smile goes tight. We've had conversations like this before. It's Gael and Jackie's first race with this level of access, but my first race ever. I could afford to go to another, technically. They don't know that. They assume my hesitance is financial, and I don't correct them because it means they don't push. But every time I look at my not-huge but respectable and scraped-for savings balance, I think about emergencies, contingencies. I'm the kid my parents can rely on. What if something were to happen to them, and I'd drained a chunk of savings for entertainment that could have gone toward a medical bill? I'd come close to buying tickets last year, but bailed last minute. Riot's sponsorship this time around is the only reason I'm here, and why, despite the ache in my chest, I don't know if I'll ever see this sport I love up close ever again.

A flash of pink catches my eye. Evan flies from the garage, his car a graceful blur as he crosses the pit exit line. He's a bobbing blob of a helmet tucked into the cockpit. The engine roars as he gains speed on the straight, then gutters as he downshifts into the corner.

I trail his progress until he disappears behind a copse of trees at the far end of the track, though the roar of his engine still echoes. "I really want to enjoy the present right now," I say.

They both mercifully say nothing and leave me to my fascination.

CHAPTER THIRTEEN

Evan

Media days are...something.

They're a part of my well-paying dream job, so I try to always bring a good attitude and energy to the interviews and the Q&As and the silly segments.

Honestly, typically, after a couple of minutes, I get into the swing of it and enjoy myself.

But I'm a bit distracted.

We got the steering wheel issue sorted, and it's always nice to get a few unexpected laps in, but hours later, I'm still processing that hidden pocket of bliss Sunny gave me this morning.

To have her wake up in my arms, to have her agree to let me undo her and give her pleasure, but then for her to show that she's as passionate about giving it back to me?

I'm the luckiest person in this entire paddock.

The thought strikes me like lightning, sudden and clear and deafening.

I need to get her a present.

I'm familiar with this kind of thought. My life can't advance in any meaningful way until I address it.

Lip between my teeth, I pull out my phone and search for a specific contact. I take a moment to decide the parameters of this gift, then fire off the request via text, which is met with enthusiasm, especially because I'll be paying for a rush order.

"Er, Evan?"

I vaguely hear my name.

An elbow finds my upper arm, and I start, blinking in the TV lights.

Fuuuuuuuuuuuck.

Thankfully, I catch the sentiment before it escapes my throat.

I clear my throat and shoot Grant, who elbowed me, a grateful glance.

"Sorry." I stow my phone and muster a disarming smile. It's a dirty trick—I was being a dick not paying attention—but it'll help them forgive me. I resettle on the couch I'm sharing with a handful of other drivers for this press conference. "Can you repeat the question, please?"

Good-natured laughs sound from the rows of journalists seated before us, their phones all held out to record our answers. "What are your goals for this weekend? You've said yourself that last season ended for you on an underwhelming note."

I rub my shoulder and consider. "Yeah, it was disappointing to walk away last season feeling like my potential didn't measure up to what the team made possible with the car. In the off-season, I focused a lot on mindset and working with the team to figure out what I need to do to close that gap. The goal is, of course podiums, and hopefully wins. I'm excited to make it happen."

There are nods and thankfully, no follow-up questions. I'm nervous enough as it is. I know what I need to do this weekend. I know I *can* do it. But there's that weird space in the middle—making it happen—that seems the slipperiest.

The interview continues without incident, and most of the questions go to other drivers.

In a break between commitments, I steal a moment to check socials. Sunny hasn't posted in a little while. I was half-hoping for something from her at the open session this morning, maybe with my car flying by in the background.

Relax, dude, don't come on too strong.

My energy can be a lot for people. My exes would probably say that when we were together, they suffered most of all. When you date a race car driver, it means lots of time apart or lots of time together in close quarters; on planes, in buses, hectic weekends in hotel rooms that get a little smelly if the prior weekend was too tight to squeeze in laundry.

It already asks a lot, and you couple that with my "big personality" as my sister lovingly calls it...

People have bailed on me before. Several times. I get it. I wish so deeply for someone who I could be a good match with, for our personalities as well as the lifestyle necessitated by my career.

Eventually, someone will think I'm worth the chaos.

Two hours later, I'm considering buying Sunny a second present.

Blair, one of Panache's top PR people, gently bops me on the head with a microphone. I take it with an apologetic smile. She knows I'll be attentive when it's important... Probably. Grant and I are tucked in the back hallway of Panache's hospitality center. He and I will do a Q&A

and photo op with some lucky contest-winning fans. Blair gives us a five-minute warning and me one of her token stern glances that tells me not to not ruin her meticulously planned day, but she doesn't even look at Grant before she turns on her heel to go make sure the snack station is properly stocked for the guests.

His eyebrows draw together a fraction and his jaw tightens.

Grant has an incredible poker face. It's one of his strongest features as a competitor. Ahead of a session, when we're both in the garage, I can never get an idea of how he's feeling about the way his team has tweaked his car as opposed to mine. I beat Grant in the points last season by a respectable margin, but I shouldn't feel comfortable. He's not a rookie anymore, and he could catch up to me if I'm not careful. Panache signed him as a racer in this series for several reasons, only one of which is the amount of money his family has.

This brings me back to thoughts of Sunny and a piece she did on teammate relationships in the motorsports world. She's covered it a few times, and it's especially clever because it's a sneaky component of our sport that people who come in from other sports fandoms get confused by.

It strikes me that I haven't heard from her since the storage room ecstasy, and I miss her. With a cheeky grin, I take out my phone.

> This morning was incredible... Why don't you come over tonight and I can show you how thankful I am?

There. More sexy than clingy. And if she comes over, that's more time to spend together and get to know each other. I've done enough therapy to know I can get ahead of myself and daydream fantasies that will let me down when they don't happen, but I think Sunny and I have amazing potential and fireworks chemistry, and I think she might think so, too. I want to date her. So, sexy flirting aside, when we've only got five days or so of stolen pockets of time, when's the opportune time to talk to her about this? Surely, I can put off that conversation for a little while. I mean, it was like pulling teeth to have her admit she likes me.

But god... when she did.

Whatever enchantment she casted over my body and soul has me staring off for a while. Long enough that Grant has to clear his throat twice when our time to shine approaches.

The Panache team member who's acting as emcee says our names, and Grant and I head out to the small stage.

I'm scarfing some delicious pasta from catering as a late lunch when my phone buzzes with Sunny's response.

For the tougher parts of the day, when the questions about my recent performance are getting old, having memories with Sunny in the back of my mind made persevering through those tough moments much easier.

First, she sends me that smiling devil face emoji, which I love. She knows she rocked my world this morning.

The second message is less exciting.

> I really need to catch up on sleep if I'm going to make it through the rest of the weekend at my best. I'm going to stay at the hotel tonight. Thank you for the invite, though.

It's a perfectly reasonable response. We met three days ago, and it's a week where we both need to focus. Still, the refusal squeezes my chest like a mechanic's wrench is trying to crush my ribs together.

All right, no worries. I'll be thinking of you. What kind of activities do they have you doing today?

A perfectly civil response. Nicely done, Evan.

And, a hopeful voice inside me pipes up, she technically only said "no" to coming over *tonight*.

My watch beeps, flashing my schedule for the rest of the day so I don't forget what else is in store.

A small smile lights my face. My next appearance is with a group of kids and staff from a nonprofit that raises awareness around and provides support for people with ADHD. Given my own experience with ADHD, I worked with Blair to bring them in for a track tour. I love talking to them. They'll load us into an open truck and give me a microphone so I can be the world's most chaotic tour guide, then we'll have a chat over ice cream after.

Then I guess I'll go home and sleep alone, which, aside from my incredible night with Sunny, is the sad status quo.

CHAPTER FOURTEEN

Sunny

The hotel's gym is surprisingly less smelly than I expected.

Lex Gotham is a firecracker rookie for Manta's racing team who won Riot's junior series by a landslide last year.

She's a ball of energy, similar to Evan but more fidgety. Her weight never stays on one foot for long and her eyes dart over all of our faces and that of the man standing next to her in quick succession.

Frances Reznik, or "Rez" as the paddock calls him, is her trainer. He's a tall, stony-faced man with legs for days and muscles to match.

While Lex gives us an enthusiastic wave and says, "Hi guys, welcome in," Rez barely inclines his head in acknowledgment. He's all business to her constant fun.

Rez's chosen wardrobe for the day is a crisp team polo and tapered joggers, and Lex wears a full Manta-branded nylon tracksuit that makes hilarious swishy noises whenever she moves.

Rez gives us a spiel on a trainer's process to help their driver be at peak performance when it comes time to get in the car. Lex chimes in to provide specifics about how they work together.

As Rez talks, each sentence efficient and thorough, Lex continues to fidget. Her eyes cut to him sneakily as he explains the types of activities that may surprise us that prove to be helpful as cross-training.

"Swimming, yoga, ice skating, video games for reflexes, martial arts—"

When he says the last one, her movement alarmingly fast, Lex spins and aims a backward kick that *should* catch Rez right in the face.

Except Rez's reflexes match hers—likely honed by him—and he catches her by the ankle when her foot is mere inches from his face. He quirks an eyebrow, his face a mask of fond exasperation, as if this has happened many times before.

Without releasing her ankle, he says, deep and stern, "Behave. We have company."

Her eyes widen for a fraction of a second, then Lex smirks and sticks out her tongue. Rez holds her gaze for a long moment, then releases her.

"Hot," Gael whispers beside me. I nod my agreement. My eyes flick to Jackie, and hers are there, already waiting. We will definitely be discussing the, ahem, *certain* variety of tension that there appears to be between these two later.

Her prank aside, the pair continues their presentation without incident. As Rez lays a thick weight on Lex's back while she's in a plank, a flash of Evan holding himself above me, smiling through a lull in our escapades that allowed us to catch our breath, hits me.

I shake myself. When I refused another sleepover, I felt both pleased and queasy.

I set a boundary to distance myself from Evan. That's good, right? Then, why do I feel so miserable?

Thankfully, our day only gets busier from here, so the odds of me thinking of him...

"Who knows what this is?"

Lex holds up the neck training device Evan referenced this morning and I nearly choke.

Rez catches my eye as I try to catch my breath. "Are you familiar?"

"Big fan," I manage.

"Okay..." He helps Lex put it on to demonstrate.

Turning red, I fix my face and get back to paying attention.

The best thing about motorsport is also one of the worst: it's loud as hell.

The fact that the karting track is housed in a giant metal building full of kids and teenagers celebrating birthdays doesn't help.

When we were all on the track, which is multi-level and lit with glowing LEDs, the sound was muted by helmets and adrenaline.

Now that I'm parked at a sticky plastic table with my leg propped on the bench and a fat ice pack over one knee, the pulse of arcade noises and general exuberance is building a matching pain in my skull.

"You're sure you're alright?" Gael asks.

Our race got a little intense and I scraped the barriers in the final turn of the track, rocking my knee against the kart's steering column.

It hurts like hell, but I made it on the podium. The silly plastic medal around my neck feels worth it at the moment.

Jackie, Gael, and I have been sat by the pizza buffet for half an hour and the swelling seems to have reached its maximum. My pain hasn't gotten any worse so I'm sure

I'll be sore tomorrow but thankfully, I don't think I need medical attention, though Cooper keeps offering to call someone. I've told him several times that I don't want this to be a whole thing. With some painkillers and sleep, I'll be fine.

My phone buzzes jarringly against the table. I groan as I lift it, my arms aching from the G-forces in the karts. They go way faster than the ones I remember from family vacations to tourist towns as a kid.

"Oh, is that your *boyfriend*?" Jackie asks. Gael says nothing but his eyes spark with mischief as he chews on a french fry.

I shake my head. Even though she won the race—and our bet—that title really needs to be reserved for safe, sensible men that don't have killer dimples.

Evan went quiet for a few hours after I declined the invitation to stay the night again. Prior to that, his messages had been in a steady flow, starting with an adorably cringey selfie of him in his helmet after he got out of the car this morning, giving a thumbs up to the camera.

How's karting?

I check my watch and type back.

> Aren't you in a driver's meeting?

We're through the important stuff. Now it's just Luke and Marco arguing about the pit lane exit. Johnny says hi. so does RJ, but she insists I should be paying attention too.

Holy shit, he's sat between two racing powerhouses, and they know about me?

> You should listen to her! (Karting is fun. banged up my knee though.)

Ouch, been there. Elevation and ice will help. Do you have that at the hotel?

> Ice and pillows are like the only guarantees at a hotel.

Fair point. ...And crappy croissants, don't forget. Let me know if you need anything. (Ex: painkillers, an orgasm.) I'll be out of here within an hour probably.

My stomach clenches at the offer and I stuff my phone in my pocket so I'm not tempted to take him up on it.

Both Jackie and Gael, and even Cooper, have their eyebrows raised, but I refuse to spill. I shove my phone deep into my purse. "Who wants more pizza?"

I'm somewhat grateful for the bruise forming on my leg. After seeing me hobble through the lobby, none of my influencer cohort blame me for refraining from their outing to the bars. I settle into bed with fresh ice and an old sitcom. I'm half asleep when my phone goes off.

I hope you're able to get a good night's sleep.

I was until you texted and ruined it.

I AM SO SORRY!!!

I'm teasing you

Takes a bold woman to tease Evan Evans.

There's no emoji that illustrates how hard I'm rolling my eyes right now.

How's your knee?

Much better. Ice and painkillers, baby.

I like when you call me baby. Wanna call me that in my bed tomorrow? We have more kink to explore…

My legs clench, which tweaks my injury.

Let me see how I'm feeling.

Right! Gotta kink responsibly.

I smirk at the screen. It stays dark for all of thirty seconds before...

Did you play sports in school?

I hesitate. He wants to talk… Do I want to? I…

I think I do.

That's fine, right? No one falls in love via text message. I'm much safer having this conversation virtually, rather than next to him in his bed, naked and blissed out from mind-blowing sex. And I do want to end up there, experiencing my fantasies come to life, but absolutely nothing more.

I reread the question. It's... friendly. And surely there's no harm in *friendly*? Say we stay friends? Having a connection with a racing driver could be a boon for my content work, like if he invited me to a promotional event or something. I imagine him dressed casually, smiling at me from beneath a baseball cap and explaining more elements of racing that I'll never have access to. The warmth in my chest that pangs in response is decidedly un-friendly. I tamp it down and pick up my phone with a frown. I can do this. I can navigate these fraught waters.

I played softball. Loved it. Not enough to pursue it though.

What's your favorite type of food?

That is far too vague a question, so I'm not explaining my answer. Breakfast.

What's with the twenty questions?

Ah, shoot, you do really need to sleep.

And you don't?

I will. Five more questions then you're off to bed. That's an order.

Um, deal?

Also, where are you? What are you doing?

Oooh, so sorry. You get no questions in this scenario. Should have read the fine print before agreeing to the terms.

You're insufferable.

You seem to suffer me just fine.

Okay rapid fire here we go.

Best rollercoaster you've ever ridden? Do you think raccoons are cute or creepy? Cats or dogs? Best pasta shape? What's your middle name?

I can't bring myself to set down the phone.

I end up texting him for too long. Long enough I avoid looking at the time. Long enough that my eyes go all bleary and my ice pack is water by the time we say goodnight.

The bastard.

CHAPTER FIFTEEN

Evan

Her middle name is Katherine.

And I definitely bothered her for far too long last night.

But... she kept texting back.

Having her not stay over again was devastating. I hope she maybe missed me, too.

What I've got planned for today is an invitation, something that could be refused. Though Blair laughed in my face when I admitted as much.

Our PR genius swings the garage pass around her finger, the thick laminate glossy in the bright light the mechanics need to see every inch of our cars. "Of course she'll come. No race fan would refuse access to a team garage."

We can only fit so many guests in the tight quarters safely, and many of the limited passes are spoken for between sponsors and other VIPs. A garage pass may as well be made of gold.

Blair pauses my protest by holding up a pristine, manicured hand. She's got gems glued to her nails. Their sparkle is immensely distracting. Her words draw my eyes back to her face. "Evan, you're a really nice guy. Please don't make me spend my limited time convincing you of that."

I smile ruefully, promising to internalize what she's said. Plus, Grant's making pleading eyes at me from his side of the garage. Whatever the issue is, he needs Blair more than I do.

I need to focus anyway. My brain is the type that's always prioritizing three or four things at once, and I make it work for me, but I need to be sure the biggest piece of my focus pie is on the impending practice sessions.

Sunny is definitely the second biggest slice, though.

My train of thought derails, and I'm bombarded by other sensations; how sweet Sunny laughs, her passionate opinions on breakfast foods, how I'd like to dive between her thighs with a can of whipped cream and...

I shake myself and adjust my race suit. Getting into the car with a boner is a nightmare. I don't know which is worse, when my left front tire tech notices and makes fun of me, or when the head engine mechanic politely averts his gaze. It's happened once before, when an A-list actor visited the garage at last year's Indianapolis Grand Prix. I'll never live it down.

I finish putting on my gear and approach the car. Gingerly, so as not to smudge the carefully buffed paint with the toe of my racing boot, I take a large step to get one foot into the cockpit. With one hand on the halo, a three-pronged titanium roll bar that protects us if the car flips over, I haul my body into the cockpit. It's a fun dance. Once both feet are on my seat, I brace myself on the halo and thread my legs into their designated channels until my feet brush the pedals, then shimmy my body into the seat's comforting embrace.

As the mechanics strap me in, Pete's in my ear to give me a reminder of the run plan and what we're hoping to learn this session. We discussed it in our team briefing yesterday, but it's important to make sure we all understand the day's purpose and touch on anything that might have changed.

My knees bounce in anticipation as the team makes the final tweaks to assure our setup is perfect. I dip my head in thanks, and finally, a mechanic steps into the pit lane to check for traffic and guide me out.

As soon as their palm drops, I'm out. I press my right foot down and the car jolts into rapid motion with the barest squeal of the tires.

When I'm free of the pit lane, I hit the gas fully and swerve onto the track, joy bubbling inside me as the wind buffets my helmet and the car roars around me. Crowds of fans have already gathered to watch practice, and though I can't hear them, I know they must be loud, too.

Pete provides updates in my ear as I start a lap, and the lights on my steering wheel blink as I shift gears and adjust the car's settings on the fly. I love thinking a few seconds ahead, knowing which curves and bumps come next.

Out here, my ADHD becomes a superpower. The information from Pete and the feel of the air around the car becomes a complicated, coded message that I understand completely. I could drive this car for hours. In this, at least, I know what I'm doing.

"Is she there?"

"Engine mode five please, Evan."

"Confirm. Did she come down?"

Pete makes a strangled noise over the radio. "Affirmative."

I want to ask more—I want to know how Sunny reacted when Blair found her—but when we're on track, our radio is fair game to all the other teams as well as any broadcast channels covering the weekend.

That same spirit of information sharing is what enabled me to check what the Crush creators had going on today. As I suspected, as the week's action ramps up, Riot has—for the most part—less interesting activities planned because team members really need to focus on what's happening on track.

The suite they set aside for the creators to watch practice is nice, but I wanted to give Sunny nearly unfettered access to the session's action.

And... if she sticks around after the session, I might get to see her.

"Thank you, Petey bird."

"Of course, man. Now tell me about the brake balance."

"Mostly good, but there's still a little bit of that, uh..." I make a rumbling noise in the back of my throat, punctuating it with a smack in the middle by popping my lips.

I know the technical terms, but Pete and I have been doing this for so long that he understands what I mean.

"Okay, let me check with the others and we'll see what we can do. How do these tires feel?"

"Eh." I consider as I steer through a chicane. "I'd say a seven."

"Out of ten?" Pete asks patiently, though he knows it's not.

"More like twelve."

"Right. Box this lap, please."

We get a lot of good running done during practice. I pit twice for adjustments and manage to keep my head forward and focused on what our team needs rather than seeing if I can catch Sunny's reflection in one of the many mirrored surfaces in the garage. Since she accepted the pass from Blair, she'll be situated behind a barrier at the back of the garage where she's got a full view of all the action. It's really cool access, and I hope she agrees. I want to help boost her reach while she's here. Riot fans who may not know her will watch stuff she makes in the garage today, then see how brilliant she is and stick around.

I also hope a small part of her can't help but keep an eye on the back of my helmet as she takes in everything else going on around her.

The team fits me with a different tire compound to test and I head out again. No one has brought up my skittish-ness in that final corner, maybe to keep me from getting even more nervous. I'm grateful for it.

Pete pipes in over the radio, interrupting my thoughts. "I think we've got what we need, Ev. No need to overdo it for the car, but is there anything you want to work out over the next couple of laps?"

I tug off one of the tearaway films over my visor, clearing my view of dust and, unfortunately, smushed bugs. "I want to try that damn turn again. I still don't have it. Three more laps?"

"Yep. Confirm."

An idea tickles the back of my brain. A bad one, which of course means I'm going to go for it.

As I breeze across the finish line to start another flying lap, I speak. "Is she on a headset?"

"Come again?"

"Is she listening on a headset, Pete?"

A heavy sigh.

"Can you turn your damn head, please, for me?" The track has gotten busier, with plenty of cars out. I bet my weird radio, which is par for the course, won't catch the attention of broadcasters right away, not with so many other drivers working through issues on their own channels. I cruise through turns three and four, nailing the apexes. In the garage, we've got a bunch of headsets available to tune into mine and Grant's radios. On the pit wall, they've got the ability to talk back to me, but everyone else can listen in. It's an awesome experience for guests visiting the garage.

Pete's grumbling, but I know he's doing as I say. I rip down a straight at a blistering pace, faster than I've gone all session. When I'm on my shenanigans, I race better. Something about the crisscrossed wiring in my brain.

"Can confirm. Your friend is on a headset and tuned to your channel, if there's something you'd like to share with the class."

Calling Sunny a "friend" hurts. It's not nearly close enough to describe what I hope we'll have.

"Is there anything more interesting than me being a dumbass happening on track right now?"

"It's your lucky day. Dean went for a spin down an escape road. He's all right, but it was an impressive error, and I bet there'll be replays from a few angles over the next half a minute."

I hug the curb perfectly as my heart hammers harder in my chest. I normally don't get this excited in practice. It's for data gathering and learning the course.

I want to be reckless. I want to give her attention in a semi-public situation, but if the media blasts our business all over the TV, that takes away the fun of the thrill. It's like when we had sex in that conference room. We were both so amped, keyed up by the risk of being caught, but if that actually came to fruition... We'd survive, but it might take all the sexy fun out of the situation.

As with racing, I think in order to win Sunny's heart, I need to just fucking send it and accept whatever consequences come as a result.

"Hey, girl!" I call like a fucking idiot.

One of the other engineers unmutes herself to snort.

Gotta commit now, especially since Sunny can't reply to me, and I'm sure Pete won't be nice enough to tell me if she flips to Grant's channel or takes off her headset. "Hope you're enjoying the view from down here."

Coming out of a slow turn, I gun it, knowing the engine's roar will make it through the line.

"I was thinking..." I accelerate more, pushing the car to its limit. "I gotta get a nickname for you. I was thinking maybe 'kit' because you're always keeping it tough when it comes to me. Those're the first letters of the words 'keeping it tough...'" I can practically hear her chiding that my reasoning doesn't make enough sense.

The turn I've been struggling with looms. Pete is happy to stay silent to prove a point, or, to not distract me. "Anyway, I'm glad you came down to see the action even more up close. And by action..." I hold the steering wheel steady, finally nailing the turn. "...I mean me." I steam over the finish line and Pete recites my time.

I've put in a lap that would be impressive in qualifying tomorrow, if I can duplicate it.

I feel my grin eating my entire face and don't attempt to hold back a triumphant whoop and some other nonsensical noises as I take a slower lap to cool down the car. I have no way of knowing if Sunny's still listening, but there's a feeling in my gut that says she is.

"Kit, I hope you stick around. I'll be back in a bit, and I'd love to see you."

CHAPTER SIXTEEN

Sunny

My cheeks are so hot, surely they're about to melt off my face.

The maniac gave me a pet name on live radio.

At least I was lucky enough that something interesting was happening elsewhere on track, so Evan's comments haven't been featured on the broadcast playing in the corner of the room. A million worldwide fans aren't wondering who he's trying to flirt with in the garage.

Not that I'm embarrassed. Not now, at least. That will come only if I fall for him like a complete fool.

To their benefit, none of the team is staring. I'd believe that Evan gets up to stunts like this on the regular. Hell, he probably brings whatever lucky person he's sleeping with down here every race. Though... the nice PR person, Blair, who brought me the garage pass, watches me out of the corner of her eye as she chats with one of the management people, wearing a smug grin.

The whir of something mechanical draws my attention. Ever since I arrived in the garage, I've hardly stopped staring. From the flurry of mechanics to the computer screens populated with data and a million other things I didn't realize went into a successful practice session. It's incredible. Whatever his motives, Evan has given me a priceless gift. There's not much I'm allowed to photograph, but there will be plenty to discuss during my next stream. There's enough for me to talk about for weeks.

During the two practice sessions per Riot race weekend, each team tries to home in on the setups that will make their car the fastest at the track they're visiting. There are many factors that contribute to a car's speed, from the engine's power to the type of tires that are fitted, as well as strategic pit stops. That doesn't even begin to touch the intricacies of needing certain settings for qualifying, and a different set of specs for the race. One of the biggest factors is a sensation called downforce, which describes how the closer a car is to the ground—we're talking millimeters—the faster it is. The car's body shape is designed to optimize airflow around it, coupled with the finely adjusted angles of the front and rear wings to essentially suck the car down toward the track so it can carve through the air at tremendous speeds.

Simply put, it's astounding.

And thanks to Evan, I'm witnessing it far closer than many fans ever will.

Not a bad hookup perk at all.

The session clock winds down and cars make their return to the pits.

Blair approaches me, a knowing look on her face. "So, what do we think?"

I can hardly form words. "There's—there's so much."

With a grin, she takes me by the shoulders as the other spectators depart and urges me further down the barrier so I'm at a spot on the wall between engineering monitors and a helmet shelf.

She holds out a hand expectantly. "Give me your phone."

Blair is one of those people that you listen to, even if you're not exactly sure you should. It explains why she's such a popular figure in the paddock, and people joke that she runs Panache narratives in the media like the Navy.

I comply, and she procures a strip of masking tape from one of her many pockets and sticks it over my phone's back camera. "You can film in this pocket of space, but selfie mode only, and make sure not to include any of our computer screens. I can buy you about five minutes before I have to ask you to go back to the paddock."

"Oh my god, thank y—"

She's already shaking her head. "Four minutes, fifty seconds!"

I fumble with my phone and go live as quickly as possible.

"Hello, Rays! This is a very special surprise for me and you. I'm coming to you live from the Panache garage. Practice one has just wrapped, and as you can probably hear from the whirring and the voices, both cars have been wheeled in. Evan and Grant both had solid runs, each getting in over twenty laps. Evan's crew had him try two tire compounds while Grant stuck with the softs, likely in preparation for qualifying tomorrow.

"Now, I can't show you a whole lot of the space per the team's regulations, but..." I angle myself to try and show the row of team helmets and the space beyond, but that puts my sight line directly facing the race car that Evan is currently climbing out of.

His helmet jerks as he answers a few questions from one of the mechanics, then he hauls himself upright, his race suit hugging him and giving me a delightful view. Drivers essentially race in fireproof onesie pajamas... Why do they look so sexy?! It's one of motorsports' great mysteries.

"Uh," I stammer, my viewers forgotten.

He steps onto solid ground and pulls off his helmet and head sock, and goddamn it, how does his hair look that good when he's been sweating in a helmet for the last hour?

My heart stutters because upon getting his HANS device off, his head whips around frantically.

He can't be… Surely, he's got other priorities than looking for—

He catches sight of me, and his face lights up like a Christmas tree.

This makes me panic. I launch into a thorough explanation of how the mechanics also serve as the pit crew who do the tire changes and why that requires them to wear full safety gear, including special jumpsuits and helmets, during the race. It's a bit dull and I'm sure I've mentioned it at least once recently in some piece of content, but I need to get this stream back on the rails because in the comments, some followers are wondering what's got me so distracted.

A few of my most stalwart followers who serve as chat moderators speculate helpfully that my visit to the Panache garage was unplanned, and that my time is short so I'm not as prepared as usual. I scan the usernames. The only one of my super fans missing is Macaron91, but that's not unusual. I have no idea what part of the world he's from, but he's said his timezone keeps him from joining during race sessions, and he instead catches me during my evening streams.

"That's exactly right," I say, highlighting one of the comments. "I wasn't expecting this opportunity so I'm still kind of taking it all in, but I wanted you guys to see it too—"

A warm hand snakes around to grab mine and gently tugs the phone from my grip. Thankfully, that means the camera turns away from my shocked, stupid face...

...and focuses entirely on Evan's pleased, stupid face.

The giraffe's hijacking my stream.

I'm still flabbergasted as Blair reappears—without getting in frame, because she's a master of her job—to make sure he doesn't reveal anything sensitive in the garage.

She grabs one of Evan's shoulders at the same time I catch the other. Together, with a conspiratorial wink on her part, we keep Evan from pointing my phone toward something he shouldn't. Evan doesn't miss a beat. He's used to being herded, I guess.

The stunned buzz filling my ears clears so I can hear what he's saying.

"Howdy, Rays. Evan Evans here. Just finished practice and got some good laps in. Very excited for Sunday and to show you what I've got. Welcome to the new Riot Racing fans. I know a lot of you are getting into our sport, thanks to Sunny. Please be sure to tell her 'thank you' for putting out such excellent content this weekend..." His eyes dart to me. "That said, I should probably leave this to the professional." He gives the phone back, and I somehow manage a coherent ending to the stream.

When I look up, those fucking giant emeralds Evan has for eyes are waiting for me.

"Hullo, kitten."

My insides melt. My pussy throbs. The man's reduced me to a pouch of writhing hormones. Ah, fuck. Apparently I have a kink for sexy nicknames.

I'm literally speechless. I manage to screw my face into a rueful grin and shake my head. Eventually, I even stumble upon a coherent thought. "That nickname doesn't make any sense." He doesn't need to know about my appreciation... yet.

"See? Exactly! Maybe 'keepin' it truthful' is more accurate."

"That's not a thing people people say," I argue.

"I said it, and I'm a people."

"He's got you there." I jump as Evan's engineer, Pete, slips by us to hand a clipboard to another team member. His apologetic smile flashes bright against his brown skin. "And arguing with him isn't worth the energy," he warns before heading back to the timing stand.

Evan simply grins wider.

I drop my face into my hands. "I'm going to strangle you."

His next words are quiet and close. He must have tucked his head down by mine. I can imagine the pleased, mischievous smirk taking over his face as he says, "Choking's never really been my kink, but I'll give anything a try for you, kit."

The flush goes from the tip of my head straight down to my clit.

He straightens, putting a casual distance between us, and clasps his hands behind his back like an obedient schoolboy. His smile still spells heaps of trouble for me, though. "You like it when I call you that, don't you?"

I cross my arms, assuring myself I still have clothes on. "I do..." I let go of the small part of me that's resisting this experience. Resisting Evan's charms and the idea of trusting him. Whatever his intentions, I'm in a real racing garage and being doted upon, and I've decided to pursue this fling through to the end for the sake of advancing my own sexual experiences. Whatever comes next, I'm grateful for this. I swallow my next sarcastic remark. "And... thank you, Evan, so much, for inviting me down here. This is amazing."

His smile widens. Someone needs to measure his mouth for a world record. There are a million people around, and I just want to kiss him.

I want to drag him back to that closet down the hall. Hell, I don't think we'd even make it that far, but thankfully, he has plans.

"No worries, kit. Come on." He offers a hand. "I've got a couple of minutes until we debrief. Can I show you around?"

I don't take it. He shrugs, and the "suit yourself" indifference jabs needles into my chest. I grimace and tangle my hands safely before me to follow him through the garage.

Evan introduces me to everyone on the team who's got a moment to spare. They're all lovely. One of the engineers gives a rundown of the telemetry graph that I only half understand, and a mechanic lets me get close to the car and eye the specific angle of Evan's rear wing that gives him extra speed on the straights. The entire time, Evan hovers behind me, adding commentary on occasion, but mostly observing. Eventually, he's pulled away by the team boss so I can watch the mechanics work, appreciating all the glinting carbon fiber that makes up much of the car's body. I've been fully zoned out for who knows how long when a warm, calloused hand touches my elbow.

I jump, bumping backward into Evan in an all-too-familiar way. "Sorry! There's so much to see."

He laughs and tugs me aside, a few feet away from the garage's bustle.

He's about to say something when a familiar head pops around the wall from the next garage over. There's swoopy brown hair, aviator sunglasses, and a Savo set of red fireproofs above a matching race suit tied around a slim waist. I stare at Johnny Trenta, who's waving like he's a regular person and not a worldwide racing superstar.

"You must be Sunny." He doesn't have the megawatt smile Evan's known for, but his small grin makes plenty of fans swoon every weekend.

Evan makes introductions, I think? I'm too starstruck to follow. Aside from the initial mishap with Evan, every other time I've met a major Riot player this week, I've had a few minutes' notice to mentally prepare.

Far too slowly, as I take in the two of them bantering, I realize this means Evan has likely told Johnny, infamously his best friend on the grid, about our fling.

"What kind of eating regimen does June have you on this year?" Johnny asks. "We tweaked mine, and I'm not loving it."

Evan's face screws up in a way I've learned means he's lost the words he wants. "It's like a... dinosaur diet," he manages.

Johnny squints and waits as Evan remembers that across species, dinosaurs allegedly ate a variety of diets, so he's essentially told us... nothing.

"No, I mean like... It's a lot of leafy greens. Like, a lot. And, uh..."

"The occasional park ranger?" I add drily.

Evan looks at me and his smile takes over his thinking face. He doubles over, cackling.

Johnny snorts at my comment, but Evan finds me distinctly hilarious. It takes him almost a full minute to recover, and he has to wipe a tear from one eye. "The occasional park ranger," he repeats.

Johnny seems to realize that we've gone off track, so his original question won't get much more of an answer right now. "So are you guys gonna make time to head to the club this week, then?"

Evan straightens and cuts a glance my way. "...maybe. Depends on timing. Are you planning to go?"

Johnny shrugs. "I don't think I'm gonna make it. I'm hoping to live vicariously through you."

Evan frowns. "If we did, you could come for a drink, or..." Evan has his lower lip between his teeth and it's like watching a train crash, but sexy? I can't look away.

"Trenta, get out of here while we have data up! And Ev, say goodbye to your friends." Blair's voice carries impressively, given the fact that she's half under Grant's car, looking at something with a mechanic. That girl misses nothing.

Johnny lifts his hands and backs away, giving me a wink as he does that makes my stomach flip.

Evan guides me back toward the garage exit with a hand that hovers at my lower back but doesn't touch me.

"What do you think?" He sounds almost as breathless as I am. The race track does that to people, I suppose.

My mouth gapes as I try to formulate an answer. Evan touches a knuckle to my chin, gently guiding my mouth closed. His eyes dip to my lips, and my face flushes. I gulp. "Ask me again in a few hours, once I've processed it."

"Okay. Come over tonight. Stay with me again."

Since I refused yesterday, it didn't cross my mind that he'd ask again. I desperately want to say yes.

"We have work to do," I start.

"We can do both."

I raise an eyebrow.

"Nurture a budding romance and annihilate this race weekend? I can do both. Watch me."

I shut down the flutter in my heart, because that's not what this is.

"Well, I can't. And I don't know that a crash course in kink counts as romance."

He crosses his arms. "Are you kidding? You're Sunny goddamn Waite. I've seen your content. You're a badass. You're efficient and whip smart. You can do anything."

"You've seen my content?"

Evan rubs his chin, and I want to trace my tongue across the scruff there. "Mmhmm, it's excellent. You're excellent. And the wi-fi at my apartment is way faster than whatever you're getting at the hotel. Plus, I won't be home till a little later, since we've got a thousand meetings after practice. You can have the whole place to yourself. I bought snacks after the other night. You could use the shower, then turn the fireplace on, watch the sunset."

"Are you begging?"

I see his muscles spasm as he physically tamps down the urge to touch me in front of his entire team any more than he already has. Everyone's minding their own business, but I've caught a few knowing glances being shot around when one of us turns away. "Sunny, you haven't even begun to see how good I can beg."

And that's one hundred percent something I need to witness. I think quickly. We have a few more events for the Creator Crush today, then dinner, but no activities scheduled after that. The other creators are finally as tired as I am, and everyone's talking about getting a good night's sleep so they can make it through the rest of the weekend.

"How're the logistics of that going to work?" The team is starting to pack up, which means lunch and a debrief shortly so they can plan for any additional running and analysis that needs to be done during the second practice session. "I don't suppose you leave a key under the mat."

"Oh, definitely not. It's a keypad. I can remember a sequence slightly better than keeping track of physical keys. I'll send you the code and call the desk to let them know to expect you."

My mouth twists as I consider it.

"There's still a bottle of wine left from the other night. And—"

I press a finger over his mouth. "You've convinced me. I'll come over. You need to get moving, and so do I."

He sets a hand on my waist, on the side facing the garage's wall, out of sight. He squeezes, digging his fingers deliciously into my side, like a promise. "See you later, then, kit."

Somehow, our schedule fits in a visit to Riot's safety headquarters, a meeting with one of the heads of volunteer coordinating, a demonstration of how teams prepare tires for sessions, and a talk with race control so we get an idea of how they keep an eye on rules and data while cars are on track.

We watch part of the second practice session, this time from the suite Riot reserved. Evan did the bulk of his running in session one, so he's only out for a few laps.

Dinner is also intense because my friends demand a thorough rehashing of everything I saw in the Panache garage. Adam poorly pretends he's not impressed as Jackie and Gael bombard me with questions. By the time we're stuffed and shuffling off to bed, I'm exhausted but excited. I duck into my room and grab what I need for a sleepover and practically skip out of the lobby. The walk to Evan's building in the brisk air makes me smile, and the person at the desk mirrors it when I give my name.

I blow a stray piece of hair from my face and hit the button for the eleventh floor.

When his front door shuts behind me and I'm standing alone in his apartment's entryway, I sag and gratefully allow my backpack to thump to the floor.

Evan will be back after I've gone to sleep, so I allow myself to flop onto his couch and scroll through my phone, catching up on all the social chatter around the race weekend and posting some of what I've captured.

I finish up a piece that will be the caption of a photo but also posted as a longer blog to my website.

Motorsport is a contest of the smallest margins, I type. I flash back to Evan spraying gravel in our initial ride-along that feels like weeks ago. We were flying. Was he driving on the edge to try and impress me? Surely not. He's a race car driver; he's always going to push the limit. I continue typing. *Champions are decided by fractions of a second, fragments of a centimeter, and best of all, with constantly changing conditions, anything can happen. If the fastest cars take a corner too quickly, a driver in a slower car with a steadier hand can win.*

A shudder works through me at the thought. I much prefer known conditions and variables. That last bit of reckless faith a driver needs makes me nauseous. I tweak and edit the piece a little bit further, then decide to let it go out onto the internet.

The reactions are immediate and overwhelmingly positive. Mac appears in the comments with thoughtful questions and glowing support.

I get so consumed replying to comments that when I look up, the sun's set outside the windows, the mountains a group of vaguely darker smudges than the sky, and the buildings twinkle. The sounds of Friday night can be heard a softly up here—a pleasant background chatter of excitement.

I pad to the bathroom for my nightly routine. I'm brushing my teeth when my phone buzzes.

Make it in ok, kit?

I'm smiling, which makes toothpaste drip down my chin. I wipe it away and type one-handed.

Yep. The strip search was a little overkill, though.

Damn. I told them to let me do that when I get back.

You can check their work.

Oh, I will. And I plan to be thorough.

A seconds-long, body-arching yawn takes me over, so I migrate to his bedroom. My toes dig into the plush carpet, gentle on my knee that's still a little sore. I think of Evan kissing it better, roaming upwards in the process, and shiver.

Now that I've got the time, I take in the details of Evan's room. It's sparsely decorated in shades of gray, with a surprising amount of fake plants and a few quirky, bright paintings along one wall. There are two super modern chairs set before a small fireplace, but what draws my attention is the display over his broad dresser. Above a bowl full of trinkets and a haphazard collection of watches thrown into an acrylic case, Evan has tacked at least thirty printed photos to the wall.

The photos are candid and chaotic and not always clear or well-framed, but they feature folks I recognize from the more formal photos in his living room. The subjects are mainly his family, with appearances by some people from the paddock as well. I spy at least five photos with Pete and several featuring other Riot racers.

What all the photos have in common is the people looking at the camera—well, maybe a few inches above it—and smiling broadly, eyes sparkling, premature laughs frozen in time.

Evan made them look like that, with something he said or did just before snapping the shutter.

My chest constricts, like someone's laced ribbons through each of my ribs and pulled them tight. He is so beloved.

Universally adored.

Including by me. *Fuck.*

I'm too tired to unpack this, and too excited to see Evan later, to be critical of myself about it. Maybe he won't crush me at the end of this weekend. Maybe we'll have an extremely civil and kind goodbye where we both agree to cherish these memories.

I make my way to the closet and snoop until I find the drawer holding his t-shirts. I take a photo, making sure to get my bare legs in the shot, still a little glowy from my lotions.

Which one should I wear to bed?

The response is quick.

Surprise me

I paw through them and make my selection, then slip into the silky sheets. I expected to be too excited to sleep until Evan got home, but his bed is so comfy and smells of him, so I bury my face in his pillow and drift off.

CHAPTER SEVENTEEN

Sunny

The bathroom door's soft click nudges me awake. I blink and see Evan's lithe, shirtless form tentatively approach the bed. I squeeze my eyes shut and even my breath, curious to see how he proceeds.

The mattress dips.

I'm face down, and his arms bracket either side of my torso. His lips trail a line of kisses along my back where his t-shirt has ridden up.

A contented noise escapes my throat, and I glance back at him with a smile. He's just wearing boxers. "How were the meetings?"

"Productive," he murmurs, shifting so he's on all fours over me, and continues talking between presses of his lips to my skin. "We're in a great spot for this weekend. This is where I turn things around. I feel it."

"Yeah? What makes you think that?" I arch, hoping to find the pressure of his hips with my ass.

He presses back, pushing me into the mattress, drawing a moan from me as I feel how ready he is. "Because..." His hands shift, exploring lower and finding the skimpy panties I'm wearing. He draws in a rough breath and trails a finger along the waistband, before letting go and snapping it, making me jerk against him. My breath is all over the place already. He quits teasing and slips a hand beneath the fabric, gently dragging over my pussy. "This week is already perfect. The only way to top it off is with a win."

I don't have to reply because he withdraws his hand and serves me a light smack to the ass, starting gently to wake me up, I assume.

I whimper, and he massages the sharp sensation away. "I got you a present."

"Really?" I shift, and he moves back to give me room to roll over and face him. "You also mentioned something about begging earlier."

He pauses, heat sparking in his eyes. "I did." He glances around. "That said..." He dips his head, eyes never leaving mine. The angle makes them look huge and repentant and adoring, like a pet seeing its owner after a long vacation. He gives a slow kiss to my knee, licking up the inside of my thigh, making my breath catch. "Will you pretty please let me give you a present?"

Eyelids heavy from the haze of pleasure he's summoning, I tilt my head. "I'm considering it."

He leaves me to open the nightstand's bottom drawer and pulls out a gift bag frothing with tissue paper. He sets it beside us and palms my ankles. He delicately drags his short nails up my shins, over my knees, and around the outside of my thighs to trace my panties as he brings his face close to mine. "I picked this out just for you, and I really want to give it to you. Sunny, please."

With an effort of Herculean willpower, I manage to remain quiet and hope that my face is some semblance of even. I watch him. The anguish on his face, coupled with the growing bulge in his shorts, is intoxicating. With a whine, he takes me around the middle and hauls me close, pulling the shirt I've borrowed up so he has full access to my breasts.

He bites my nipple as he rubs his hard cock against me, the clothes between us providing magnificent friction as a partner to the tiny pinch of pain his lips provide.

I can't form a coherent thought. My entire body is a flood of addictive sensation. He presses me to the mattress, switching from one breast to the other, never easing his cadence of thrusts rubbing us together. A keen wails from the middle of my chest at the torture of this almost-fucking, this concerted effort focused all on me, the intoxication of an incredible man working so hard to make me happy and to get me to agree to let him do more.

"Evan—Ah!" He gives my nipple one last, intense suck before halting his onslaught. His hips stop moving, but he's pressed hard against me. My chest heaves like I've just finished a sprint.

"Ask me again," I say. The command is breathless. Toothless.

He finds my mouth for a lingering kiss, one endless, promising slide of his tongue, then, "*Please.*"

"Okay."

He moves back onto his knees, leaving my soaked panties exposed to the air. I give an indignant noise that he ignores. He presents the bag. "Open it."

Tentatively, I explore the clouds of tissue paper with one hand till my fingers wrap around a cool, slim surface.

My confusion must be sprawled across my face because Evan's grin goes wide and devious.

I pull out a hot pink paddle a bit larger than one used to play ping pong. A picture of the sun wearing a smirk and sunglasses is etched into its service.

It feels like all of the blood in my body rushes to my pussy.

"You like it?"

I gulp. "I think I'm going to like it very much."

"Flip over, kit. Right now."

I scramble to acquiesce. Before I can settle, Evan hauls my ass up and sinks a finger deep into me. Quickly, I'm a mindless, writhing thing, matching the tempo of his strokes.

Then comes the contact—a sharp slap of the paddle against my ass. It's a more intense sensation than his hand, and I love it.

He gives me a moment to assess the pain, and I wriggle for more. "That's so good, Sunny. You can take more, can't you?" He increases the cadence of his spanking and brings me to a quick orgasm, but doesn't stop his movements, instead, sliding a second finger into me. I'm trapped between his hand and his firm body, overwrought with blissful sensations.

There's no sound except for my harsh breath and the smack of the paddle against my skin. I turn my head and catch Evan's laser focus on the perfect rhythm that makes my body sing.

A second orgasm comes, and in its wake, his fingers are not enough and the fire blooming across my ass is too much.

"Evan." My words are a mewling plea. "Evan, please."

His lips press to my neck. "Tell me, kitten. What do you need?"

He plunges his fingers deeper, and I cry out, then bite my lip.

"Anything you want, Sunny," he says, dark and grave as a blood oath. "Tell me what you want me to give you."

"Fuck me," I gasp.

He moves back and flips me over. I haul the shirt over my head as he slides my panties down my legs. When I toss the shirt away, he catches it and shakes it out.

"PNW Junior Karting Championship. What a throw-back."

"It's soft."

"Keep it. I like seeing you wear it." Evan stands to re-move his boxers and put on a condom. He's beautiful as he moves. I spread my legs and slide a finger between them while he works. His eyes glaze and his movements slow. "Keep my shirt, and when you're missing me and needy in your own bed, you video call me to take care of you. I want to see you hike it over your tits so you can touch yourself while I talk dirty to you."

My throat is tight, my inner walls tighter. "What will you say?"

"I'll tell you all the plans I have for when I see you next. And I'll ask you to tell me how you touch yourself so I can learn a thing or two for the next time I get my hands on you."

The next time. A fantasy, surely?

Except, maybe not?

That stupid, gorgeous smile of his doesn't fade the entire time. He climbs back into bed and braces himself above me. "Fuck you? That's all? Such an easy request, and a gift for me, too." He moves my hand aside and drags his thumb up my core, eyeing my pussy and licking his lips. "You sure you don't want anything else, first?"

I shake my head vehemently. "Just your cock. I've been waiting all night. All day, really."

"Oh, yeah?" He dips forward, nudging the head of his cock at my entrance. "You were thinking about fucking me today in the garage? While you watched me work?"

"I was thinking about a lot of things." I lift my hips, taking him a little deeper, but nowhere near deep enough. He's got plenty of cock left and if I'm not full of him in the next thirty seconds, I might die.

With a firm grip, he presses my hips back to the bed and gives me a little more, while peppering soft half-kisses to my lips. "If it wasn't obvious, I was thinking about you too, in the car. Imagining what you would look like bent over it. If I made you wait, naked, while I looked you over. The voices of people in the paddock echoing around us. We'd have to be so quiet. I don't think you could manage that. I'd have to cover your mouth. Gag you, maybe."

I can't take any more teasing, so I surge up to capture his mouth, and what started so gently turns savage. Evan meets me with teeth and tongue. I bury my hands in his hair as he grips my hips and works his full length into me with long, strong strokes.

The kissing is bliss, and at some point, we break for air, and I'm babbling. "Fuck, I love being full of you."

The words set his eyes glinting in the night. Evan buries his head in my shoulder, nipping the skin there. His fingers dig deeper into my ass on one side, and he braces his other on the mattress to drive into me harder. I hike my legs high around his ribs.

"You gonna come for me, Sunny?" he speaks into my skin. The question feels like an order. "I want two more before I fill you up."

Oh, his bossy tone. My body is happy to comply. My clit is a lit fuse where it rubs against his stomach, and pleasure barrels through me. I cling to Evan and ride it out, relishing each wave of pleasure.

Evan's thrusting slows. He lifts his face to cup my chin, kissing me gingerly. I take his lip between my teeth for a second before I pull away. "Two?" I confirm, slightly intimidated. I feel like if I'm filled with any more pleasure, I'll explode.

He slips a hand between us to rub my clit with his thumb, melting me into the mattress. "C'mon, Sunny. Think of it as strength training. Wait till I demand eleven."

"We're not aligning my orgasms with your brand identity." I roll my eyes. The bastard winks. I cross my ankles and attempt to tug him closer. "I can take that many, though."

"That's my kit," he rumbles, ransacking my mouth again. My next orgasm is hard won by Evan, and as I peak, I swear I feel his tip inflate before he comes, too.

His fingers are desperately tight around me, his movements jerky. Amid my own noises of release, I hear him babble: "God, Sunny, I'd do anything for you, you know that? How is that possible already? I knew we'd be good together but *fuck*, you unravel me. It's like you've got me on my knees and on a leash and I never, ever want to get free."

Immediately, my thoughts are overriding what he's said. *It's the high of the sex*, I convince myself. *You've been babbling like an idiot, too. He doesn't know what he's saying.*

Waves of pleasure work through us both, and I repeat it fervently. *He doesn't mean it. It's a trick. A trap. A lie. He doesn't mean it. He doesn't mean it.*

In the comedown, as we're plastered together and breathing hard, his words come back to me, though.

It sure sounded like he meant it.

The night gets much softer and slower after that. Evan wants a shower, and I'm more than happy to accept his invitation to come along. There's an easy sleepiness to the minutes we take to get settled.

Other words of his from earlier stick with me, too. I pause as he fluffs the pillows. "What club was Johnny talking about earlier? Did he mean one of the premium fan areas?"

Evan tugs me to him, tucking me into his side. "No, he was talking about Skirt."

I blink. The name means nothing to me.

"It's a sex club," he says, squeezing my side.

"Oh." I flush all over again. I'm getting used to the sensation. If I weren't so bone tired, the mention of such a place might have me ready to go for another round. "That's something on my list, you know... of things I want to try."

"Really? Well, now it's on my list of things to show you."

I sigh. It's a fun thought, but I definitely don't think either of us has the time for that this weekend. I turn to my other burning question. "You and Johnny have gone?"

"You're asking if we've played together." I don't argue. He kisses my temple. "Sometimes. Sometimes our relationship is like that. Never more than friends emotionally, but we're a good match when it comes to sexual tastes.

He's in an open relationship, so sometimes he and I scene together, the two of us or with others."

Somewhere along this explanation, I've begun squirming. It's gotten so dark, I hear the sexy wickedness in Evan's voice more than see it on his face.

"Does the idea of that make you hot?"

I nod. His scruff scrapes my cheek as he kisses me there. "Yeah? You like the idea of watching, or maybe being shared?"

My "yes" is a squeak. His laugh is a dark rumble. "Noted, kit." He changes the subject smoothly, his brain veering into a new lane. "Are you excited to present on the broadcast tomorrow?"

"I will be. Right now, I'm nervous."

"You'll crush it. Can I come watch?"

"Do you even have time?"

"I'll be there." His promise is solemn.

I clear my throat. "We have to go to sleep."

"Ugh, I hate that you're right." One more kiss. This one was meant for the tip of my nose, I think, but he misses in the dark and gets the corner of my eye.

I snort a laugh and snuggle into him.

We fall asleep curled together, and I drift off with the pleasant, foolish supposition that maybe this bliss will last.

CHAPTER EIGHTEEN

Sunny

I'd do anything for you.

I knew we'd be good together.

You unravel me... I never, ever want to get free.

The words swirl in my mind all night, pleasant and ethereal. It's when I wake with Evan's warm arms banded around me and my face pressed to his mango-scented chest that I consider them literally.

The bliss lasts all of twenty seconds before my subconscious kicks into overdrive, blaring the alert that something is WRONG.

Hard to believe in the morning sunlight with the pleasant smell of brewed coffee leaking in from the kitchen.

Sunlight. Shit.

I roll over and grapple for my phone, startling Evan awake behind me. His sharp intake of breath sends pleasant shivers over my body.

My phone screen reflects my horrified face. I slept through both alarms.

A warm palm rubs my lower back. "Good morning, k—"

"We slept in," I say tersely.

Carefully, Evan untangles himself from me and grabs his phone. "Are we late? Am I late? Are you late? What day is it?"

"Very, *very* late!" I swear and scramble from the bed, tugging my fingers through my hair. "There's that networking brunch, and I need to rehearse my segment again. And it's qualifying! Go fast day, giraffe man!"

"Right." He hauls himself out of bed and nearly falls over, yanking on his boxer briefs. His hair is a mess but still adorable. He grabs his watch and eyes it. "I can make it if I rush. What about you?"

"Yep." I'm already digging in my bag for clothes.

"You use this bathroom. I'll take the spare." He whips into the bathroom, emerges with a toothbrush, and sprints for the closet. "Give me five minutes and I can drop you at the hotel on the way to the track."

I don't answer because I'm frantically sprinting through the apartment, searching for the note cards I'll be using for my feature later.

In a blur, we make it into his car. Evan stops a block from the hotel in case of paparazzi scouting out the front to catch any drivers that might be staying there. He leans over the console and presses a delicious, albeit sloppy, kiss to my mouth. "Thank you for a great evening."

"Likewise." I'm halfway out the door and breathless when he speaks again.

"Don't forget your purse. And break a leg at your presentation. I'll see you there!" He passes it to me. I babble my thanks. "Will I see you tonight?"

His question halts me. Tomorrow is race day... and my flight home. Surely, he needs to focus?

If this trip is all I get with him, I'm going to squeeze every last moment from it. "I'll text you later."

I'm lucky enough to have a few spare minutes before I'm officially late. I make a quick pit stop in my room to put myself together—the mirror says I look a tiny bit frazzled—before I head to the bus. Thankfully, this late in the week, with all the activities, excitement, and consequential partying, I don't look out of place at all among my media peers. Jackie has the most impressive bags I have ever seen under her eyes that she's doing her best to hide with a huge pair of sunglasses.

"Hey..."

She holds up a hand. "Can't talk. Too hungover."

Apparently, some of our cohort rallied and did make it to the bars last night. "Impressive," I murmur.

Gael rubs her back and gives me an apologetic look. With a frown, I realize I'm the last to arrive and the only seat left is directly behind them, alongside Adam.

My butt barely makes contact with the seat's edge before he talks to me. "Hey, we should do a collab. I bet your followers could use an introduction to sports betting. I'd be happy to do a takeover or something."

His tone is warm and friendly, his smile charming. My internal defense mechanisms rear their heads like impatient warhorses. I'm not in college anymore, and I've learned to see maneuvers like these for what they are. He wants exposure to my audience. In the creator world, I firmly believe that a rising tide lifts all boats... unless the boat in question is an asshole.

I lean forward, effectively ignoring Adam. "Can I get your opinion on something?"

Gael swivels my way. "Of course."

"I've prepped a few posts on the more complex, technical aspects of racing, but I don't have space in my queue this week for all of them. I want to save some for the summer. Which topic would be most digestible and important for newbies to the sport? Diffusers, hybrid engines, or oversteer versus understeer?"

He tugs the small gold hoop in his earlobe in thought. "Hm, not diffusers... The engines, I think. It makes sense to start with the process that makes it possible for the cars to actually go, you know?"

"You're so right, thank y—"

Adam's head pokes over the back of the seat. His hand dangles a breakfast burrito perilously close to Jackie's hair. She groans and puts her head between her knees.

He doesn't seem to notice that he annoys her, or that Gael and I are mid-conversation.

"Hey man, can you explain your social handle? I don't get it."

Gael's eyes catch mine for a second, wide in a "can you believe this guy" kind of way. He clears his throat. "So... it's gael_force_wind, right?" he starts. "But people often mispronounce it, like 'gale' instead of the two vowel sounds together. I'm taking ownership of how people mess it up, and trying to make them reflect on why they wouldn't take the time to learn to say my name properly. The play on gale force winds has to do with my interest in aerodynamics."

Adam frowns. "I still don't get it."

There's not much for it but to blink at him, which we do. Each rattle of the bus over a pothole fills the silence.

Adam finally stares into his burrito. "Er, it's cool that they put tater tots in this." He slinks back into his seat.

Gael rolls his eyes and Jackie white knuckles the rest of the ride. The moment we step into the paddock, we're ushered into a tent to network. It's a blur, but I go into focus mode and crush a handful of interactions with folks from various businesses affiliated with the racing series that will hopefully manifest into opportunities down the road, half-noticing Adam boring people to death in the corner.

After that, they've secured us another special box to watch qualifying with an epic appetizer spread. We're all just happy to sit down, I think. I'm dozing off in the minutes leading up to qualifying when my phone buzzes.

> Are you feeling up for a game?

I'm typing back before I can even think. He should be in the car by now!

> There's hardly a time more important than this for you to be paying attention to your job.

> A clear yes or no please, kit.

> I'm going to need more info on this game.

I slipped another present into your purse this morning.

With a frown, and with Jackie snoring lightly beside me and the boys nowhere to be seen, I dig into my purse until my hand closes around something unfamiliar. I pull out a slim, slightly curved disc a little wider and longer than my thumb. It's pale blue and silicone with a tiny button on one side and a raised nub on the other. With growing suspicion, I flick the switch and the thing starts vibrating.

Flustered, I turn it off and drop it back in my purse before typing back viciously to Evan.

How is this even possible? Your hands are *occupied*.

Let me worry about that. Do you trust me?

You, sir, are a menace.

I like it when you call me sir.

So the game is, kit, will you wear that during qualifying for me? You can experience the thrill while I do. I'll accelerate you and the car at the same time. Say yes.

My legs clench together from thigh to ankle. My entire body has flushed hot reading his message. He can't be serious. But... I want him to be.

It's a terrible idea, and I'm fully on board.

I glance around. We're all tucked into cushy seats. Jackie is snoring softly, her head on a rolled-up jacket a few seats down, and no one else is in our row. The others opted for lower seats and a closer view, though many heads are lolling, halfway to snoozeville already.

Anyone awake will be paying attention to what's happening on track. If I have a... *moment*, I'll have to be quiet. A thrill licks up my spine.

> Deal. Send it, Evans.

All I get in return is a salute emoji.

I dash to the restroom to secure the vibe in my underwear.

Once I'm reseated, I snag one of the blankets provided to stave off the breeze coming through the front of our box.

There's a large TV secured to the wall sharing the broadcast of today's qualifying so it's easy to understand what's going on. There are a few timing stands scattered around the course in view of the fan seating areas, but it's nice to have the supplement of seeing every corner of the racetrack and the graphics that pop up on screen.

Right now, it's showing the Benji garage, and Hendrix's dreamy eyes beneath his helmet's open visor. He finds the camera and winks.

That's Evan's ex, but claws of jealousy don't sink into my chest. I'm the one he's chosen to split his attention with today. I'm the one he wants to bring to the brink of ultimate pleasure while he's doing a very important job.

Because it's inevitable, the coverage heads to the Panache garage. It starts on Grant, who's already in the car and reviewing data. Then, Evan appears.

He's not in the car, but chatting with Pete and adjusting his radio earpiece. It could be my imagination, but he looks particularly happy.

I wriggle in my seat. He hasn't even done anything yet.

The commentators wonder if he'll be able to pull off something miraculous today to put him in a good position for tomorrow's race.

I double-check my phone to make sure my scheduled post explaining how qualifying works has gone up. All of the drivers take to the track at once. There are three rounds during which every driver puts in the fastest lap they can manage. Each round, a few of the slowest cars are dropped.

Drivers want to make it to the final session, as the front of the starting grid is determined there.

Evan makes it out of the first round easily, and I'm half relieved there isn't a whisper of movement from the vibrator. Maybe his plan won't work.

In the second round, Evan has a tricky moment in his first flying lap that costs him half a second, but he makes a cleaner pass on his second try and slips into the third round by the skin of his teeth. I relax into my seat as they prepare for the final round.

Evan takes an easy out lap, trying to build some space between the other cars zipping around. Since the team was picky with exactly when to send him out, he'll only have time for one fast lap this session. As he crosses the line to start his fast lap, the vibrator buzzes between my thighs. I jump, my yelp of surprise covered by Jackie's snore.

The first buzz is quick, like he's giving me a moment to know what to expect. A few seconds later, it buzzes again, slow and grumbly, and doesn't stop. My toes curl. I clutch the blanket close to my chest. The remaining cars rip around the track and their tires scream against the tarmac beneath our box.

The sounds are followed by increased intensity from the device in my panties.

I manage not to jump this time, and enjoy the early waves of pleasure lapping at my core. I resettle the blanket over me and grip the armrests.

On the broadcast, the camera follows Evan's car, and the pink graphic illustrating a radio message of his pops up.

"Alrighty, let's go fast," he tells his team.

It strikes me how desperately I want a good result for Evan.

Jenna Bow and Luke Boltek, who I usually root for, are also in this group and doing well so I don't feel too traitorous.

I can see maybe a quarter of the race track from this seat, and the TV broadcast alternates coverage of each driver, so I pull the live track map up on my phone and watch the little pink dot that is Evan progress around the track.

As he passes the halfway mark of his lap, the vibrations taunting me increase in fervor, mimicking Evan's blistering pace.

I eye the timing table nervously as I squirm, half my brain numb from this slow build of heat, the other half frustrated that Luke just set an impressive lap time. He's currently got pole by two tenths of a second.

Evan can beat that, I know it. And that's not coming from a part of my brain that's been dickmatized—he's been excelling all weekend.

The vibrations increase in intensity. With only a few turns to go, the pattern shifts to two shorter buzzes followed by a much longer one.

Tension twines my body tight. I grit my teeth. The graphic showing Evan's time flickers between green and red in the moments he's ahead of and behind Luke's time.

He approaches the track's final sector, and I'm so close. Delicious, torturous pressure builds, and I fight not to arch out of my seat. I'm so close, and Evan's so close... I breathe deep when the pleasure spikes, forcing myself to keep quiet as I come, demanding my eyes remain open and on the timing screen.

Evan doesn't quite nail the last corner, but it's better than he's been doing at that spot in practice, and he was extra quick in the other corners, so it should be enough.

The crests of pleasure ease. I shove a hand beneath the blanket to remove the vibrator and turn it off.

Evan crosses the line, a blur of pink and black. He zips below our box.

Those of us who are awake hold our breath.

His name jumps to the top of the timing table.

My screech of joy fits in with the roar coming from all the stands and the Panache garage. I realize I've stood and thrust both hands into the air, including the one holding the vibrator. I quickly shove it into my pocket. Jackie startles awake, alongside everyone else. I temper my excitement because no one here is freaking out as much as I want to.

We cram to the front of the box to lean over the railing and watch the celebration.

Evan gets to park just before the starting line, and he's joined by the second and third place starters, Luke and RJ. Jenna is lower down the field, the commentators lamenting that her car isn't up to snuff this week, and her team's been struggling to get a feel for the track.

The crowd's roar is deafening. He's so beloved and... my heart swells. Now I know why.

Evan hauls himself from the car. He stands atop and pumps both fists in the air.

I shake my head. Reporters swarm him and the lead Riot presenter asks him questions as he's awarded with the week's polesitter medal.

"Evan, a great run there. Tell me how you pulled off that last lap."

His smile huge, Evan speaks into the mic. "You know... the whole team's been working really hard to get here and..." His eyes dart, a tell I'm beginning to recognize when he gets a silly idea. "Sometimes you gotta know when the machine will do the job. I'm just the pilot, you know. I'm pressing the right buttons."

He looks directly to the camera and gives a feral smile, his tongue lolling out as his eyes flash.

My knees actually go weak.

Other reporters are allowed in, and the action is so loud between all the fans and the hustle and bustle of the crews rolling the cars back to their garages, I can't even hear his answers.

As the excitement starts to ebb, we realize that we're a bunch of exhausted influencers, and everyone begins to grumble and pull back to their seats.

Cooper clears his throat a few times at the door before we all see him.

"Um," he starts, "we have this space for another twenty minutes before it needs to be cleaned for the next group, so please be sure to clear out by then. Report to the media center for your presentations by two. If you're late, you will be skipped." He departs the room, his duties for the week apparently done, his whole body sagging in relief.

Jackie grimaces. "Guess since we're almost to race day, some of the more hospitable experiences are done, huh?"

I nod morosely.

Gael's reappeared and feels no need to reply to our raised eyebrows, wondering where he's been. "Fine by me. This week has included quite enough socializing for my tastes.

There's too much here that isn't science." He elbows me gently. "Any new updates on *your* chemistry?"

My eyes widen. There's no way I'm sharing about what went down with the polesitter and the rabbit-y machine in my pocket.

"Er, he wants to come see my feature. Promised, actually."

Gael gives a knowing look and opens his mouth to say something, but Jackie interrupts with a yawn so wide it makes her jaw crack. "Maybe Sunny's endured enough of our pestering this week, too." She stretches, and I'm relieved for her misinterpretation of my distress. "That nap means I'll at least get through this presentation looking somewhat presentable. Are you ready?"

I want to believe the twinge in my stomach is mostly nerves for this pinnacle of what we've been working toward—the chance to share our specific styles of content to a broader audience on a bigger stage. But now it feels like a harsh reminder that after the race tomorrow, the entire series packs up and moves on without us.

I set my jaw. Best to make the most of it while we're here.

We make a pit stop at the bathroom to freshen up and then head to the media center.

It's so exciting to enter a space we've only seen on TV. We got glimpses of the rest of this building earlier in the week but this room is iconic to Riot fans. Every week, drivers and team leaders are interviewed here before and after races to talk about all the action on track and the rumors happening off it. It's a cavernous room with a velvet couch in front of a branded backdrop and a smattering of large, fake plants.

Usually, the rows of plastic seats staring down the couch are full of reporters, leaving unfortunate latecomers to crowd at the back.

Now, a single Riot staffer sits in the middle row, typing away on some other project. There's one sleepy camera operator and a sound tech who must have gotten the short stick to do our session.

Thankfully, the Riot commentator we'll be volleying with, the talented Ivy Graham, seems committed to keeping up her energy as we each do our segment with her.

We file into the seats and wait our turn.

Jackie crushes it. She stuck with a topic she's covered many times, citing to us earlier in the week that she wanted to set herself up for success and stay firmly in her comfort zone. Gael's a little stiff, but he wasn't thrilled about this part anyway. He's more than happy to stick with his small, curated community chat rooms, but could always use a boost in subscribers.

Adam says something initially to offend Ivy so she gives him basically nothing as they talk and his piece falls flat, but not without him mentioning, for the fifth time this week, that just the other day, he made eight hundred dollars with a single bet, and you can, too!

It's overall very lame, but he doesn't seem to think that, of course.

Finally, it's my turn.

My knees quake when I introduce myself to Ivy. This is kind of the capstone of the Creator Crush program, a chance to engage with a journalist on the more traditional side of motorsport reporting and bridge the gap with whatever concept we bring. All of our segments will be shown on the TV broadcast after the race, too.

I've prepped this segment for weeks, tweaking and fine-tuning. They let us do a quick rehearsal right when we got in, but it didn't feel comforting. We each get three minutes. I've got all my notes memorized, which is good because I basically black out.

As if from far away, I hear my voice, pretty evenly and at a decent speed, explain my chosen topic: fandom and accountability. Risky, maybe, but Riot approved my brief. My point is that fans have the power to influence a sport and should be vocal about holding their favorite series accountable. I cite how fans flocked to Riot when they committed in their first season to recruiting drivers from backgrounds traditionally underrepresented in other racing leagues.

"In sports, league organizers too easily forget that fans are often the most powerful partner in a sporting relationship. We buy the tickets and the merch. We share the graphics on social media. We spread the word. As fans, we can make sure they never forget, by using our voices and the power of our dollars and our attention."

Before long, my voice is going a little hoarse, and I'm definitely speaking too quickly when Ivy gives me softball questions to answer, but something I close with makes her laugh, and the camera light blinks off.

Ivy shakes my hand. "Nicely done, Sunny. Clever, engaging and effective. Just needs a little polish. You have a knack for this." She pulls out her phone, searches for my account, and hits the 'follow' button. "I'm gonna keep my eye on you."

I giggle deliriously, unable to process that at the moment.

I shuffle back to my seat, and Jackie grips my wrist. "Damn, girl, you really put some nitro into that delivery."

I'm having an out-of-body experience, so I only half hear her. "You think?"

Gael pipes in. "Oh yeah, and we're not blowing smoke up your tailpipe. I think yours was the most organized, and definitely the most passionate. You were so clear on what you wanted to do."

I allow myself a breath. A smile. "Aw, thanks. You two crushed it, too." I crane my head around, searching the far corners of the room. Despite his promises, Evan is nowhere to be seen. My heart sinks like Excalibur to the bottom of the enchanted lake. "That's something to be pleased with about this week, huh?"

Though I've tried not to think about it,

Gael's brows draw together. "What are you— Nothing? Nothing since quali?"

"Radio silence," Jackie murmurs.

Sure, qualifying hasn't been over for that long, but if the man could operate a vibrator from within the cockpit, he could have sent me a text by now.

I shake my head, accepting the slow sinking feeling in my chest. After all, I knew this would happen.

CHAPTER NINETEEN

Evan

For a pole sitter at their home race, I'm pretty irritated.

Pete's politely ignoring my jittering knee as he guides us through the engineering debrief. Its usual slot got adjusted because the engineers needed to address something on the car, and the last-minute change has me confused. Now I can't figure out how my schedule aligns with Sunny's.

This stuff is so important. The analysis of how I got that lap today and what it means for what I can do to try and secure success tomorrow, especially with so many fast cars stacked right behind me at the beginning. Starting first is one thing. Keeping that position is a whole different beast.

And I'm missing Sunny's presentation, I'm sure of it.

I knew the odds of me getting over there were slim, but on a high like today, I felt like I could accomplish anything, and was sure I could maybe sneak over and hide behind a plant or something to not attract attention while she presented.

That, of course, didn't work. I was stupid to not have thought it through. Sometimes I trick myself into thinking I'm invincible and can do anything, though the rules of time and space and my brain wiring won't allow it. Race weekends have repetitive patterns, and they almost always start with the comfort of routine and get more stressful and chaotic as we approach Sunday.

Sometimes I get this way, so hopeful that things will work out that I forget to check in with the reality of the situation, which right now is that she has a commitment at the same time I do and I can't bail on mine.

Worst of all, in the flurry of all this, it totally slipped my mind to even text her good luck. And I'm not going to disrespect all the hard-working people who want a win as bad as I do by pulling out my phone.

I grind my teeth. I'll be able to see Sunny and apologize soon enough.

I'm convinced that the social media admin across the entire paddock purposefully don't give us drivers much instruction whenever they have games they want us to play, because it goes even more haywire when we don't know what's going on. Drivers plus being confused equals many, many views on the internet. I don't blame them at all if it's true, but I can't be sure because if there's one driver who will likely get confused by directions or isn't paying close enough attention, it's me.

I didn't realize that this activity is a grand finale of sorts for the Creator Crush. All the drivers and the creators have been bustled into a large gymnasium that's part of the broader sporting complex the track's a part of.

I've been handed a goddamn paddle-and-or-racquet-type-thing, and I have no idea what's going on.

I'm fully to blame for the latter problem, because I wasn't trying hard to pay attention to the instructions. We were assigned influencer teammates at random and Sunny's not in my half of the room, so I keep searching for her whenever the ball is volleyed to the other side of the net.

And for whatever reason, there are water balloons involved?

I'm trying to be a team player while gawking and looking over heads to try and spot Sunny.

Finally, I see her telltale curls tied up in a ponytail as she jumps.

She swats a ball to the side while she dodges a water balloon, setting up a perfect shot for her partner, I guess. I catch a short wall of muscle and a glinting blonde haircut. She's paired with Jenna. My heart warms. I was worried she'd make it the entire week without talking to her favorite racer, at which point I would have arranged time for them to chat myself.

A boisterous laugh echoes from all the way at the end of the room. I curse, not only because a water balloon has exploded against my thigh, but because they're playing against another influencer... and Hendrix, who likes to flirt with every person he ever encounters and has plenty of thoughts about the kind of romantic partner I am, if Sunny were inclined to ask. He isn't spiteful, but he loves to stir the pot, and Sunny and I don't have time for that.

I swear again and miss the ball... again. I smile apologetically at my partner and they give me a good-natured smile back. I refocus because as much as I need to talk to Sunny, it's not worth being a dick to this person who's also trying to have a nice conclusion to their weekend.

Further, Geoff is the driver my teammate and I are paired against, and as Hendrix's new boyfriend, he's not threatened by me, but he doesn't mind ribbing me on occasion, or in this case, pelting icy balloons at me, even though I'm fairly certain those are not the rules.

The energy in here is familiar. Judging by the frazzled air radiating off each of them and the bags blooming beneath their eyes, the Riot staff charged with putting this on are exhausted, and there's still a full race day left.

I hope Sunny's holding up okay. She was more restless last night as she slept than I've seen her.

I force myself to pay attention and help my partner. We still lose, but at least by a respectable margin. By the time we all shake hands and get a picture, I've searched the space frantically but find that Sunny has already left.

I don't see Jackie or Gael, the friends she told me about, so maybe they're off to do something together.

No worries. I'll text her because I really want her to come over tonight.

I dip into a corner and there's a sinking feeling in my chest as I grope at my pocket and don't feel the familiar weight there.

My ADHD Kryptonite has snuck through my armor of careful plans and systems.

The last time this catastrophe occurred, it took me three whole days to remedy.

I've lost my phone.

CHAPTER TWENTY

Sunny

I nearly pull a muscle with how quickly I escape from the gym.

After making sure to be as far as possible from Evan in the group photo, I made a run for it. I couldn't stand it if we were to awkwardly make eye contact and I saw the fading interest in his face.

Thank you so much, creators! We hope you had the best time. Enjoy the race tomorrow!

Riot's parting words echo in my head like an endless funeral dirge. Dramatic, I know, but the comedown from possibly the best week of my life hurts.

The gloom is mirrored by the paddock's unfamiliar quiet. Teams aren't allowed to make changes to the car between qualifying and the race except under very special circumstances, so nothing drowns out the sound of my panting as I tuck myself against a wall and drop my face into my hands.

A Riot staffer passes and says, not quietly enough, how relieved they are that this program is over. I know deep down they mean because it was a bitch to organize and had so many moving parts, and an opening race week is already difficult enough. A less wise part of me clings to the fact that the ruling group of this race track is pleased to be free of the responsibility of entertaining us.

Those feelings quickly meld with my thoughts about Evan. He still hadn't texted by the time we arrived at the gym, and I couldn't bear to look at him—to see him probably trying not to make eye contact with me because the fun is over and now he really needs to focus.

I only spiral for another moment before Gael and Jackie find me.

"Wow." Gael brushes his hair out of his face. "That was our send-off with fanfare, huh? Thank god we've still got a race left. Going back to work on Monday will be brutal."

At least I'm not the only one feeling the cracks in the fairy tale that was this week.

Jackie tries to shoo away the melancholy mood when she slings her arms around our shoulders. "Luckily, I've planned for exactly this and booked us a big table at the nearest barcade for tonight. All our new creator friends can come, too. We'll drown our sorrows in beer and nacho cheese."

We hit the hotel for a power nap before heading out.

I hate that I'm still hoping Evan will text, even though I'm pissed about how this morning went down. An epic orgasm and then radio silence? I knew it. Classic.

I texted him right after the session, sharing my thanks for and approval of his sexy stunt.

So, after checking my phone for the tenth time in the rideshare on the way to the bar, with Jackie raising her eyebrows at me but saying nothing, I decided that was that and I didn't care. I stuffed my phone in my purse and smoothed my dress. Arm-in-arm, Jackie and I saunter to the bar to toast to a life-changing week. Gael's already there in a shirt unbuttoned extremely low and strong opinions about which shots we should start with.

Neon lights, craft beers, and good company make a potent medicine. I place second in a heated Skee-ball tournament, and the least bashful of us find the small dance floor in one corner. I laugh until my throat hurts, and as the evening winds down, I help Jackie and Gael make sure everyone has ordered their rideshare back to the hotel and has at least downed one glass of water.

The stragglers gone—some unlikely ones paired up—Gael leaves and I swear I spot Cooper sneaking past the bar's front window when he does, Jackie and I sag in the massive booth our group shared, picking at scraps of appetizers.

"Nightcap?" she asks.

"Yes, please. My treat." I flag down a server and order our drinks.

As I stare into a third beer, I realize I don't want it. I watch the tiny bubbles pop. "What's surprised you most about actually being here?"

Jackie considers for a moment. "How loud it is at the track in the mountains. It's constant sensory overload with the sound bouncing. Our home track isn't like that." She means her and Gael. They both live near LA and have been to races together before. Familiar jealousy seizes my stomach. They already have plans to meet up at the California race later this season. They invited me, but I don't know if I can make it work. "Everybody must get used to it after a while. I can't imagine how intense it must be at a track that's super hot or cold. What about you?"

I bite my lip and consider the week, but the tone of today especially. "How down-to-earth it feels. Yes, it's this big, exciting spectacle of entertainment but still, all of the Riot staff and the team personnel are simply doing their jobs.

Cool jobs, exciting jobs, but jobs nonetheless. It's kind of awesome that this is how they make their living."

Jackie smothers a yawn. The side of my purse buzzes. "Have you not checked your phone since we got here?"

I gulp. "I'm afraid to."

She gives me a flat stare.

I crinkle my nose. I haven't taken the phone out all night, counting on all the photos and videos I'll be tagged in by the other creators. We all know the importance of logging off sometimes, but this isn't that.

"It's probably my mom demanding proof that I'm alive," I hedge.

Jackie taps her lip. "Evan could surprise you, but only if you give him a chance to."

My traitor heart is in my throat as I check.

"Fuck me, you're *right*."

Jackie throws her head back and cackles.

From an hour ago:

> Hey sunshine, I'm so sorry that I missed your presentation. I got stuck in a meeting, then lost my phone for a couple of hours and just found it in one of my spare shoes in the driver's room. How was it? Did you crush it? I'm sure you did. I AM SO

SORRY I WASN'T THERE WHEN I SAID I WOULD BE.

Actually you don't have to tell me I know you nailed it CONGRATULA-TIONS!

I'm glad you appreciated my stunt with the vibrator. I enjoyed it, too. Though I'm jealous I didn't get to watch your face in person. Maybe I can have the opportunity tonight…?

The final text is shorter.

Come over, please?

The "please" kills me. Seeing him is a bad idea, but I'll take any bright spot to chase away these awful feelings about the week ending. I shoot Jackie a look and type back.

Need me to comfort you through the pre-race jitters?

His response is near-instant, with a bubble appearing a few times to suggest he's having trouble deciding on an answer.

Yes, kit. I need your soothing touch.

My legs clamp together.

Time for one last rodeo with the giraffe.

CHAPTER TWENTY-ONE

Sunny

Even though I'll see her tomorrow, I hug Jackie fiercely.

She usually has a response for everything, but this time, she just lets me squeeze for as long as I need.

She hops in a car, and I point my sneakers toward Evan's building. Jackie picked a bar weirdly close to where Evan lives—surely not on purpose. The short walk along the streets bustling with race fans, tourists, and Seattleites will be nice. My thoughts aren't the most soothing company, though, so I pull out my phone. Beneath the twinkling lights and hooting of late-night meet-ups, I dial.

"Hey, Honey."

"Hi, Dad." My shoulders immediately drop at the sound of his gravelly voice. They inch back up when I hear my mom's voice rise over whatever TV show they were watching.

"Why hasn't she called more often? She knows how my poor nerves are, thinking of her alone in that big city!"

The sound dampens, and I wait as my dad soothes her. Then, I hear his heavy steps move through the house.

"How's Seattle?" Beyond his voice, I hear the hum of machines in his workshop, a jazzed-up shed in the back-yard he's spent years expanding, weatherproofing, and filling with the accoutrement of a thousand hobbies.

"It's amazing…" I pause. It takes a moment to find my breath. "It's going to be hard to come home."

Whatever machine he's using quiets. "That doesn't sound like you."

"I know." I swallow. The beginnings of a dozen statements stir in my head, but I can't bring myself to voice any explanation.

"You really love this racing thing."

"Yeah." I've made it to Evan's building so I'm shifting on my feet on the sidewalk, a little chilly, staring up at the lit windows. "I've never felt so ignited by something before."

"Hmm." He makes the sound of a supportive father entirely out of his depth. "Maybe your gut's trying to tell you something."

"It's not being very clear," I scoff.

"I guess you gotta keep on listening, then."

I shift my weight. Though the buzz of booze is long gone, my head starts spinning when I see Evan erupt from the elevator through the building's glass doors. I press a hand to my stomach, where nerves flutter. "I'm gonna head to bed, Dad. I wanted to let you know things were going well."

"Okay, honey. Have a nice time. Call us before your flight tomorrow... And when you land. You know your mother's worries. She means well."

"I will. Love you." I fumble to tuck the phone away as Evan bounds toward me.

I don't tell my feet to move, but they do.

The tiny creak of the opening doors. The squeak of my sneakers on the freshly buffed tile. Murmured conversation coming from the person on the phone at the desk. Pealing bells portending the arrival of my Icarus flight and fall.

This last time with him will be so good, as all the others have been. But when it's over... I'm pre-grieving, I guess, preparing for the hurt.

Despite all the boundaries and reasoning and preventative measures, I like him so much.

Evan nearly slips as he approaches me. I catch and steady him. His arms surround me and the breath vacates my body. His presence causes an overwhelm that dispels my drama.

He sounds as breathless as I am. He's only wearing sweatpants, and his abs cast shadows on his skin in the dim light. His eyes are ravenous as they flash from my face to the little dress I wore to the bar.

"Hi."

He steers me toward the elevator. "How was your walk?"

"Uneventful. I called my dad."

"Nice. Did you tell him I say hi?" He tugs me into the elevator and then his arms. I comply, twining my arms around him and meeting his mouth for a kiss.

"I did not."

"My sister would love you."

The doors close and the arrival at Evan's floor is shortly announced by a *ding*, but my eyes are squeezed shut so I can fully enjoy the feel of him. His skin beneath my hands, his tongue sliding against mine, his breath releasing as we kiss. One arm is looped around my waist, tugging my already short dress higher. Evan digs his other hand into my hair, gently pulling so he can explore my mouth.

I vaguely remember planning to try and create space between us tonight, but that's been derailed. I just want to *feel*. There's an unfamiliar force in my chest driving my movements. I'm scared, and I'm mad, and Evan's going to disappear tomorrow. So really, why would I want to dispel this sweet, passionate flurry?

We break for breath, and Evan presses his forehead to mine. "Missed you today, kit."

I back us into the hall, running my hands up his chest. The intensity in his eyes is like being under a spotlight. "It was amazing to watch you qualify."

Bundling me under one arm, Evan gets us through his door. When it closes, he crowds me against it, caging me in. My breath catches as he brings his face close, his eyes locked on my mouth. "Did you like my game earlier today?"

I give a shaky nod. "Very much. Are we... going to play more tonight?"

His smile is wicked. "I think you'll love what we try. It's a hell of an apology."

"You don't have to apologize," I grumble. What I mean is that it won't make any difference. I know that racing is Evan's *job*, but he insisted he'd be there, and I believed him.

He pauses with a knuckle under my chin. "Of course, I do. Sometimes it's all I can do. Even with all of my processes and reminders and failsafes in place, sometimes, with my ADHD, I forget things, ot make promises I should know better than to make. I know it's going to happen on occasion. Sometimes, it's not a big deal. Today was, though. It was your big moment, and I missed it, and I'm sorry." He kisses me again, holding me close. Our kisses slow till he gently pecks my mouth a few times before pulling back. "Are you hungry? Do you need anything?"

I dig my nails into his pecs and shift us into the safe territory of kink-instead-of-feelings. "I need your cock inside me right now, or I feel like I'll faint from wanting you all day."

Evan's eyes widen. "Can't have that." He swings me into his arms and sprints for the bedroom.

I'm plopped in the middle of the bed. Evan crawls on top of me, inching my dress up my body as he does. "I'm very disappointed," he muses between kisses. "I missed seeing whatever you got up to in this dress earlier."

I arch my back, partly in response to the way he runs his tongue over my stomach and partly to help him get the dress over my breasts and all the way off.

"You didn't miss much," I say, batting my lashes. "Drinks at the bar, and maybe I bent over to play a few arcade games..."

He moans in appreciation, continuing to lick every inch of my skin he can reach.

"And maybe I danced a bit, and my skirt rode up a little while I wiggled under the neon lights."

His hands find the sides of my underwear and grip, pulling them tight against my swollen and sensitive pussy. "I would have gotten a glimpse of these, huh?"

My voice goes breathy for the next bit. "And I definitely played one of the racing games. A motorcycle one, where I had to kick my leg over the seat and ride it. The vibrational feedback was great."

Evan groans and bites my nipple. I arch further, letting out a moan.

"You were running around, being my little sex kitten, and I missed it," he murmured. "What if I rode on that bike behind you, and everyone thought we were being cute, but really, it was so I could slip a finger beneath your panties and rub your clit for you, and you'd have to fight so hard to be quiet so no one knew."

I nod somberly, threading my hands into his hair. "Mmhmm. But you didn't. Poor me, all wet and needy from the long-distance orgasm you gave me, with nothing to follow it up."

He groans again, tracing the tip of his tongue around my other nipple. My hips buck against his grip, searching for friction.

He sits up and I make to follow, but he stops me with a warm palm pressed firmly in the middle of my chest. "Don't move."

It's an order. I swallow and settle back to the mattress, though it's hard with my muscles taut like bowstrings, aching for release.

"Very good." He steps from the bed and retrieves something from a bag on the floor. I watch, but I can't see what he's unwrapping. His eyes dart to mine. "Tell me your safe word."

"Halt." I say it clearly. He won't continue if I can't demonstrate I understand this machine's brake pedal.

He grins. "Thank you. And before I forget, if at any time tonight you can't say the word because your mouth is full, two taps with your fingers will do the trick."

"Copy," I breathe, which draws his grin wider.

"You're so brilliant. Now, put your hands above your head for me."

I do as he says. Being my own binder—that is, keeping my hands away through my own willpower—is sexier than I thought it would be, and the movement arches my back and lifts my breasts.

Which must have been his aim, because Evan shows me a small, clear package of nipple suckers.

I writhe as I watch him unbox them, then examine the little rubbery contraptions. He sticks the open end of one in his mouth, and I moan watching him wet it. Then, he bends over me and squeezes the air out before pressing it to one nipple that's still wet from his earlier attention. When he releases it, it attempts to refill with air, but instead sucks my nipple into a perky point. I moan and squirm.

"You want the other?"

"Please."

He repeats the process, brow furrowed in concentration. The waiting is torture. I feel like I could catch his sheets on fire, but he continues moving slowly, drawing it out.

"Hmm. I should've seen if they had something like this for your clit, too." He swirls a finger around it, drawing whimpers from me. He tilts his head. "Do you want to hear what I think we should try next?"

"Yes." It's a high-pitched whine.

"You're familiar with the idea of a sub earning a reward from their dom?"

My head bobs voraciously. I've only read about it—dreamt about it—a thousand times.

"You want to earn one from me, Sunny? Please me, and I'll give you whatever you want."

I haven't stopped nodding. "Please. Yes. Show me."

He eases my arms from over my head and helps me slide from the bed to my knees beside it. Each subtle movement sends my breasts swaying, and the sensation from the suckers ratchets up my pleasure. I'm panting as I settle on the carpet before him. I fight the urge to grind on the floor like a mindless thing.

Evan stands there, arms crossed, eyebrow raised. He's devastating. "You want my cock, kit? Take it out."

My shaking fingers curl into the waistband of his sweatpants. I rise on my knees to kiss and lick the trail of fuzz covering the muscles of his stomach. The smell of mangoes and sex floods me, an addiction I'll never be able to sate again.

He fists his hand in my hair and tugs gently. "I'm the only one doing any teasing tonight, kit."

I free his cock and waste no time taking it deep, allowing it to bump the back of my throat. Evan's head falls back, and his fingers tighten in my hair. As I settle into a rhythm, the heat between my legs coils, burning brighter as he praises me. It's criminal that I can't get much friction like this. It drives me to please him faster, to earn my reward, which only ramps up how enjoyable it is to make him come undone.

He watches me now, and when his eyelids flutter as my tongue massages a certain spot, I know he's close. I repeat the motion over and over, getting faster until his thighs quake where my fingers dig into them and his breaths come harsh and loud. With a groan, he spills over my tongue. I'm light-headed with joy and sensation.

With an impossible combination of gentleness and speed, he whisks me back onto the bed.

Evan settles on his knees between my legs and painstakingly draws my panties down my legs. He unhooks them from my feet and tosses them aside. His hands catch the insides of my thighs and spread them wide. "How wet have you been for me all day, baby? Let's see."

I whimper. It's all I can manage.

Evan traces two fingers across my stomach and down to the entrance of my sex, brushing back up to spread me obscenely. He grunts in appreciation at what he finds—that I'm soaked and needy for him. He eases two fingers inside of me, pumping a slow, steady rhythm.

"Evan—Evan, please." I fist my hands in the comforter.

"What, kitten? How can I reward you if I don't know what you want?" he asks, sounding entirely unbothered, though he knows what he's doing to me. He curls his fingers up and inside me to press against the perfect spot. As he probes deep, his knuckles knead against my ass while he still holds me wide open with his free hand. I'm fully at his mercy. "Please fuck me," I gasp.

He removes his fingers and shifts, and I think I'm about to get the miraculous relief of his cock deep inside, stretching me, but instead, he lowers his beautiful head and takes a long drag up my pussy with his tongue. My breasts tingle and ache with every movement I make.

I scream. It's too much after a long day of needing him. My pleasure has been too drawn out since the orgasm earlier, and I realize I'm ramped up with the terror of saying goodbye to him, too.

"Come all over my face, Sunny. Give me a taste and then I'll give you what you want."

"Yes, yes," I'm babbling. I'll do whatever he says. He's hypnotized me into the subliminal space of sheer pleasure, and it's freeing to know I'm safe at his mercy.

His tongue probes my clit, and I give in to making animalistic noises as he strokes me, stoking my pleasure higher until I'm about to explode. He twirls his tongue around my stiff clit and then sucks, and I shout again as his lips knead the pinpoint of my pleasure. My hips rock and my pussy clenches, desperate to be full as I come. The waves of reaction roll seemingly endlessly, and once my tremors ease, Evan busies himself licking every inch of my pussy, coating his face and mouth. He's somehow gently ravenous, insistent in his mission but careful not to stress my overly sensitive parts.

I'm gasping still as he crawls up my body, hovering over me and staring at my face with a wicked grin. He squeezes my side. "That's right, breathe. Excellent, Sunny. Are you good?"

My hands shake as I grab his shoulders and nod, unable to speak. He smiles wider and kisses up my neck, evidence of my pleasure in the scruff that scrapes my skin.

"You said..." My voice cracks because my mouth is dry from gasping and screaming. I swallow and try again as Evan pulls back to eye me with concern. "You said you'd give me what I want."

His laugh echoes around the room as he stands at the side of the bed and rummages for a condom. "I did, you're right. I got distracted by your delicious pussy. I'm sorry." I shiver. His cock is hard and throbbing at my eye level, and Evan cuts a heartbreakingly beautiful picture at the edge of the bed. I need to snap a picture of him on my phone—not naked, if he's not comfortable with that—something so I can remember the brief time I had him.

"Now..." Evan's rolled the condom over his hard, thick length, and he bends over the bed to kiss my nose. "How would you like me to fuck you, Sunny? I know you like it hard and rough, so I'll be sure you're sore tomorrow, so you remember me whenever you move, but tell me how. Where do you want my hands? My mouth? How do you want my cock to stretch your sweet pussy wide?"

"From behind," I say, breathless. "And spank me."

A dark chuckle. "Dirty girl. Just like our first time, but this time, we don't need to be quiet."

I scramble to turn over, but my movements are sluggish. Evan takes to the bed and helps, grabbing me firmly by the hips and flipping my over. He's closer to the foot of the bed, and he hauls me back so my ass and pussy are right where he needs them. His cock teases against me as he reaches forward, snagging a pillow and setting it beneath my stomach to keep my rear hiked up. He notches his head in my entrance and leans forward, not going any deeper.

"Hold still now, Sunny. I'm driving." He gently shifts my hands in front of me. "Hands here, very good." He grabs my hair and guides my left cheek until it's against the covers. "There. I need to see that beautiful face, so I know how much you like this." One big hand smooths over my back, squeezing my ass, then sliding up to press between my shoulder blades, further pressing my chest to the mattress while my ass is in the air, wet and waiting for more of his cock. The friction tugs off the nipple suckers, and I moan long and low as my blood flow returns to normal there.

A soft smack against my skin. He's brought out the spanking paddle again, and I moan low as he gives my ass a few more swats.

For a moment that feels eternal, Evan admires me, his thumbs stroke soft circles over my skin, his cock stiff a few inches inside of me. I'm panting; he's appreciating. "Are you ready, kit?"

I moan again, but I know he wants more. "Yes," I manage, catching his heated gaze out of the corner of my eye.

"More importantly... are you mine?"

The word is the tip of a sword at the base of my spine, demanding my surrender.

"Yes," I gasp, betraying myself, throwing the battered scraps of my emotional shield aside.

A sound of wonder from Evan, and his hands are at my waist; he thrusts.

I cry out at the first stroke, at how full he makes me and the small bite of pain at how his size is just-almost-too-much. I am a raw, naked soul. I have to be to experience this nirvana.

His momentum is relentless as Evan blindly chases his pleasure. Surely, he must know that I'm a vessel of swirling sensation at this point. In this moment, my entire existence is bliss.

Evan spanks me again, sending a zinging wave through my body.

I alternate shouting "yes" with his name and unintelligible cries.

Evan's thrusts grow frenzied, and he grips my hips so tight I'm sure I'll bruise. He shouts my name and then he's coming, his dick twitching deliciously inside me, wringing one last orgasm from my spent system.

I lose all sense of time, but eventually, two minutes after we catch our breath or twenty, I hear his voice.

"All the energy I just put into fucking you? To giving you—*us*—pleasure, Sunny? That's how sorry I am for letting you down."

CHAPTER TWENTY-TWO

Evan

Sunny is a bundle of boneless contentment in my arms. We've been snuggled together for a few minutes, sweat and pleasure still slicking our skin. It's the most comfortable I've ever been, the most relaxed. I don't want to move.

But Sunny should pee, and I definitely left the oven on. She arrived while I was waiting for it to preheat so I could chuck in some chicken tenders for a late night snack.

With a heavy sigh, I nuzzle her neck, murmuring her perfect name into her beautiful skin.

Adorably, she grumbles back. It's incoherent, but has the tone of a question. She's coming out of subspace, but I've learned she's stubborn enough that I need to ease her into aftercare, rather than dominating it upon her.

"You should use the bathroom, Sunny. Get ready for bed. Can you manage it yourself? I'll meet you right back here."

She mumbles—possibly begrudging that I'm right—and uncurls, sitting upright and leaning in for a kiss. I love that she does that, that she wants that from me.

When she withdraws, her brow furrows. "Do you ever stop smiling?"

"Why should I?"

Her lips quirk but she doesn't answer. I watch her hips sway into the bathroom then dash from bed. I turn off the oven—Sunny's wrung every need from my body—and start my electric kettle. My night-before-the-race-ritual is a long one, but that doesn't stop me from trying to stave off the sleeplessness with some calming tea as a small effort.

I brew a cup for each of us, my heart squirming behind my sternum in apprehension. She said she was mine. Under the influence of epic sex hormones, yeah, but there must be a hint of truth there. It's a lot to ask of someone to date you when you travel full-time for work, but I would do everything in my power to see Sunny as much as possible.

I rehearse the last bit mentally as I carefully return to the bedroom, only spilling drops of steaming hot tea on my bare foot twice.

"How are you feel—"

I assume Sunny is the lump beneath the comforter. I tiptoe around to set the mug by her side, and her eyes are open... and narrow.

"Everything okay?"

"I don't need a call girl goodie bag."

"What?" Oh, she must mean the travel-size versions of my mango routine I left on the counter for her. I thought the bow leftover from Christmas was cute. "They're another gift."

She heaves up onto one elbow, swiping her messy curls back. "Yeah, but you left the lowest drawer cracked. It's full of those. And toothbrushes... and... and I don't need a thank you for being your sex toy of the week!"

Her cheeks are aflame, and I'm mortified. "That's not what this is. That drawer is for me, since I travel so much. I need a stash of the small sizes to get through the airport. I'm constantly leaving them in different cities and needing new ones." I perch on the edge of the bed.

She tugs the comforter higher, eyes glued to the mattress. "What about the garage pass?"

"What about it?"

"I can't be the first person you've brought down there."

Ah, she thinks I'm a fuckboy.

"Like, ever? No. I've brought people I'm interested in there before, yeah. I've been a racing driver for a long time, and it's the best seat you can give someone you care about."

I want to touch her, soothe this fear, but I'm afraid of making things worse. We're on the edge of a precipice here.

"You didn't give me insider access so I'd sleep with you?" She sounds uncertain.

I sigh. "No. Did you sleep with me to get insider access?"

"Of course not."

I take a risk and cup her hip through the blankets. "Exactly. I take your word for that. Can you take me at mine?"

She squeezes her eyes shut and doesn't open them for a long time. "You're right. I'm sorry I assumed. It's been a long day—a long week." She takes a shuddering breath. "I really need some rest."

She rolls over, and I try to douse the worry kindling in my chest. No chatting tonight, then. That's alright. We can talk in the morning over coffee, or after the race.

Maybe I can pull off something elaborate before her flight home, like a meal at one of my favorite spots, or a trip to the aquarium... Though if I had to bet, I guess her flight's in the morning on Monday. A lavish breakfast in bed it is, then, with roses and mimosas and a proclamation of... Well, I need to be careful of getting ahead of myself.

It'll be alright, I try to tell the clenching in my chest.

I leave her mug and cradle my own. I need to finish my routine. The faster I review data for tomorrow and calm my mind, the sooner I can climb into bed and wrap my arms around her.

There's no way I'll sleep long, if I fall asleep at all, but it'll be worth it to hold her for a while.

We have tomorrow and a scrap of Monday, I remind myself. And then, if I can convince her, we'll have longer.

CHAPTER TWENTY-THREE

Sunny

A coughing fit jerks me from sleep. My throat is nearly wrecked from so many days of talking and cheering and moaning.

The clock says it's well after midnight. I sit up carefully, only to discover that Evan isn't in bed with me. The realization makes my heart feel like it's sunk to the bottom of the ocean.

More importantly, are you mine?

The memory of our last fuck sends shivers down my spine. It felt different, more intimate. I admitted the hold he has on me. So much for all of my defensive efforts. I fell for my fling.

And then lashed out about it. This is why I don't take risks.

On the nightstand, I spy a cooled cup of tea, bitter-smelling from sitting for too long. Light catches my eye. Subtle blue flashes wash the wall beyond the bedroom door, echoing from the living room.

Evan's out there. He famously has trouble sleeping the night before races.

My insides go tight as I realize these are the last hours I'll spend in this apartment.

I remind myself of the chaos of the track. That's what's real, and it's his life, not mine. My reality is a gray apartment and a grayer office and a sleepy town and uneventful weekends spent watching movies with my parents and helping to guide my sisters. Evan and I have been playing an adventurous game of house this week, in this apartment he barely visits. I've gotten comfortable in a fantasy that's nearing its end, and the hangover will be brutal.

I'm exhausted and as prepared as I can be for the hurt that's coming. Arguing with Evan didn't feel good, especially when it turned out I was wrong. I'll give in to my traitorous feelings that got me in a bad position again and try to see if there's any joy left to wring out of this thing.

Steeling my nerves, I pad out there. Evan's situated in his sim racing rig, a series of metal pipes holding a mock race seat, replica steering wheel, and pedals, playing the Riot

Racing video game in a simple t-shirt and shorts. His hair is tousled, still sticking up in places from where I pulled it.

He notices me and pauses the game.

"Hey, kit. Are you okay?"

I dip my head. "Don't get up. I just need some water."

Still, his eyes follow me as I grab a glass and fill it at the sink. He only continues playing when I hesitate at the island and take a sip.

I scooch around the counter, captivated watching him race on a game I know and love, too. We even have the same brand setup of wheels and pedals, which makes my heart swell with pride. As he races, I move to stand next to him, unconsciously resting a hand on his headrest.

He slides a hand around my thigh and presses his face against my hip, driving impressively with one hand and no eyes on the road.

"I hope I didn't wake you," he says, even though the volume is a soft hum from the soundbar.

"Nah, just thirsty," I murmur. "Have you slept yet?"

He pauses again, turning in the seat to look at me. "No, but with you, I think I will for a little. That will be a nice change."

A smile springs to my face, and I nod at the TV screen. "Practicing for tomorrow?"

"I'm more nervous than usual. Home race jitters."

"Want to talk about it?"

"Nah, there's not much more I can do to prepare, but the repetition helps me get sleepy after a while... Want to have a go?"

I sidle onto his lap, preening at the shocked and pleased expression on his face, especially when his hands tighten on my hips and he situates me perfectly in his lap. As I nudge his feet off the pedals, he scoots the wheel back a few inches to give me room. I navigate to begin a new race. He wraps his arms around my waist and rests his chin on my shoulder to watch. He's a warm, centering tether as I begin. I pick a short time-trial setup, something that would finish within a few minutes. Evan's quiet and lets me focus. After a few laps, making sure I have the track down as well as I remember, I begin a flying lap. When I hit a corner's apex perfectly, Evan perks a little. "That's good," he murmurs, nuzzling my neck. "That's really good."

As I wing through the last few laps, bringing down my average lap time, Evan has gone completely speechless, his jaw hanging beside my face. I can't help but giggle as I take the checkered flag and my average lap speed flashes across the screen. I haven't come close to beating his best time—he is a professional, after all—but I've taken a top ten spot on his console's records.

"I love this game," I whisper.

Evan's hands run up my arms, trail up my neck and grip my face. Gently, he turns it to the side so our faces are inches apart. "That was *so* sexy," he says, and then his mouth is on mine.

I try to turn to wrap my arms around him, a needy noise erupting from my throat. As we kiss, our tongues battling, Evan gently topples us to the floor.

The soft carpet draws goosebumps along my heated skin as Evan plunders my mouth, one hand cradling my head, the other wrapped around my waist. I wrap my legs around his. I only wearing his t-shirt.

My blood rushes, trying to keep up with his kisses. He moves to my neck, ravishing me there as I hang on to him for dear life, my hands buried in his hair and the meat of his ass.

He pulls back to grab a pillow from the couch to tuck beneath my head. Our hands are frantic. He shifts the shirt up, revealing my breasts, and buries his face in them, placing biting kisses over every inch. With a moan, I scramble to ease his shorts off. I manage it when he takes a breath. "Condom," he says, and stumbles up and back to the bedroom. His goofy bare ass glows in the light from the TV, and he nearly trips over a table in his rush.

I reel from the wave of fondness that floods my system. The thought of leaving him hurt before, but now it nearly knocks me breathless, and maybe it's the exhaustion, but I struggle for air.

Evan's back fast, pulling the condom on as he kneels. I grab his neck and tug him back to me. He slips a hand between my legs and moans when he meets the wetness there, remnants from our earlier fucking.

I find his cock and give it a firm stroke before guiding him to my entrance, whimpering when his head brushes against me. I remove my hand. Evan sinks into me slowly. His eyes close and his head rolls back. "You feel so fucking good."

His next thrust bumps my G-spot, and I can only moan in response. Evan swallows it, his deep plunging kisses matching his thrusts. Our franticness eases into something slow and sweet, incredibly earnest.

I can't get close enough to him. I hold him because of the pleasure, but also because as this next orgasm comes for me, I recognize the feeling brewing beneath it. I've fallen for him. I've fallen head over heels for this beautiful idiot, just in time to say goodbye.

Another orgasm crests right after the first, and this time Evan comes with me, his pleased noises twins to mine.

A gentle kiss, then he's gone. I gasp, panic sucking me under like some evil orgasm from a mirror dimension. I hear the faucet, then he's back with a warm washcloth to clean me up.

As he does, I notice the notes he's written himself on the fridge whiteboard. The biggest one says TEXAS! My heart drops. The location of the next race. It's where he's headed next, where he's looking ahead to. Somewhere I'm not.

When he finishes wiping my skin, I wrap my arms around him, hauling him to me. He squeezes back with a laugh. "You liked that, huh, kit? Maybe I'll actually be able to sleep now. Maybe you were the missing ingredient."

At some point, tears have leaked from the corners of my eyes. I loosen my arms and try to wipe the moisture away subtly, beneath the cover of the darkened living room.

But this idiot is so damn sweet, and he's already set aside the cloth and taken my face in his hands to kiss me again. But before he can, he notices the tears.

"Are you crying? Sunny, what's wrong?"

"I'm okay," I insist, trying to swallow. Evan fumbles around and gets a lamp on. The concern carved into his face is heartbreaking.

"Did I hurt you? What happened?"

God, I have to lose him *and* suffer the embarrassment of him seeing how invested I've become.

"I'm okay," I say again, silently begging my body to make it real.

"I don't think you are." Evan pulls me into his lap, his voice soft and edged with worry. "Won't you talk to me, Sunny? What's going on?"

A steadying breath highlights the sorrow lacing my body. What's the use of explaining this to him?

"Sunny, please. If you're upset, I don't want to be the reason why. I want to be the one to help fix it."

My small laugh is strangled. Evan really thinks he's invested—that his affection won't fade in the flurry of passing days. My tears are embarrassing, as my confession is about to be. The only comfort is that he'll likely forget within a few weeks.

"This..." I try and gulp, and try again, laying a hand on his warm chest. "It's really going to hurt when this is over."

His eyes leave mine for a moment, the gears working as he tries to understand. Then his arms go tighter around me. "Wait, you mean us? Why does it have to be over?"

"Why wouldn't it end, Evan? This week is a fluke, a special occasion, a once-in-a-lifetime opportunity. I'm not supposed to be here. We have different lives, in different worlds."

He's quiet for a moment, until... "I disagree."

I wipe my eyes. "I know we've had fun this week, but the shine of me will wear off, Evan. It won't work when we're apart and there are people trying to flirt with you at every corner and I'm not top of mind, I'm not the most interesting thing. You'll realize that it's not worth the effort when you could have whatever else you want easier, even if it's no one. And I won't be able to handle it. I can't handle the stress of trying to keep you interested but not bothering you and not being too clingy, but god forbid I don't answer the phone... if you call at all." My chest heaves. Evan rubs my back till it eases, his face a twist of concern.

As my breathing slows, he cradles my head and guides it to the pillow. He takes a steadying breath himself. "Sunny, why do you think that? Did I do something to make you think that's what would happen?"

"You didn't." He looks relieved for an instant. But I have to be reasonable and protect myself. "But plenty of other boys with nice smiles did. They gave me attention and made me feel special and taught me it would happen."

"That's not... That doesn't..." Evan strokes my cheek as he finds what to say. "Can't I prove how I'd treat you? Let's talk about this more tomorrow, after the race. We'll make a plan before your flight on Monday. When is it? This doesn't have to be over for us, Sunny. I—"

My sigh sounds pitying as I press a thumb to his lips.

"See, this is why it has to be. I don't leave Monday. Riot booked me the cheapest ticket home, right after the race. I leave tomorrow." I find the clock in the corner, its readout bright against the dark. "I leave later *today*."

CHAPTER TWENTY-FOUR

Evan

Panic. That's all I feel, aside from the impending doom of heartbreak I'm insistent won't happen.

Sunny's clammed up, her wet face buried in my chest.

We were having such a perfect night, a perfect week, but I didn't take the risk to talk to her about this sooner. Now we're out of time.

Sunny works out a few hiccupping breaths as I hold her.

I am so stupid for thinking that it could be this easy, that she would want this as badly as I do. I knew she'd have concerns, of course, but I thought I'd handle them easily.

I'm such an asshole.

She pushes gently at my chest.

God, is she trying to leave? I'm an idiot, assuming she'd fly out tomorrow. Why would they keep the creators an extra night and pay for the hotel? I thought we'd have time, at least a little *more* time, to talk about this. About... our future. It seemed so easy and logical to me, but now that it's time to confront it, and the knowledge that Sunny hasn't thought about it, I'm worried. "We can see each other again."

She closes her eyes. "You travel constantly for most of the year. Your life is so busy."

I roll so I'm on my side facing her, sharing the pillow. "You can come to other races. As my guest. As my... person. I'll fly you out. You can stay with me."

"I can't ask you to foot a bill like that."

"You're not asking, I'm offering. I want to."

Sunny's not looking at me anymore; her gaze is fixed pointedly on my chest. "I can't keep up with your life."

"It could be your life, too. You're built for this. No one is doing it like you. Through your content, you're bringing so many new fans to this sport, making it enjoyable and accessible. You're thriving in the paddock, close to the action. A career in motorsports is chaotic, but you adjust."

She scowls. "You started this career with a bank of raw talent, your family's support, and the drive to make a name for yourself."

I'm dumbstruck. "Sunny... what do you think *you* have?"

She looks away. More tears squeeze out, and no matter how I try, I can't catch them all. "Don't sell me that dream. I can't take it."

"What have I done this week that makes you think I don't mean this? I want to have a relationship with you. I want to travel the world and rank mediocre hotel croissants with you."

She's shaking now. "But it'll hurt so much when you change your mind. Worse than it does now."

I draw her close, letting her breathe into my chest. I'm so serious about her, but it would be silly to promise that wouldn't happen. A definite promise wouldn't mean anything to someone as ruthlessly practical as Sunny. "All I can say, Sunny, is that if you do this with me, I can promise that the only reason we'd break it off is because you or I don't want to be together anymore. That our spark's gone and it's not a good fit. Not distance, not thirsty fans making a pass. You have those too, remember? I've seen the comments on your bikini pics." She snorts. That's progress, I guess.

Her crying eases, but she's so worked up. I don't want to leave it like this, but I've already deprived her of so much sleep this week, and I know it's hard to focus on falling for someone and committing to your job at the same time. "How about we sleep on it? Sounds like we could both use a solid night's rest, or what's left of the night. Let's revisit this in the morning."

She wipes her eyes, and her gaze still feels distant. "Okay."

I stand and carry her to bed. She's quiet but snuggly as I tuck her in. I'm dying to know what she's thinking, and I'm trying to put every ounce of sincerity and devotion I have toward her into my touches. But as she falls asleep curled against me, it's hard to keep hoping that she'll give me a real chance.

When I wake up, all the sunshine has left my bed. In a daze, I tumble into the hall, trailing sheets, and find Sunny pouring a cup of coffee.

She glances up. "Hi. I was up before the alarms. Coffee?"

"Hi. Yeah." I dislodge my tail of bedding and stumble to the counter across from her. I hate having it between us, but I don't want to crowd her.

She slides a mug to me. "Sleep okay?"

"Yes." *Once you were in my arms.* Panic's got my throat in a vice, and I can't say anything else.

"I've got to get going," she says.

My stomach plummets, my mouth goes dry, and Sunny soldiers on, somehow keeping her eyes locked with mine. "I need to pack."

She wants to leave.

"Listen, Evan, this has been so fun. Thank you so much for hosting me, cooking for me." Her voice cracks, and her fingers trace lines on my counter. "For taking care of me. This... fling was so excellent."

She's named it. A fling. Casual. Here and gone.

She's decided. She's giving up on me. On us. She doesn't want to give it a shot.

She doesn't share my feelings.

I committed the cardinal sin of assumption. Thinking that because she loves racing, she'd grow to love me, too. I definitely lulled myself into a sense of comfort with the belief: *Who wouldn't want to date a racing drive*r? My fucking pride has landed me in trouble.

As she's halfway to the door, I realize the mug Sunny poured was for me. Is there an empty one in the sink she drank while waiting for me to wake up?

How am I supposed to face today when she's walking out the door and taking all the breath in my body with her?

It's only a few seconds after the click of the door closing that I realize I'm naked, and Sunny's walked out with half my heart.

I didn't realize I'd given it to her.

CHAPTER TWENTY-FIVE

Sunny

I get my crying out on the walk to the hotel. It's early and rainy enough to go unnoticed.

I keep waiting for a wash of relief at cutting Evan out of my life. Now I don't have to worry about getting hurt beyond the soul-shredding pain I just caused myself.

It aches so much worse than I imagined. I don't want it to linger. I did what I was supposed to—the responsible thing. With gritted teeth, I wrestle the ache away to some quiet corner inside me where it'll shrivel, forgotten and unfed by my attention.

And my prejudice truly hurt him. That was unexpected.

By the time I reach the hotel, I've stopped my stuttering breaths. I book it to my room to clean up and mask any signs of distress. The Crush is over, and I can enjoy the best part of the weekend—the race.

And try not to pay too much attention to the eleven car in the process.

I'm strong, and I'm excited to be here. I can handle it.

And then I'll go home.

Logically, my life is so good, but there's a part of me, tiny and raging in my chest, influenced by Evan but not dependent on him, that's begging me to acknowledge that it's wrong.

What do you think you *have?*

He sees me as someone who belongs here.

I'm the last person who does.

My fake smile is enough to placate the other creators over breakfast, and we're all tired and excited enough to keep our talking to a minimum. It's race day. Bigger than the rest of the week combined.

The chaos of a busy paddock is the distraction I need.

My heart aches again, this time at the realization that over the past week, I've gotten used to certain details that surround me, and now I notice smaller ones. The smell of rubber and fuel and dust. How no matter what team they work for, every staffer seems welcome at Cyber Ward hospitality, which must offer the best coffee, judging from the steaming cups that keep departing in the hands of folks wearing all different team polos.

Our paddock passes are still good, so we take the time we have to get last-minute photos and memories of everything we want to see. I flit among our boisterous and somewhat recovered Crush colleagues, so Jackie and Gael don't have the opportunity to ask about Evan.

There are screens showing pre-race coverage everywhere, and I begin to sweat when the camera cuts to a view of Evan in the back of the garage. He looks resplendent... and miserable.

Surely, that's not because of me.

The commentators remark that it's odd to see him so morose, speculating that maybe he's hyper-focused, especially because there's a small chance of rain toward the end of the race, which would upend every teams' strategy.

Someone calls my name. Gael taps his watch impatiently, wanting enough time to track down the grandstand seats Riot has booked us. The accommodations are nothing compared to the access we've had all week, but the views of the track are good and that's all that matters.

We hustle toward the paddock exit—or try to, as the crowd is the biggest we've seen all week.

While some of my peers are looking for photo ops with different team members and others are visiting the garages they've befriended since the week began, I'm trying not to make it obvious that I want to give the Panache garage a wide berth. If either of my friends mention it, I'll distract them with a proposal for one last visit to the gargantuan merch tent.

"Sunny."

The deep voice startles me, as well as the insistent tug on my elbow.

Pete appears, hat pulled low and a denim jacket over his Panache polo. His eyes are shifty. "Enjoying race day?"

Sweat beads at his temples, though it's chilly. I blink rapidly. "Don't you have somewhere to be right now? Like finalizing your run plan with..." I swallow.

"Yeah... about that. Can you follow me, please?" Gael and Jackie are both staring, and I hear the crowd around us murmuring. Pete's seconds from being recognized, and as soon as people decide his photo is worth getting to their seats late, he'll be swarmed.

"Is Evan okay?"

Pete's responding laugh is choked. "Physically, yes, at the moment. At least, until I strangle him."

"What are you talking about?"

"He won't get in the car."

My breath catches. "He can't be that stupid."

A hollow laugh. "You know that's not true. Can you come with me, please?"

My eyes pinch shut. So much for my attempted clean break.

I know Evan isn't stubborn enough to miss the race... probably. And it's not my responsibility to make sure he does his actual fucking job... but... I didn't really give him a chance for a rebuttal when I fled his apartment this morning. I don't owe him one.

But he's been nothing but wonderful to me, so maybe letting him have a little more closure is a kind thing to do.

Kind, at least, to Pete, who's barely fending off a complete meltdown.

"Lead the way." I follow him numbly as he weaves through the crowd with a perfect, far-off stare so people know better than to stop him. The team garages have been cordoned off, and he leads me past Panache, where a few feet of open space between it and the Matthews garage are blocked by a handful of giant potted shrubs.

Pete gives me a gentle shove behind them, and then he's gone.

"What the—?" I trip over what I initially expect are some Panache storage crates, but the pink and black mass unfolds to save me from my fall. "What the hell are you doing?"

Evan fully straightens, glancing shiftily between the plants. "Hiding from everyone except you."

He's in his form-hugging fireproofs under layer, with his firesuit zipped just over his hips, the empty sleeves tied around his waist until it's time to get in the car and he'll pull it on entirely. One warm hand steadies my shoulder.

"I'm sorry to disrupt your race day, but I wanted to talk to you, and I only asked—well, had Pete ask—because I think you want to talk, too."

I cross my arms. "He said you're refusing to get in the car."

"What? No—I wouldn't let the team down like that. I'm just... stalling a little."

I frown. Evan's hair is a mess. A flush swamps his cheeks, and the corner of his lip is chewed and puffy. His eyes are tight and downcast. He looks... heartbroken.

I've been trying to protect myself, but in doing so, it sure seems like I'm the one who's devastated him.

If he's this affected, then that means...

"We're not done, Sunny. We can't be."

I can't tear my eyes from him. Gingerly, he takes my hands, and I don't pull away. He gulps. I don't know what to say. My heart aches just looking at him.

"I don't want this to be the end, Sunny. It's the beginning of something great, I can feel it, and I think you do, too. You trusted me in the car at the beginning of this week. I'm asking you to trust me again. Don't take your flight home. Let me book you another, tomorrow night. Wait for me after the race, so we can figure this out. So we can figure *us* out."

"I—I...." I stammer, my voice breathless. "You can't be serious."

"You know that I'm rarely serious, but I am about you. You don't want to be hurt, I get it. I don't either, but it's a risk I'll gladly take to truly know what my life can be like with you in it. I think of the joy I can bring you, the chance at more mornings hearing your takes on racing, on life... Sunny, it's so worth it to me. I can treat you well. I can worship you and make you so happy. I can prove there are people like that, Sunny, but only if you're brave enough to give me a chance."

"*Time's up!*" Pete's harried voice floats between our skimpy shield of branches.

Evan hits me with the full force of his hopeful cow eyes. "I'll call you after the race. Don't take your flight home. Think about it, please?"

Thinking about it will be easy. It's the final decision that will wreck me. "I'll think about it."

His hands squeeze, and the tightness in his face eases a little. Seconds pass. He's fixated, staring at me. Pete lets out an angry sigh.

I step close, tugging Evan's chin down till our faces are close together. "I said, I'll think about it. I promise. Now, go drive the damn car, you idiot."

I think his eyes crinkle with pleasure, but I'm not sure, as he finally goes.

"I love it when she yells at me," I hear him tell Pete.

My heart pounding, I take a few steadying breaths and step from between the plants.

Another jumpscare in pink and black awaits me.

I curse at the ambush, and Blair gives a satisfied smile, dangling a garage pass in front of my face, the one with my name on it. "You left this last time. It's good for the entire weekend, you know." I begin to protest, but she crosses her arms, a formidable wall. "It makes me look bad if guests refuse our invitation."

With a scowl, I snatch it from her. "You're impossible to argue with."

"It's why I'm so good at my job." She places a hand on my shoulder and guides me into the garage. "Hurry up. We're gonna miss the formation lap. If it makes you feel any better, I already gave a handful to a bunch of kids decked out in Panache merch, so you'll be behind at least three rows of yelling pre-teens. I doubt the cameras will find you there."

I slip the pass over my head and grumble. "I didn't mean to be ungrateful."

She pats my shoulder. "Don't worry. His smiles make most people go crazy if they're not used to it, and I've never seen him smile at someone as much as he does at you."

I can't think of a response. Luckily, she deposits me behind the aforementioned youngsters, hands me a bottle of water, and disappears deeper into the organized chaos of mechanics and officials swarming the cars.

I wring the bottle nervously between my hands.

"Careful, or you'll make a mess and they'll never invite us back."

Mouth agape, I turn to find Jackie and Gael grinning contentedly from where they lean against the viewing barrier, brand new Panache caps on their heads and glossy garage passes around their necks.

Jackie tugs me over to them. "So, funny story. The loveliest Panache PR person appeared right after Pete whisked you away and gave us these passes, courtesy of one Evan Evans. Can you believe it?"

"No," I manage.

Gael smooths his hair. "She said, and I quote, 'Evan said you're Sunny's two besties here, and he wanted you all to be able to watch the race together.' I know we're doing that thing where we try to give you space to make decisions for yourself, but girl, that man is a gem."

Jackie smacks him on the arm. "And now we go back to leaving her alone about it." She bounces on her toes. "Sunny, this is the coolest thing that's ever happened to us."

I gulp and nod, turning my focus to the rest of the garage. Evan's fully suited up now, his helmet gleaming. I have no idea what I'm going to do about his proposition, but the cars are about to head to the track, and we have a race to watch.

CHAPTER TWENTY-SIX

Evan

My heart's never pounded this fast before.

Usually, a blissful calm takes me over this close to the race start. All the preparation has been done, and now it's time to execute. Shifting from one type of hard work to another. It's all so electrifying and satisfying.

I muster a smile and wave to the cheering crowd as I follow my team, who carefully push my car to the front of the grid. The fans get even louder as my machine is situated in the frontmost starting position.

I join Pete's second-in-command in front of the car's nose, since Pete's already situated on the pit wall. The engineer's usually-serious game face is replaced by a broad smile as she surveys the stands. "They all want a win from you today."

I wave again. "I'm gonna try my hardest to give it to them. Whatcha got for me?"

She runs over a few things she's noticed in the data from earlier sessions, and the mechanics pitch in their two cents, but we all land on the same conclusion: we've done all we can.

It's the same as I've done with Sunny.

At least with the race, there's something productive I can do—drive the wheels off this car.

I swing one leg into the cockpit.

As I get settled, I let thoughts of Sunny fully occupy my mind before I need to compartmentalize and focus on the race. I close my eyes as the mechanics buckle me in, imagining Sunny's head tucked beneath mine in bed last night, how her warm scent soothed me to sleep.

I almost bailed on trying to talk with her again. I don't want to distress or coerce her, but her reasoning for wanting to end us before we can even start doesn't have anything to do with who we are as people, but rather the circumstances we live in and how some assholes have treated her in the past. I'm committed to making those circumstances as easy as possible and proving the guys in her past were wrong, if she feels the same way I do.

So much of racing is the tricky, fluid art of trusting your instincts, and mine have been absolutely screaming that she's the person I'm meant to be with. To love and to care for and change the world with, even if it's just by making each other as happy as possible.

After the race, I'll be elated or devastated. It's too late to brake now.

The engineer gives me a thumbs up.

The car, my partner on this track, rumbles comfortingly around me, cradling my body. I eye the readouts on my steering wheel, tap my feet against the pedals. Run through the final steps of my pre–race rituals.

"Radio check, Evan." Pete's voice is a comfort in my ear as the mechanics flee to the sides of the track before we start the formation lap, which allows us to warm our tires.

"Radio's good," I reply. "And thank you again, for earlier." When I dragged him from his preparations on the pit wall to go find Sunny, it looked like his head was gonna explode.

"Anytime," he says. "Reminder, Ev, we're sticking with strategy A today, unless something goes sideways."

"Keep the car un-sideways. Copy," I mutter as the lights signal me to lead us out. I ease from the line and build up acceleration, weaving to get some heat in my tires as soon as I'm through the first corner.

A heavy sigh sounds in my ear, fuzzy and blown out across the radio. It occurs to me that around this time, I'm usually cracking jokes to lighten the team's tension before the green flag. Pete speaks again before I can ask what's up.

"Listen, man, you've done all you can. We've got faith in you. You've gotta have faith in everyone else, alright?"

Everyone else. Not the team.

He's talking about Sunny.

"I understand," I answer, as I come around the final corner and head back to the grid, slotting the car into the first grid box at an angle that will give me the best jump to block the hungry drivers behind me when the lights go out. This is a starting position I've clawed for, one that will give me the slightest edge to win this race.

I don't have time to be distracted. Luke's like a coiled snake alongside me. He's an annoying threat to my right and situated a little ways back in second place. His silver helmet glints threateningly.

RJ and Johnny are right behind us, with Grant on row three, alongside Jenna. Hardly any of us have had an edge on each other in earlier sessions. Today is going to get deliciously spicy.

I remember what I told Sunny. I can do both. So I put my hopes and dreams and worries about her in a little pocket of my brain that I won't open until later, after she's made her choice.

I shift my focus to the beautiful stretch of clear track before me.

I lift my gaze to the bank of lights suspended over the starting line and force a smooth exhale.

Whatever happens, this has been one of the greatest race weeks of my life, and I plan to enjoy it to the finish. I need to get this car to the final lap quickly and in one piece, though I'm wondering if I'll have as much luck with my heart.

CHAPTER TWENTY-SEVEN

Sunny

There's an engine cylinder stuck in my throat. Or a wheel nut. Any of the myriad car parts I've learned about this week would accurately describe the feeling.

From our spot in the garage, I can see out onto the grid, where the nose of Evan's car pokes past the pit wall. Watching the race from here will be a torturous thrill, with our only actual view being the blistering blur the cars cut down the main straight. Happenings elsewhere on the track are being reported on the broadcast playing on monitors throughout the garage.

"I didn't expect it to be so quiet in here," Gael whispers.

Jackie and I nod. The engineers stare mutely at their data screens, and the mechanics have changed into their fire-suits and helmets to be ready for a pit stop at any moment, but for now, they sit quietly in chairs they've pulled out and set where the cars usually go.

It seems everyone's jaws are clenched tight, mine included.

The wait is tormenting. I crouch to eye the bank of starting lights poised before Evan and the rest of the grid. My breath catches as the first light goes on, red like the main color in Riot's logo. Then the orange light next to it lights up, and then the final, yellow light.

The last scrap of waiting feels a year long. Then...

The lights go out. Instantaneously, the roar of two dozen hungry cars blares around us. I blink and they're gone. Even seeing sessions live this week hasn't prepared me for the rush of a live race start. I'm dumbfounded, staring at empty air where a line of cars just was.

Jackie's sudden grip around my elbow, stress emanating from her fingertips, is the only thing that tethers me to reality. I seek out a screen to see if Evan made it through the start okay.

He got a great jump, keeping a small but crucial distance between him and Luke as he leads the field into turn one.

Every car makes it through the first few turns unscathed, which is something for a race start. Drivers fight to make passes early so they're not playing catch-up later, and all the moves are finished cleanly. My friends and I watch with various emblems of stress—my fingers are going white where they grip the barrier, Jackie's are tangling together beneath her chin, and Gael shifts from foot to foot while chewing his lip. Our heads move in tandem, from watching the broadcast to attempting to follow the cars when they shoot past the pit lane. One car nearly loses it taking a turn too wide, and another two almost crash as they tussle through a chicane. Through it all, Evan keeps his head down, staying seemingly calm, with Luke a sliver of a second behind.

My palms are sweaty and ache from gripping the barrier, and my stomach is a boiling mess. The clouds grow darker and threaten to slick the track with rain. It's going to be a long race.

My heart is actively splintering into pieces.

This is the part of fandom I struggle with. It means so much to you that when the going gets tough, the pain is so incredibly difficult.

An ill-timed safety car has lost Evan the lead.

Seemingly in a tussle with her last-minute replacement strategist, RJ went off at turn five while trying to hold off a rookie. She managed to save herself from a collision with the wall and get back on track, but lost her good position and ended up at the back of the field after having to come in for a new front wing.

It resulted in essentially free pit stops for much of the field, including Luke, as debris was removed by the stewards. Now the time advantage from Evan stopping earlier in the race is gone. The slower pace lasts only a moment, so Evan can't sneak in for a fresh set of tires. Sometime before the end of the race, he'll have to stop again.

There's buzzing from the engineers as the call is made. They bring in Evan right away to give him the most time to try and fight for his lead spot back. The tires he had wouldn't have made it to the end, putting him in danger of slipping off track or being overtaken by other cars with fresher tires who were able to sneak in for new ones under the short safety car period.

Blood pounds in my ears when he stops in front of the garage. The crew swarms, changing the tires with alarming quickness. They've got the old tires off and new ones situated in a blink, then the tires squeal and he's off again, rejoining the race in fifth place.

"This whole fiasco has really put Evan on the back foot," Ivy comments on the broadcast.

"How much can he recover over the next twenty laps?" the other commentator wonders.

At least the drama has negated any dull, action-less laps, where, against my efforts, I return to Evan's proclamation, his plea from before the race. I don't know what to do. My head and heart are in direct conflict, and both seem fine with my destruction as they joust.

"Holy shit, holy shit, holy shit." I have to bite back a shriek as Evan makes a gutsy pass and gains a spot.

I wince an apology at the kid who glances up at me. I'm bouncing on my toes, gaze ping-ponging between the screens showing the broadcast along the garage wall and the top cars zooming by every lap. Evan inches toward the lead pack. Once again, he, Luke, and Jenna fly past, bunched together, engines and wheels screaming.

There are only a handful of laps left, and the garage is tense and quiet, interspersed with elated noises whenever Evan staves off one of his pursuers' attempts to pass.

The commentator's voice cries from the TV speakers. "It looks like this one is going to be tight to the end, folks. Grant Colby's tires' grip has faded off. He's got no hope of making the podium. Luke will be difficult to catch for the lead, but could this be the end of Evan Evan's trophy-less curse?"

Evan has to hold Jenna off, but fighting back and forth is wearing out both their tires. And Johnny, the racing veteran he is, probably knows it from his spot a few meters back. He could be biding his time to pass them both at the very end. He's wily enough and has done it before.

On the screen, I watch the pink car fly through turn four, chasing Luke's. Jenna goes for Evan on the inside. He leaves her just enough space, but jerks wide, his right rear tires scraping the gravel and sending a fine dust flying so her move on him sticks. We all gasp. He's a bit behind now, at risk of Johnny stealing the final place on the podium with only a few laps left.

I swear, all I can hear is my heart pounding as Evan gradually draws the nose of his car even with Jenna's down the back straight. He has so few chances left to get her.

We hear the echo of thousands of fans gasping somewhere further down the track a few seconds before the footage hits the TVs. Something happened, and RJ's car is smoking in the gravel, the rear wing crumpled against a tire barrier.

"In an uncharacteristic move, RJ had made a costly second error and put it in the wall!"

"That's her first race as a full-time Riot Racer done, Simon. You can see her hitting the steering wheel. Good to know she's all right, but oh, that heartbreak must be fierce.

I wonder if this has anything to do with this morning's last-minute strategic change-up."

My heart thuds as the field settles into the slow clump of a well-behaved, safety car-led field. Evan's still in third. Hardly a comfortable podium spot with the field now bunched up. Everyone's tires are new enough to make it to the end of the race, so no one will risk losing position by coming in for a change. It'll be a mad, desperate dash to the end.

Gael frowns. "Wait, what happened with RJ's strategist? Tracy, right? I slept in."

Jackie doesn't look away from the screen as she explains. "Tracy is sick, the reports are saying, and Savo brought in Owen Stang to call strategy for RJ."

"The old guy she replaced when he got hurt last season? That can't be good."

I snort. "Old? C'mon, Gael, He's like, forty."

"Old, for an athlete. You know what I mean."

Jackie massages her neck as the safety car leads the pack into another lap while the safety team moves RJ's car. "He's easing into that tasty silver fox territory, if you ask me."

An appreciative sound hums from the back of my throat. Owen Stang is a handsome legend with a surly, bad-boy vibe.

A thought rises, unbidden. I prefer Evan's unique brand of silly seriousness. His darkness in the bedroom while still making me laugh.

I gulp.

"Safety car will be in this lap." The call comes, and we all promptly quiet down to watch the screens.

The cars hit the start line and jump back up to speed.

Luke builds a gap, and Evan's occupied holding off Johnny, who's finding every scrap of life left in his tires.

Evan fends off his friend successfully and builds a few-second gap that will be nearly impossible for Johnny to eclipse. Just a couple of laps left now, and while Luke is looking like he'll win, Evan is within striking distance of the car in second place.

The garage buzzes with excitement at the prospect of Evan's podium finish.

"While third is a commendable result, Evans sees an opportunity here..."

"Agreed," Ivy says. "He wants this so bad. And if he wants that spot, he's going to have to nail it three times in a row for these last laps in that corner he keeps struggling with. This is where we see: can he do what he says he can? He's made all the preparations and set himself up for the best bet of a good finish. Now he needs to trust himself and commit and believe it'll work out."

I get tunnel vision, glued to the plume painted on the top of that bouncing helmet. Luke is going to win, so the cameras are trained on Evan as he inches closer to Jenna. Her tires are nearly dead, and she struggles to keep her car on track.

I realize I know that Evan can do this. I...I trust he can.

He hits that final turn and... nails it.

I jump, not realizing how nervous I was.

"He's gonna go for it, isn't he?" I ask.

Gael's voice is breathless. "Of course, he is. The reward is worth the risk."

"If he messes up, he can have another go next race," Jackie murmurs.

I shoot them a glare. "We're talking about the race, right?"

They ignore me. A light sheen of rain begins to fall. There's no time to change to wet-weather tires. The drivers will need to be extra careful to keep their cars on track.

Evan does it again the next time around. This time, his car's rear wiggles slightly, but he saves it and continues hunting Jenna into the final lap. Sprays of water plume from their tires.

On the broadcast, they cut to show Pete, who isn't speaking into his headset. There's not much he can say anymore. It's all on Evan.

The entire lap, Evan seeks an opening, a crack in Jenna's armor. He makes a move on the straight, but she blocks it brilliantly.

They approach that damn turn, and Evan wings through it flawlessly, right on Jenna's tail.

He exits neatly and flies around her flank, finding a pinch of speed somewhere and overtaking her. He crosses the finish line ahead of her by half a car length.

The garage erupts into wild shouts. Mine blend with everyone else's as we bellow and scream and pound the walls.

No one can hear the commentary. The Panache team floods out the front of the garage, a joyous mass of limbs careening for the podium area to celebrate Evan breaking his streak to receive another Riot trophy. To congratulate him and celebrate their amazing day. Grant finished fifth, adding to their nice haul of points for the team.

The other lucky fans around me follow the team. Security relaxes a touch during podium celebrations as everyone swarms. I'm awestruck, joyous and conflicted. Gael and Jackie are already at the front of the garage.

I follow, and a different, slower swarm of neon and orange shirts catches my eye.

The packing team has already been deployed. While most of the team is celebrating, these stalwart folks begin the breakdown, popping screens off walls and securing tool chests in companionable silence. This is a traveling circus, after all, and they need to be efficient in moving on.

I might cry.

One of them catches my eye. "Go on then, girl!" she says. "We're not doing anything interesting. We prefer the quiet work. You better get out there, or you'll miss it."

I hear *or you'll miss him.*

I catch up with the crowd. Jackie and Gael have been swept away in the crush of thrilled bodies.

With shaky hands, I remember myself and lift my phone to start a stream.

"Hey, everyone," I start, then pause as I catch sight of my face. A little blotchy, extremely forlorn. Oof. I look like I'm about to cry. I switch to my phone's other camera and narrate the top finishers of the race, recapping the most exciting parts. Slowly, I make my way to the podium area, which at Seattle's course is a raised platform right over the track. Luke's winning car has the honorary parking spot on the platform that's raised underneath.

The crowd is dense. I get as close as I can, but everyone's packed in. With a grumble, I search around and spot that the barrier at the edge of the track has a bit of a concrete ledge on the bottom. I push through the crowd and make my way over, heaving myself up the six inches that will help give me a height advantage. I twine one arm through a break in the fence to keep myself stable and get my phone situated with a good view as a drumbeat blares through the speakers, announcing the ceremony's impending start.

Jenna takes the stage first, a rueful smile in place as she hops onto the third-place spot. I've followed her for so long, I know how she feels. She'll be pissed to have lost to Evan, but thrilled at the good, hard fight they had.

The thoughts disappear from my head when Evan appears, all gleaming teeth and squinted eyes as joy floods his face. He literally bounds across the stage, playing to the cameras and pointing at his team.

Honestly, everyone else on the podium could have skipped the entire production, and I wouldn't have noticed. My eyes are locked on Evan and his uninhibited happiness as he accepts his trophy, then poses with the other two, before they spray each other with champagne.

He looks at me like that.

I'm suddenly dizzy. I sign off numbly and end my stream, let go of the fence and stumble back the way I came. I'm sweating, and my chest is heaving. I'm definitely going to cry. I can't be here. I can't do this.

As fireworks release from the other side of the track, barely visible in the early sunset, I leave. The adventure is over, and I need to be home.

CHAPTER–TWENTY EIGHT

Evan

The moment is nearly perfect. Second is a solid step on the path to first place, and this trophy is something to be proud of. With Grant's commendable finish, Panache is leading the team championship for the first time in years. I'm overjoyed. The team's ecstatic and hollering below me. I scan the crowd, and my smile falters. There's a familiar figure with their back turned to me at the rear of the crowd.

Sunny's leaving.

The podium celebration wraps up in a flash. I smile for what must be a million photos and then I'm whisked back to track level where I'm attacked, lovingly, by my team. My back is pounded, my cheeks are kissed, and lots more champagne is procured.

I thank everyone—sure to look them in the eye and say their name when I do.

The entire team is over the moon as they sip champagne and take photos and pass around the trophy and holler my name over and over.

Through it all, it feels like half my chest is filled with helium, and the other half is weighed down by rocks. I keep up my smile during the post-race whirlwind of media and celebrations and quick debriefs, but there's a growing part of me that's terrified that what I said to Sunny wasn't enough, and I can only hold my grief at bay for so long.

I need to call my family. One of Blair's staff is waiting patiently to film posts with me for socials. I need a fucking shower. I have to apologize to my PR handler—a junior staffer, as Blair is with Grant—because I'm jumpy and impatient and clearly not in as good a mood as the rest of the team regarding my result. I need five seconds. I need to call Sunny.

But I've already pushed her today.

I find the first moment that doesn't feel entirely rude to ask after June. During races, she's the keeper of my orange "go everywhere" bag. The PR person points, and I see a flash of orange a dozen yards away. June has the drawstring bag securely across her back... But *she's* been hoisted atop a mechanic's shoulders and is dousing them both in champagne.

It's gonna take me forever to get through the swarm of people to her, so I grit my teeth and start the journey.

I get stuck behind a never-ending parade of Riot folks wheeling carts of tires when an elbow digs into my side. I glance over at Grant, whose eyebrows are raised. "Are you going to go after her?"

This guy never ceases to surprise me. He's quiet but perceptive as hell, in addition to being a great driver and… maybe a good friend.

"I think she left," I hedge.

When I admit it, it's like one of Seattle's clouds is wrapped around my heart, dampening my spirit and making my insides cold.

"Finding out if she did is the only way to know for sure what choice she made."

I chew my lip.

"You don't want to screw it up," Grant says. "Trust me, it's worth it to check." My eyes track his gaze across the tarmac to Blair. So I haven't been imagining that Grant's eyes go all crystal ball-ish when he looks at her.

"Thanks, man." I'll give my team and this success as much of my attention as I can spare, and then I'll go find my girl.

CHAPTER TWENTY-NINE

Sunny

I am a gargantuan idiot. The grandest sucker this world has ever known.

Jackie eyes me, but doesn't say anything. The glass of wine she's offered me is untouched.

I'm sitting on the edge of the bed in a short black dress, looking like an absolute fool in the fancy room my friend sprang for to stay an extra night.

A dress I had to borrow from Jackie because I didn't pack enough clothes to stay this long.

My ribs still ache from the blistering hug we shared with Gael when he left to catch his flight.

It's a good hurt, knowing I'll miss my friends but that we'll see each other again. We want to meet up at a race later in the season, and I told them I'd go, the hits to my savings account be damned.

It was also a shock to see the person giving Gael a ride to the airport was Cooper, three hours early and dressed handsomely. Sneaky boys.

I glance at the clock on the wall, my stomach clenching. If I sprint, and if the rideshare gods smile on me, I could still make my flight home.

"What if—"

"No," Jackie cuts me off. "The only thing you're allowed to pick up that phone and do is call out of work tomorrow. Most likely to spend it with your dreamy new beau who adores you. And if not, to cry into your pillow all day and eat take out for every meal like a normal person."

I chew a nail. "But—"

She grabs my hand and squeezes. "He said he'd call. You said you'd trust that. This is an exercise in letting go." I frown. Jackie looks at her own phone. "The team celebrations are just ending. Give him some time."

"How do you possibly—"

My phone rings. Our faces snap to where it's buzzing, lit up with mine and Evan's selfie from the beginning of the week. That first fateful day.

"ANSWER IT, YOU SILLY GIRL!" Jackie shrieks and chucks a pillow at me. God, I love her.

With shaking hands, I answer. "Hello?"

Evan's breath is a whoosh of relief. "Are you still here?"

"Yeah," I hold back a hysterical laugh. "Yes, I'm still here. I'm at the hotel."

"Thank fucking god. You're amazing. I'm the luckiest man alive. Can you— Hold on." I hear glass clatter and Evan swears and thanks someone. "It can't be a real celebration if you're not part of it. Come downstairs, please?"

I'm staring, dumbfounded, at the headboard. Jackie gesticulates, eyes wild, while I try to form a response. She gets impatient and snatches the phone. *"She'll be right down!"* she screeches.

She slams the end call button and drops my phone to the mattress, where we both stare at it.

An entire week of dreams coming true finally catches up to us. We collapse on the comforter in twin fits of hysterics, giggling till tears leak from the corners of our eyes.

"What did I tell you, Sunny? We were destined for adventure this week."

I roll to my stomach and take her hands, shoving my hair out of my eyes. "You did, and you were right. I'll never doubt you again."

"Terrific. Now, respectfully, get the fuck out of here and go see your antelope man."

"He's like a giraffe, actually."

My smile hurts my face as I fix my dress and head for the door. I whip it open, making sure I've got my purse and suitcase, and I nearly run head on into a solid chest.

I look up into the eyes of... "Pete?"

He's standing sheepishly in a sweater and slacks and carries a bouquet of roses.

Desperately slow, I turn to eye Jackie. "Surprise," she mouths.

"Oh my god," I sputter, maneuvering around Pete and failing to not run over his shoes with my bag. "Let me— Sorry. Have a good time! Er, night? Time. Whatever. Call me later, bye!"

My excitement builds as I try not to sprint through the hallway. The elevator moves too slow for my taste. I spill into the broad lobby, searching desperately for disheveled hair and a big smile...

It's getting late, so there aren't a million people here, just some sleepy check-ins and folks turning in for the night.

My sneakers squeak as I cut through the space, searching.

A frantic wave and glint of teeth catches my eye.

Evan's beyond the front doors, his grin blinding.

As if in a trance, I step outside and join him. He paces the concrete. He's breathless, with color high on his cheeks. He's wearing a collared shirt that's tucked crookedly into black pants, like he got dressed in a hurry.

He carefully sets the two bottles of champagne he carries on the sidewalk and comes for me.

I meet him halfway. He sweeps me into his arms.

When we break apart, he breathes, "You stayed?"

"You're worth it. Worth how hard it is to be brave. Worth the risk that we might get hurt."

He spins us around, eliciting a shriek from me. "I told you I knew it! We can't be out long. It's cold, and I assume on your first official night as my girlfriend, you'd prefer to not get swarmed by paparazzi the minute someone spots me—"

"I don't care," I interrupt him. "That's part of it. Part of being with you. You're worth it." I say it again. "You reminded me how to feel *alive*, Evan. That I have a hand in it. That it's not just for rare special occasions like a race week or the ren fair."

This is officially the biggest I've seen him smile. It spreads impossibly, surpassing its earlier length when he stood on the podium by a millimeter.

He huffs a laugh and pulls his sunglasses from his pocket, popping them over those brilliant emerald eyes. "God, Sunny. You're too bright, I can't even look at you." He lets me go to pretend to shield his face from the sun, except...

"It's literally raining, you dork," I snort, wiping the drops from his lenses. "Let's move. We don't want to get sick."

He shakes his head. "Right, absolutely. Okay, what was my plan?" He searches around for the champagne. "So," he says, "Quickly, I want you to know what it feels like. I wanted you up there with me, on the podium." He tugs me toward a large stone planter with a broad rim and helps me up. I stand there awkwardly while he fetches the bottles and opens them, offering me one. "There's some disagreement regarding who started this tradition of spraying champagne on the podium, but I say it doesn't really matter who started it because it's awesome and it's here now." He grins at me triumphantly from his spot on the ground. "Are you ready, kit?"

I nod, at a loss for words.

Something clicks in me, acceptance that this is happening, that this is real. The joy rushes to my head. I snag the bottle and shake, beating Evan by half a second. Champagne erupts from the bottle and I angle my finger to spray it directly in his face. Laughing like a maniac, he returns the gesture, spraying me all over. Out of breath from laughing, I finish by dumping the remainder of my bottle over his head. He smiles, closes his eyes, and lets me.

All too soon, my bottle is empty and Evan snags me around the waist, dragging me off the planter.

Our kiss is... God, it's like ancient alchemy. The magic of two grand, powerful entities coming together. I lose myself in him and his warmth and his steadiness. It doesn't matter that my feet are off the ground. He'll catch me.

Halted footsteps. Sudden murmurs. "Oh my gosh," someone exclaims.

Evan reluctantly lifts his lips from mine and glances over my shoulder.

"Busted," he mutters. "We better move." He makes to shield me with his arms.

"Worth it," I remind him. "Evan, I mean it. I don't care if people see. I don't care if the media knows."

Maybe I imagine it, but his eyes look a little misty. Could be the light rain, though.

He grabs my hand and urges me into a brisk walk that, as the rain comes harder, becomes a full-blown jog to his building.

Somehow, we hold off on the messy kissing in the lobby.

The attendant waves with a knowing grin and lets Evan know that he's had some packages arrive. "Lots of macs up there, Ev. The ones you like."

Evan nods his thanks. He's breathless and hasn't let go of my hand. "I was looking at flights earlier. Are you open to a late flight tomorrow night? That would give us a full twenty-four hours to make a plan." He pauses from where he's fumbling to enter his door code. "And it gives me plenty of time to show you how much you mean to me."

My entire body flushes. "This time tomorrow is fine and I– Oh, wow."

Evan's opened the door and there's a trail of frilly boxes from the kitchen that's bleeding into the entry hall. It's stacks and stacks and stacks of...

Macarons.

I pass him to enter the apartment and stare. Many of them are in Panache colors. They're from a broad variety of Seattle bakeries and tagged with congratulatory messages from family, friends, and folks within the paddock. Bottles of champagne are scattered amongst the arrangements, as well as cards and some flowers. There's even a giant moose-shaped balloon.

Evan follows me, stepping carefully amongst the towers of clear boxes. "Would you believe that there's a bouquet of sunflowers somewhere here for you?"

I stare, trailing my fingertips over one exceptionally packaged batch of the delicate French cookies. "You're a big fan of macarons?" 'Macs," as the guy downstairs called them. Some things start clicking together. Bits he's said over the week. I haven't had time to mull them over but...

Evan rubs the back of his neck and eyes me. His cheeks go red and not in the way they do when I kiss him. He looks... guilty.

The pieces click together, and I gasp. "You're Mac91! You're a *Ray?!*"

He waves his hands in front of himself. "I swear, I am not a stalker. Last year, one of your videos came across my feed, the not-public account I have. It was about the IndyCar weight jacker they use on ovals. I learned a lot from that video, and I thought you explained it so well that, of course, I gave you a follow. And then I started keeping track because your content is so good and I—I had this inkling that we would get along and, well, to be honest I had a little crush on you and you had weird feelings about me, so I thought it would be important that we meet, and I asked very nicely to be paired with you for the hot laps. And... here we are. I never expected this though. This is... a dream come true."

He looks so worried, like his knobby giraffe knees are clacking together beneath his champagne-soaked slacks.

I start chucking macarons at him. "Why didn't you tell me?!"

"That I was a fan? That I was practically in love with you already? When the whole internet knew you didn't like me? What was I supposed to do?"

I blink, processing, then dissolve into giggles of delight. "That's amazing. I'm so flattered."

"You're not... mad?"

"No. You enjoy my work. That's a solid reason to want to connect with somebody."

He seems unsure, so I step closer and wrap my arms around him. He sets his chin on my head and breathes. "Good. I'm sorry I didn't tell you sooner. I couldn't figure out a good way. And then everything got so crazy this week and I forgot... I feel like I've known you for a year, and I really wanted to see what you would think if you got to know me."

"I think you're wonderful."

He leans back to kiss me and amidst it, we start shivering. Not the sexy kind.

"Let's get out of these clothes..." Evan says. "For our health."

I snort, and he nuzzles the spot where my neck meets my shoulder.

"How about a long bath, kit? I think we deserve it."

In pleased and companionable silence, we make our way to the bathroom. Our movements are slow and appreciative as we continue to nurture this thing between us.

Evan starts the tub, and I propose a quick shower first so we don't stew in champagne and rain.

Evan washes my hair and body. When I aim to return the favor, I don't want my arms to ache. "On your knees, giraffe."

With a glint in his eye, he obeys.

I carefully wash his hair and massage his scalp. He groans, pressing his forehead against my stomach and wrapping his arms around my thighs.

When I attempt to step back to rinse his hair, he lets me but tugs me against him after a moment, inching my legs apart. I let my head fall back and enjoy him devouring me. We've got time, after all.

We make it to the bath eventually, our legs tangled and smiling at each other like idiots across the scented water. Another bottle of champagne made it in here and it's already half empty, sat on the floor next to a plate of macaron crumbs.

Evan traces his fingers over my calf beneath the water. "You make me so happy, Sunny. I'm so grateful to you—for you—for giving us a shot."

I twist my hands together, making ripples that travel from my chest to his. "When it came down to it, it was kind of an easy decision... when I got out of my own way. I judged you."

He grabs my foot and tweaks one of my toes. I half-heartedly splash him. "And I made assumptions about you. We're both guilty."

"And absolved," I counter. He nods.

After a quiet moment, he raises his eyes to mine. "So… are you buying what I'm selling now?"

I hesitate. My fears resurface at the prospect of taking this final leap. But while I know there are times to be careful, what feels more important in this moment is to be honest. Honest with Evan and honest with myself. My voice is quiet but sure as I lift my gaze to his. "Absolutely I am."

I swear to god, I will never tire of watching Evan smile as long as I live.

He reaches for me, gently pulling me across the tub and into his arms. "Well, that works out nicely, because I'm gonna fall in love with you real soon, I can feel it."

One Year Later

Evan

I really should bubble wrap every breakable item in the apartment.

I'm bouncing around so much that Sunny banished me from the bathroom after I knocked over four different hair products.

She's back from Australia!

I mean, she took me there with her, but her schedule was packed, so it sort of felt like the times we're apart, which are my least favorite times.

Thankfully, she moved in before the holidays, so for the past few months, amazingly, this has been *our* apartment. And it's going to be *our* apartment for possibly, like, forever!

The idea of forever reminds me to check my list of reminders, which is longer than usual. With a sigh of relief, I confirm everything is set for tomorrow, so I can be present tonight, with her.

She emerges from the bedroom in a cloud of mango scent, and I swear to god, her face is somehow sparkly.

And... a wire in my brain melts.

She's wearing a new dress that is absolutely sinful.

It's dark blue and filmy, clings to her body, and I— Is... Is it see-through? Kind of? In places?

I gulp. "I think I'm having a heart attack."

She laughs—she does it so easily with me now—and steps into the circle of my arms. "The dress is a winner, then?"

I bury my face in her neck and bite gently. "It's only a bad choice if you're hoping for us to make it out of this apartment."

She steps back, ignoring my whine of protest. Her eyes brighten at the mention of heading to the club. "Let's get moving then. Think of it as delicious, torturous antici-pation. Especially since I'm not wearing underwear." She bites her lip, and I know she's suffering the same affliction I am.

"That flight was long, and you're a tease." I aim to give her a quick spank, but she dodges, and we're torn between quiet laughs and affectionate nuzzles as we make our way down to the lobby. In the car, we quiet down. A fog of lust begins to build, as it does anytime we make our way to Skirt.

We started going not long after we got together. Sunny's interest was piqued, and I was dying to take her. Turns out, our fateful first fuck in that hotel conference room was an indicator of our tastes... We love the tiny element of danger involved in semi-public sex.

So clubs like Skirt allow us to indulge in that interest among a group of people who have consented to others fooling around in their vicinity. Spaces like it are a gift.

The driver takes us to a side entrance, a more private and secluded way to enter. While neither of us is ashamed of our preferences, Sunny has put up with a lot of invasiveness over the past year. Getting together brought a lot of attention, most of it good, but there's always a troll or a hater prepared to make a snide comment or suggestion of how she won my affection.

She masterfully never responds and somehow, neither do I, after many lectures from her and Blair explaining why it's not a good idea for me to pummel someone who's screamed in Sunny's face that she got all her success by spreading her legs.

I tug her closer as we enter the hallway that's all cool air and purple-veined, white marble walls. The surroundings are a familiar and arousing comfort.

Since the Seattle franchise is our home club, we breeze through the registration and security area, our preferences and hard limits already carefully documented alongside payment methods.

Lighter marble melts into dark the further we go into the building.

We skip the main lounge area, where you can have a cocktail and engage in foreplay and dirty talk or catch up with friends. It's been too long since we've gotten to indulge in this particular fantasy, so we head straight for one of the playrooms.

Sunny tugs me into the darkened room, this one themed with cool gray statues and tufted-velvet furniture and heavy drapes, all in deep shades of blue. The lights are low, just bright enough to keep us from bumping into others as she finds us a small sofa tucked against one wall.

I sit and draw her into my lap, tilting her chin and eyeing the curves of her face and how the strange lighting brings out facets I don't often notice.

She just looks back, her heart in her eyes and also pounding in her chest.

The soft murmur of the others in the room quiets as the lights flash once and a spotlight comes down on a raised dais in the center of the space.

Sunny's breath catches as four beautiful people step up, wrapped in artfully draped fabric teasing at the shapes of their bodies. Their hair, necks, wrists are accented with pearls.

A slow, thrumming music permeates the air. They weave among each other, trailing chaste kisses and fleeting touches. Every so often, a button or clasp will be undone and gradually, they all become naked except for the pearls. The kisses linger longer and tongues join lips and hands land more firmly on skin, exploring. By the time one of the people has a woman's arms clasped around his neck, another person sinks to their knees before her and teases her legs open...

I mimic the movement on Sunny, shifting her and sliding one leg open so I can slip my fingers inside her at the same time the woman on stage experiences it.

The orgy unfolding on stage is beautiful, and from what I can tell, the other people scattered around the room on chaises and chairs are watching with rapt attention or devolving into similar dances of their own, but it'll keep my focus for only a moment longer as Sunny's soft, restrained moans escape her beautiful mouth.

I can't think about anything else except for the feel of her skin, the drape of her hair, her pussy pulsing around my fingers. I whisper, making the filthy promises she likes.

"Better be quiet, Sunny, or someone will hear you." Funnily, it makes her moan a bit louder. She loves these veiled threats, this fake danger.

I spank her clit with my free hand. She comes apart in my arms, and I can't take it anymore. The sounds around us are a beautiful symphony of joy and pleasure, the air thick with anticipation and contentedness that repeats in an intoxicating cycle.

I lift Sunny, her muscles soft, and shift her so she's facing me. She snaps back to herself and meets me, movement for movement, tugging at my belt, her curls a mess around her face as she draws out my cock.

I pause her with a deep kiss. As soon as she's breathless again, I guide her on top of me and bring her down. We both shiver as we seal together. It doesn't matter how many times we do this, I'm starstruck every single time.

As Sunny rocks in my lap, wrapped in my arms, the straps of her dress slip off her shoulders. Her head falls back, her lips parted as she loses herself in pure ecstasy. I hold her tight and guide the rhythm, never taking for granted the gift of her pleasure and witnessing her vulner-ability, here, tucked in the shadows just for me. I squeeze her ass and try to keep my eyes from rolling back in my head at how good she feels. I try to hold out coming until she gets a few orgasms first.

God, I love her.

I don't know what greater power helped me convince her to give me a shot... Fate, gods, fairies, the fucking moon?

Whoever it was, I try to show them and the world every day that I'll never take Sunny for granted.

I'll never forget the pull in my stomach the first time I saw her, even through a phone screen... That instinctual feeling—the rightness of it, of her and me.

And for all their sublime, heavenly perfection, tonight's aren't the plans I'm most excited for.

SUNNY

Evan's already gone to the track by the time I wake up. I pout at the empty, mussed blankets beside me, but internally, I'm proud of this trust I've developed that Evan won't just disappear.

It didn't take long to get here, with all the work Evan and I put in on the emotional side of our relationship, but still, nearly a year later, I'm proud.

Evan implored me to consider sleeping in, and after the chaos of covering a race week halfway across the world, I agreed.

He's left me a warm half-pot of coffee and a sticky note with hearts scribbled all over it.

Our cat, Chassy, returned from her vacation with Evan's sister, curls up on my stomach while I hatch in bed with my caffeine.

I smile as I stroke her tortoiseshell fur, then my eyes track to the art above our bed. To most, it looks like an abstract, squiggly line across a bright canvas, but Evan and I know it's the soundwave from the first orgasm he ever gave me, the one I accidentally recorded.

This past year has shown me the difference between joy and contentment, and the importance of both. I thought I experienced them both at my old apartment, my old life, and in a way, I did, but I'd been holding myself back out of fear. It's been a few months since I quit my job, and I don't regret it one bit.

I sigh a long, easy breath, happy to rest a little longer. I wouldn't leave bed all day if Evan were here, but as today is a pre-season test for some of the Riot teams, including Panache, I get to see him in one of my other favorite situations—driving a race car.

With a reluctant groan—I'm still a little sore from our visit to the club last night—I rise from bed and start getting ready. Chassy curls up in my abandoned warm spot.

Abby always wears one of her signature cute dresses, so I opt for a jumpsuit patterned with pink flowers in the spirit of supporting Panache and matching her vibe.

I call a rideshare and catch up on my socials on the way over. I've got so many comments to respond to now that my Australia content is posted, but when I open the first app, a video of Evan appears at the top of my feed. I haven't seen this one yet, from when he visited friends on one of the Formula 1 teams at their garage while I was covering the grand prix. He got caught in the crossfire of one of the TV broadcasts in the paddock between sessions.

"Evan, you weren't necessarily supposed to be here this weekend, right?" the interviewer had asked. "You've been busy prepping for Riot's next season."

His exuberance practically leaks through the camera. No amount of PR coaching by Blair could keep him from practically dancing as he talks. "Yeah, I think in the midst of all the prep that goes into a season, you get really consumed, so it's amazing to have a week away. It was generous of Sunny to invite me."

"And Sunny, of course, is your lovely partner, for viewers who may not know. Though how could they not?

She's been running around the paddock all weekend doing coverage for the series. Could you tell us a bit about that? You had a chance encounter at the Seattle Grand Prix last year, is the word on the street."

Evan pauses to think this question through. We're not the most private of athletic couples because, honestly, it's a pain in the ass to try to be. We reserve all of our privacy efforts for our trips to Skirt because I like to keep those preferences between us.

"Honestly, I'm obsessed with her." I press a hand to my chest. He means it, and I feel the same way. Our brief time together has been amazing, but lately, especially since I moved in, there's a swelling inkling inside me that he's the person for me... forever. I'd like to tell him that, and the opportunity should arise now that we've got a couple of weeks before the start of the Riot season. And while we'll both be busy, we'll at least be mostly together. Jet-setting to all the races is its own kind of chaotic but comforting routine.

"I'd follow her to the ends of the Earth. I mean, I kind of have, haven't I? How far are we from Seattle?" Evan continues. "Is it halfway around the world? Have we already started heading back towards the States, technically?"

The interview derails from there in classic Evan fashion. The audio even picks up the camera operator's laughter.

The car pulls to a stop outside the familiar gates of the course, which I now think of as my home track. Abby's just outside, adorable as usual, and gives me a friendly wave.

I thank the driver, slam the door, and run to give her a hug.

She's new to the Riot circuit and had a recent, whirlwind introduction, so I try to make her feel welcome.

She seems a little nervous, jittery. She wasn't even familiar with the world of motorsports until one of the final races of last season.

"Are you excited to see your first pre-season test?" I ask as we head toward the garages. The paddock area is quiet since it's not set up for full race festivities. I don't even see anyone besides a duo of Panache people and one Riot safety officer. In fact, I only hear the roar of a single engine out on track.

"Are your boys here yet?" I ask, scanning for anyone in a yellow and black Benji kit.

She loops an arm through mine. "Hurry, someone's out already!"

Her statement is punctuated by the sound of tires squealing. My heart beats a little faster just hearing it.

"Can you show me the Panache garage? Since it's a little less hectic than a race weekend, maybe you can fill me in on some of what's happening? The data and telemetry and stuff?"

Abby is like a teddy bear made of cotton candy. It's no wonder that not one, but two drivers decided to keep her. We're new friends, and I'm hoping we get a quiet minute so she can give me the full, delicious story because the rumors I've heard... Well. Evan and I want to take some inspiration from their alleged bedroom antics.

I gulp and avoid swerving into a pillar. Evan and I have talked about trying a threesome, and I'm desperately interested. He seems thrilled to give that to me, but I don't know how to pull the trigger, and we have more to focus on right now.

I clear my throat and go into Riot Racing 101 mode. "I'm happy to show you whatever you like." I squeeze her around the shoulders and guide her to the garage.

Blair shoots me a wry look when we arrive and I give her a small wave before we settle. We're the only two at the viewing barrier. Evan is whipping out laps. Grant isn't here today, which is a little odd, but maybe he'll join us for another test, or his team could be opting to do this at a different track closer to his home.

I mean to ask someone what Evan's goals are for the day or what exactly he's testing, but everyone is dutifully focused, the air in the garage a little tense.

Abby keeps up a steady stream of questions.

As I'm animatedly explaining the difficulty of keeping the car from overheating during a run, Evan pulls into the pit box, his car gleaming.

Abby's eyes flick between me and his car, her smile stiff, but I'm on a roll. This is something I only began to truly understand late last season after Pete and I got tipsy and he gave me a college-level lecture on racecraft around a bonfire in Nashville.

As I finish my explanation, I realize the garage is too quiet. The mechanics haven't rushed to the car to bring it in, and Abby looks a little panicked.

I glance over my shoulder. Blair looks ready to burst into laughter.

"*Sunny Waite!*"

I whip around, and Evan's got his helmet off. His hair is disheveled, and he's got one foot on the car's rear wheel well. His car also seems strange. The colors are correct, but something's weird about the sponsorship logos, as well as the car's proportions.

I squint and gasp. There's no way I'm seeing it right.

The car is a two-seater, and all of the logos are the official, branded size and font, but... none of them say the actual names of companies or financial services or brands of energy drink.

They all say, "Marry me, Sunny."

I gape. Evan's got his arms spread wide, matching his smile, though I notice tightness at the corner of it. He's nervous.

Blair opens the little gate in the barrier's side and clears her throat, nodding for me to go through.

Hands shaking, I do. People make space as I head for him, seeing his question poised in myriad ways across the car's livery.

Evan meets me. He takes my hands and guides me into the sunshine that's decided to appear just for us.

"You're serious?" I ask him.

"I have been from the start. There are so many things I admire and love about you. You're my favorite person in the world. My deepest wish is that I could somehow possibly share the rest of my life with you and witness how amazing you are every day, and help make you happy." He gets a little choked up at the end.

I wrap my arms around his waist and bury my face in his chest, thinking of all he's organized to get this done, thinking of all the people who have sacrificed a Saturday afternoon and traveled who knows how far for this surprise.

I don't have words. Deep gratitude and awe take over my body, and all I can do is follow the instinct to grab

Evan's face and kiss him. He dips me, holding me steady and taking time to explore my mouth.

The garage erupts into cheers, and I hear familiar yells coming from the VIP box situated above it. Evan buries his head in my neck, and his shoulders tremble. I squeeze and breathe and look to where the voices come from. He brought my parents, and my sisters even showed up. His family is here, too, and some more of our friends. I hear whooping that is Gael's signature and Jackie's cackle.

When Evan finally brings me upright, I've got tears running down my cheeks. Evan wipes them away. "So, are you gonna marry me or what? You have to answer before you get in the car with me. Also, there is a ring. Pete has it, so I don't misplace it."

In the back of the garage, Pete waves a small velvet box above his head. "After the hot laps!" he shouts.

I turn and take Evan's face in mine, tracing the smile that's mine forever with my thumb. "Yes, you beautiful idiot. I'll marry you."

Want more?

Thank you for reading the first installment of the Riot Racers series!

Want more Sunny and Evan?

Sign up for the newsletter at delaneyandrews.com/news to receive a bonus epilogue and discover what, or more importantly, *who*, Evan has in store for Sunny on their steamy first anniversary. (Subscribers will also be the first to know when the next Riot story is on the way!)

More Riot stories are on the way!

Delaney also writes action-packed superhero stories (with a little spice) under the name Delaney Andrews.

The Silhouette Series

Silhouette and the Shadow
Silhouette and the Monster

Acknowledgements

The idea for this book hit me like a bolt of lightning on a plane to San Diego in 2023. It felt like a wild, impossible dream at the time, and I was only able to see it become a reality with the support of many incredible friends.

Dustyn, you happened to be trapped in my vicinity when I was struck by the aforementioned lightning. I couldn't guess what anyone's response would be when I blurted "I think I need to write a horny race car book." While everyone has been supportive, you were the first, with a response that went something like... "Hell yeah, *Formula Fuck!*" Thank you for the hype. (Hi, Carm!)

Thank you, Lindsey, for being a terrific beta reader and fellow lover of unhinged romances. Your comments saying that you always understood whose body parts were going where were especially helpful.

Thank you to my sisters for being early readers and letting me bounce ideas off of you. Thank you to my brother for cheering me on even though you have no intention of reading this. (#boundaries) Thank you, Mom, for your endless support even though you have no idea what to expect in the contents of this book. You're welcome and/or I'm sorry?

Thank you to Marissa and Nora for providing feedback on the synopsis. In the hellscape that is corporate America, true friendship is a gift. I'm so grateful for you both.

Oodles of thanks to Hannah G for providing a sensitivity read regarding Evan's ADHD. Bonus thanks to James Briscoe for sharing with me how sometimes ADHD feels like a superpower.

Thank you to Vicky Skinner for a thorough and thoughtful edit. This book is stronger because of your involvement! I'm so glad the universe brought us together. Alonso fans simply must stick together.

Z, thank you for splitting the weight of life with me. I love our adventures and that this ludicrous sport has become our shared hobby. There's no one else with whom I'd rather serve on the front lines of Papaya Army.

Atreyu, thank you for keeping my feet warm while I wrote smut, judgmental looks and heavy sighs aside.

Lastly, I have to thank the hoards of motorsport fans that populate my digital and corporeal worlds. Racing wouldn't be nearly as wonderful if there weren't lovely people to share it with. Friendship bracelets and outfit compliments and retweets are the lifeblood of this dysfunctional family. Extra special thanks go to my personal creator crushes, Matt, Brian, Jeni, and the Gen Z interns at the Red Flags Podcast (Daddy loves you, Vankahs!) and Elizabeth and Ash from the Elizabeth + Ash Show. I'm a solitary creature, and the insight and entertainment you all provide week over week feeds my sanity.

Extra lastly, thanks to you, readers. I hope you adore my beautiful idiots. I have so many more to show you!

About the author

Delaney Jean accidentally watched the 2022 British Grand Prix and has never been the same. Each June, she can be found watching IndyCar race along the streets of Detroit. Her waking hours are also consumed with all things superhero, and you can read about *those* beautiful idiots under the name Delaney Andrews. You can scream about motorsports with her on most social platforms at @dj_rhetoric. *Too Late To Brake* is her first romance novel.